IN THE DARK

VIKKI PATIS

BLOODHOUND
— BOOKS —

Print ISBN 978-1-913942-28-1

ALSO BY VIKKI PATIS

Girl, Lost

The Wake

For Marcel, the light in the dark.

1

CAITLYN

I *am a bad mother.*

The words reverberate around my mind as I stare down at the floor, and the small red stain blemishing the white carpet beneath my feet. It is new, this carpet, laid only a year ago when I'd finally had enough of the original dull red. *At least it would hide the blood better.* The thought is unbidden, horrific, and I push it away.

I close my eyes, trying to regulate my breathing. In, one two three. Out, one two three. Inhale, exhale. The next thought is louder, so loud it makes my heart skip a beat: *She's done it again. I'm too late.*

I push open the bathroom door, knowing, deep down, what I will find. There is a distinct lack of urgency; my body feels heavy, and my movements are slow as I step inside to find what I have been expecting to find for almost a year. The body of my daughter.

As soon as I see her – her eyes closed, one hand dangling over the edge of the bath, blood dripping from her fingertips – my heart speeds up, beating so hard that I start to feel dizzy. Sweat prickles along my forehead; my jaw clenches so tightly I hear a crack. And then, movement. Her fingers twitching, a low moan coming from her lips. She is alive. She is *alive*.

'Isabelle!' I say, rushing towards her, dropping to my knees beside the bath. 'Isabelle, wake up!' I press my hand over her wrist to stop the bleeding, though the wound is not too deep. I have learned how to tell. I reach over and grab her other wrist, and here, the wound is deeper. She is right-handed, and she must have cut her left wrist first, the razor opening the skin like a hot knife through butter. Blood is pulsing out of it, coating my fingers. She moans again, her eyes flickering.

'I'm going to call an ambulance,' I tell her, letting go of her left wrist and fishing in my back pocket for my phone. 'It's going to be okay, darling. You're going to be fine.'

'It's all for attention,' Michael said when Isabelle first started cutting. 'A cry for help. She'll grow out of it.'

But shouldn't we be answering her cry for help? I thought but didn't say. He had already gone back to reading the newspaper, his glasses balanced on the end of his nose, while Alicia made hot chocolate for her younger sister and I perched on the armchair, my hands clasped between my knees, feeling out of my depth. That was the first time.

I am still out of my depth now. This is our second hospital visit in the past twelve months, each 'cry for help' getting more and more serious. This time, Isabelle has swallowed a pack of the amitriptyline I was prescribed for insomnia a few years back, as well as cutting her wrists, and so the pace is faster this time, the hospital corridors whizzing past as I run alongside the stretcher on which my daughter lays, wishing Alicia was here, glad she doesn't have to see it this time.

'You'll need to wait here,' a nurse says, holding a hand up in front of her. I stop as if she has activated an invisible shield, blocking me out. I watch Isabelle disappear through the double doors, my hands clenching and unclenching at my sides. The nurse's eyes soften as our gaze meets. 'Just take a seat here. We'll keep you updated.' And then she is gone in a flash of blue uniform and rubber-soled shoes that squeak on the polished floor.

I sit in the hard-backed chair, picking at a groove in the armrest, thinking of Isabelle's last words to me as the ambulance flew down the motorway, blue lights flashing. *There's a photo. They shared it. Everyone's seen it.* A photo. What kind of photo? I get my phone out, tap on Alicia's number, then put it down again. Michael is in Italy on a business trip; he only left yesterday, and isn't due back for another five days. What time is it there? What time is it here?

The clock on the wall reads 4.16pm. $4 + 1 + 6 = 11$. $1 + 1 = 2$. The same as Isabelle's life path number. Sensitive, emotional. The mediator. The peacekeeper. Michael has always frowned at my dabbling in numerology and horoscopes, calling it 'mumbo jumbo' and 'that weird, hippy shit'. He is a man of business, only believing in what he can feel in his hands and see with his eyes. But numbers have always made sense to me. I find comfort in them in a world full of chaos, feel myself drawn to them when everything else is a mess.

Alicia's life path number is 5. Resourceful, wild. Never still. She is away at university now, studying and partying with equal relish, turning from the child I reared to an adult in her own right. Will Isabelle have the same opportunities as her sister? Will she even make it to university? Will she make it through tonight?

I think back to the last attempt, the one which I managed to thwart by being at home when I wasn't expected to be. I had planned to visit a friend for coffee, our usual monthly catch-up, but her father had had a fall and needed her help. And so I was in the bath when Isabelle came flying through the house, her feet stomping on the stairs as she headed for her bedroom. Music blared from her speakers almost instantly, and so I slid down in the water, hoping to avoid another row, until I heard the rattle of the bathroom door.

'Mum?' Her voice was full of tears, so much emotion in that one word, and I got out of the bath, hurriedly tucking a towel around myself, and took her in my arms, holding her like I used to when she was small.

I wrap my arms around myself now, desperate for comfort, staring at a scuff mark on the floor. She will get through this. She will be fine. I won't let her be anything else.

2

LIV

I'm scrubbing at a stain on the kitchen counter when Seb jogs down the stairs, his hair still damp from the shower. A waft of aftershave follows him into the room.

'Morning, love,' I say, drying my hands and nodding at his cup of tea cooling on the side. 'Sleep well?'

'Like a log,' he says, as he often does, grinning his usual grin. I smile back at him. 'Any bread left?'

I shake my head. 'There's a box of cereal in the cupboard. Chocolate rice pops or whatever they're called these days.'

'Yes!' Seb says, taking the box out of the cupboard and pouring a generous bowl. 'I love these ones. Thanks, Nan.'

My smile flickers as I remember the 'reduced' sticker I ripped off and threw in the bin as soon as I got home. You'd never notice the price of gluten-free cereal unless you had no choice but to eat it. When Seb was diagnosed with coeliac disease back in primary school, I felt utterly overwhelmed. 'BROWS,' a woman in Tesco told me once when I was staring uncomprehendingly at the back of a packet of biscuits. 'Barley, rye, oats, wheat, spelt.' She ticked them off on her fingers. 'And may contain. Stay away from anything that says it may contain gluten, it's not worth the risk.'

In the years since, both Seb and I have learned a lot. We've learned that first and foremost he is a teenage boy, and he gets easily frustrated by having to be different to the rest of his friends. More than once, he's spent a few days in the bathroom after one of his 'just a little bit won't hurt' moments, or not checking if the food is suitable for him. I suppose he'll learn the hard way.

He wolfs the cereal down now, dribbling chocolatey milk down his chin. 'That's a clean shirt,' I say, handing him a tea towel. 'You've no more until I do the washing.'

'Better get on with it then, Nan,' he says, winking, and I pretend to swat him. He dances past me and places his bowl in the sink, before grabbing his lunch and water bottle from the fridge. 'See you later.'

'Have a good day!'

The front door slams and he is gone. I breathe out. He's a good boy, Seb, though cheeky beyond belief. He's always been that way, ever since he was a child. Always happy, and willing to lend a hand. He has never shown any sign that he is like his father.

I was thirty-four when I became a grandmother. I had been a young mother myself, falling pregnant at fifteen, swiftly marrying Harry as soon as I turned sixteen so our daughter was not born out of wedlock. It seems such an old-fashioned word, wedlock. Locked into marriage by a few vows and the magic words: *I now pronounce you husband and wife.* But when you're sixteen, without qualifications or any real-life experience, what do those roles really mean? My mother was never going to be a good role model, what with her fondness for staying out late most nights, coming home stinking of booze and cigarettes and men's aftershave, and her aversion to housework and cooking anything more complicated than bangers and mash. My father had left a long time before, when I was three and had barely formed an impression of him or who he was to me. One day I had a dad, the next I didn't, and because he hadn't been around all that much to begin with, I didn't particularly feel the loss.

Six months after we married, Paige was born. It was a bright day in August, which started with blue skies and searing heat and ended in a storm so powerful the roads flooded and the thunder shook the car as we drove to the hospital. She came quickly, not wasting any time in announcing herself to the world, slipping out in a rush of heat and blood. Her cries filled the room instantly, her tiny fist reaching toward the sky as the midwife cleaned her up as if in triumph. *I made it. I'm here.*

'Here she is,' the midwife said with a smile, placing my daughter on my chest. 'Congratulations, Olivia.'

'Liv,' I said automatically, forgetting myself. Harry didn't like nicknames. 'I mean, thank you.' I stared down at my daughter, taking in her red, wrinkled skin and tuft of dark hair. 'Hello, Paige,' I whispered, waiting for the advertised rush of love and feeling only pain and exhaustion.

'You need to rest,' the midwife said, taking Paige back and placing her in the cot beside my bed. 'A rested mum is a happy mum, and a happy mum means a happy baby.' My eyes were closing before she finished speaking, fatigue taking over and pulling me under. But when I woke hours later to Paige's deep-blue eyes staring at me, her tiny fingers reaching for me, that wave of love engulfed me, washing away all the pain and the doubt. Well, some of the doubt.

I would repeat those words eighteen years later, when Paige laid in the sweat-soaked sheets, baby Sebastian cradled against her chest, her eyes tired but triumphant. Though I'd had dreams of her going off to university and doing all the things I never managed to do, in that moment, I was bursting with pride. My daughter had given birth to a perfect baby boy, with dark curls and tiny fingers that took hold of mine the first time I held him in my arms. And for him, for Paige, I accepted Brad. I opened my heart to a man I did not trust, sat across from him while we ate Sunday lunch at my small kitchen table, watched him hand Seb to Paige for nappy changes. Countless times I gripped the phone in my fingers, listening to him shout in the background while Paige told me not to worry. 'Everything's fine, Mum,' she would say, whispering into the receiver before hanging up. But it wasn't fine. By the time Seb was four, Paige would be dead, murdered by the man who was supposed to love her, and keep her safe. The father of her child.

3

SEB

Seb is in English Literature when the message comes through. He feels his phone vibrate in his pocket, but he doesn't pull it out. His nan will kill him if a teacher confiscates his phone again. So instead he pretends to listen to Mrs Hall drone on about *Of Mice and Men*, a book he curses because his so-called friends have started calling him Crooks, which, though it is light-hearted, stings in a way he doesn't quite understand. Not yet anyway.

When the bell rings, Seb shoves his books into his rucksack and hurries out of the room, jogging down the stairs until a voice shouts, 'No running, Taylor! It isn't a race.' But it is. He has to get to the bus before it leaves, else he will have to walk across town and up the hill that feels more like a mountain. And that will make him late for dinner. His nan isn't strict about many things, but she is especially keen on punctuality, and they always eat dinner together, unless she is working a late shift.

Outside, Seb almost runs straight into Josh, who has stopped in the middle of the path.

'Beep!' Seb says, laughing, as he passes his friend. But when he glances at his face, something makes him stop. 'What's up?'

Josh is staring down at his phone, his eyes wide. 'Have you seen this?' He turns the phone around so the screen is facing Seb, but he's too far away to see it properly and he can't waste any more time.

'I've gotta run, mate. The bus driver won't wait.'

'Check the group chat,' Josh says, his eyes back on his phone. 'There's something you need to see.'

Seb feels a flicker of concern as he turns and jogs towards the front of the school, his eyes on the bus that will take him home. Once he's on board, he pulls out his phone and opens Snapchat. There are seventy-two messages waiting for him. He scrolls up, looking for the beginning of the conversation, and pauses, his thumb hovering over a photo. A sense of dread fills him, a premonition that he cannot explain. His heart begins to race as he taps it and the photo fills his screen.

It takes a moment for his mind to catch up to what his eyes are seeing. A girl stands before a mirror, her long hair trailing over her shoulder. Her phone is held up before her face, covering one eye, the flash of the camera reflected in the glass, bright like a firework.

Those are the first things Seb notices. The second is the fact that the girl is naked but for black underwear and thick fluffy socks. And the third, the thing that slams into him like a fist, is that he recognises the bedroom behind her, the unmade bed with the colourful blanket thrown over the end, and the desk in the corner he knows is littered with eyeshadow palettes and fluffy brushes and blunt eyeliner pencils. The bedside table which has four or five books stacked on top of one another, the lamp with the purple lampshade and silver base covered in fingerprints. The rug that curls up on one end, which Seb has tripped over almost every time he's been in that room. His girlfriend's bedroom.

~

'Hiya, love,' Liv calls from the kitchen as Seb opens the front door. 'Good day at school?'

'Fine,' he says, slipping off his shoes and stacking them on the rack. He hangs his rucksack on the hook and goes into the kitchen.

'Curry tonight,' she says, stirring a large saucepan with a wooden spoon. 'I managed to get some gluten-free naans the other day. Get them out the cupboard for me, will you?'

Seb opens the cupboard and rummages around on the top shelf. 'We'll need to get you a step,' he jokes, placing the pack of naan bread on the counter.

'None of your cheek, young man. Respect your elders.' Closing the oven door, she turns to face him. 'Good day?' she asks again.

Seb shrugs. 'All right. Got a merit in biology today.'

'Well done, love,' she says, her eyes crinkling as she smiles. 'It's a big year for you.'

Liv has been going on about his *big year* ever since the end of his last *big year*. 'Every year is important,' she says whenever he rolls his eyes at her. 'Your schooldays will set you up for life.'

'I know,' he says, leaning against the counter. 'Exams.'

'That's right. Only two months to go.'

He glances at the calendar on the wall, which has been showing the month of May since last September, with all of Seb's exams written out in his nan's neat handwriting. He knows she left school 'without qualifications', as she puts it, and that she'd hoped her daughter, Seb's mum, would have gone to university.

'But it wasn't meant to be.' She sighs whenever she talks about his mother. 'And she gave me you, the most precious gift of all.'

Seb isn't sure if he's a precious gift. He thinks of the photo on his phone, and feels his skin prickle with shame. What would Liv say if she knew? He cannot tell her, cannot bear to see the look on her face if she looked at the photo. She has always liked her, called her a 'lovely young lady'. Would her opinion change now? Would she blame Seb?

Something is telling him to keep quiet, to cross his fingers and hope it all blows over. But, somehow, he knows it won't. Somehow, he knows this is just the beginning.

4

CAITLYN

I am sitting at my daughter's bedside, watching her breathe deep and slow. She has finally stopped throwing up after the doctors gave her something to act against the amitriptyline, and her wrists are wrapped in pure white bandages. She is sleeping, her dark lashes fluttering gently as she breathes in and out. She is *alive*.

'She's just exhausted, poor lamb,' the nurse told me when she showed me into the cubicle. 'The doctor gave her something to make her bring it all up. We'll let her rest for a while.'

It is almost eight o'clock now. My hands are clasped on the bed in front of me, my head bowed as I whisper my silent prayers. They are not proper prayers, I suppose, not to an omniscient deity I doubt exists, but rather a mantra, a wish that I could stop the demons from haunting my daughter, that I could tear the bullies apart with my bare hands.

Isabelle stirs and I lift my head, my eyes searching her face. Her eyes flicker and then they are open, staring straight at me.

'Isabelle,' I whisper, reaching for her hand, feeling the rough bandage beneath my fingers. 'Isabelle, it's me. Mum.' I don't know why I feel the need to clarify who I am; it is something I do all the time, as if each time I am reasserting my place in the world. 'I know, your name came up on the screen,' she would say whenever I called her with my usual, 'Hi darling, it's me, Mum.' I am Mum. But what does Mum mean?

'How are you feeling?' I ask, wrenching myself out of my cyclic thoughts. 'Shall I get the doctor?'

She shakes her head, swallows. Water, I think. She must be thirsty. I reach out for the tumbler on the side, holding the straw to her lips while still clutching her wrist with my other hand. The memory of how I found her flickers through my mind and I feel myself start to withdraw, my fingers tingling as I trace where the wound is. Where the new scar will be.

'Slowly,' I tell her, watching her throat move as she swallows the water. 'Little sips.' She drinks until it is gone, the straw making a loud noise against the bottom of the empty cup. I put it aside. 'How are you, Isabelle?' This is the only question I can ask. The only question I want to ask. It's too early for *What happened?* or *Why did you do it?* I just need to make sure my daughter is okay.

She turns her head, her eyes fixed on the blue curtain surrounding the cubicle. She doesn't speak, doesn't turn to look at me again, even as I rise from the chair, my back stiff. 'I'll get the doctor,' I say, patting her arm before slipping through the curtain.

A nurse follows me back in, her dark hair pulled into a tight bun that would give me a migraine. Her smile is bright as she approaches the bed.

'Hello, petal,' she says warmly. 'How are you?'

Isabelle doesn't respond. I glance at the nurse, panic flashing through me. 'Is she... I mean, could–'

'Don't worry,' she says, placing a hand on my shoulder and lowering her voice. 'She just needs to rest for a while, don't you, petal?' She raises her voice again at the end, once more addressing Isabelle, who stares blankly at a spot behind the nurse, her eyes dull. 'How about a nice cup of tea?' the nurse says to me. 'While we wait for the doctor.'

The tea is lukewarm and the exact opposite to *nice*. I clasp the plastic cup between my fingers, trying to draw on its warmth as I sit in silence beside my daughter. Her eyes are closed again, but she isn't sleeping. This is another thing I know about my daughter, how to tell when she is pretending to be asleep. She and Alicia used to do it as children, leaping out of bed and running into one another's bedrooms as soon as I'd gone downstairs, then scurrying back when they heard my footsteps. I remember listening to their giggles, their whispers filling the air as I paused on the stairs.

The memory makes my eyes burn, and I close them for a moment, forcing the tears away. I cannot afford to think about the past, about when everything was so much easier. Before this chapter of Isabelle's life began. But oh, how I wish I could go back. If I could change one thing, just one thing that would change the future, that would stop her from hurting herself. But I could never make myself go far enough, to that time I have buried deep inside me, the lid firmly shut. That was the beginning of it all, and it was my fault. It is all my fault.

A noise from beyond the curtain startles me, and my eyes flick open to find Isabelle staring at me. She averts her gaze, and I turn to see a woman standing there, a clipboard in her hands. 'Mrs Bennett?' she says, looking at me.

'Yes,' I say, standing to offer my hand instead of correcting her on the surname. She shakes it with a slightly bemused smile, and I curse myself for being so formal. 'Caitlyn, please.'

The woman nods. 'I'm Kira, a nurse from the Mental Health Liaison Team. Is it all right if we have a chat with Isabelle?'

I turn back to look at my daughter, whose eyes are suddenly wide and fearful. A memory comes to me then, the first time Isabelle tried to take her own life. *Please don't call them, Mum. I don't want to be locked up. Don't let them lock me up.* I watch Kira as she steps into the cubicle, perching on a chair on the other side of the bed. She looks like a small bird, her fingers long and delicate. This woman cannot lock my daughter up, can she?

'We just want to assess your needs, Isabelle,' Kira says. I note the use of *we*, as if she alone is not responsible for what may happen next. 'I can see from your record that this isn't the first time you've been in here.'

I blink, taken aback. Am I imagining her confrontational tone? Isabelle doesn't speak, and when the silence becomes uncomfortable I answer for her. 'This is the second time,' I say shortly. 'Isabelle is... She's having a bit of a hard time.'

Kira doesn't look at me. 'Can you tell me about it, Isabelle?'

Isabelle closes her eyes in response.

'There's been a bit of bullying,' I say, lowering my voice as if my daughter wouldn't be able to hear me. 'Usual teenage stuff.'

Now Kira's eyes shift to me. 'I wouldn't call this *usual*, Mrs Bennett. We need to think very carefully about what your daughter needs, don't you?' She turns back to Isabelle, tapping her pen against her notepad as her questions go unanswered.

When Kira finally gets up to leave, I stand too, reaching out as if to grab her arm. 'Please,' I say, glancing back at my daughter, who is staring up at the ceiling. 'She'll be fine, really. It's going to be dealt with.'

Kira stares at me for a moment, and I can almost feel the judgement coming off her in waves. 'What is going to be *dealt with*?'

Another glance at Isabelle; she has closed her eyes now, but I know she still isn't asleep, so I step outside of the cubicle, closing the curtain behind us as if it will muffle our words. 'The reason she... She's being bullied. At school. But I'm going to speak to the school, enough is enough.'

Kira arches one eyebrow. 'Has Isabelle told you this? About the bullying?'

'A little.'

'And how long has it been going on?'

'Oh,' I say, swallowing. 'A while. Too long, really. I–'

'And do you know what caused the escalation?'

'E-escalation?' I stumble over the word.

She sighs. 'The attempt. Did something in particular trigger it? I believe last time...' She checks her notes. 'Last time there was an incident at a sleepover, yes?'

I nod, remembering. 'Yes, a misunderstanding, but teenagers can be cruel, can't they?' I try to smile, but even I know it is less than convincing. I don't really know why I'm trying to brush this off. My daughter, my beautiful, clever, wonderful daughter, has tried to kill herself. Again. But I know that Isabelle's words – *don't let them lock me up* – are the driving force behind my pretence. I cannot let them take her from me.

I take a deep breath, trying to compose my erratic thoughts. 'She was having counselling until about three months ago, when she said things were improving. And they did seem to be. She was going out more, had friends over, was engaging with the family. And she has a boyfriend, a lovely boy she's known since primary school. So I really don't know. I suppose something must have happened, but I am her mother, and I'm going to get to the bottom of it.'

5

IZZY

She listens to the sounds around her; the heavy breathing of another patient beyond the curtain, the gentle whoosh of a fire door opening and closing, the squeak of a nurse's shoes on the linoleum. These noises are different to what she is used to at night, the surroundings unfamiliar, and she lies awake, staring at the ceiling, trying not to think about why she is here.

Her mother has gone, though Izzy can still feel the imprint of her lips on her cheek, the faint scent of her perfume. She tries not to think about the look in her mum's eyes, the worry etched onto her face. *I caused that. It's all my fault.*

She thinks of Seb, wonders whether he is lying awake too, staring at the messages she refuses to open. She is so full of her own emotions, a tangled web that has created a knot in her stomach, a hard, heavy lump that weighs her down, that she doesn't have space for Seb and his feelings. She knows she has made a huge mistake, one she doesn't think she can ever come back from, and she fears what will come next.

Izzy closes her eyes, tries to focus on her breathing. She doesn't want to remember the way she had stood in front of the mirror before taking the photo, pinching at the flesh on her hips, turning this way and that, trying to find the most flattering angle. She doesn't want to remember how she had undone her bra and stood looking at herself, wondering if one breast was bigger than the other, if her nipples were normal. Were they too dark? She had seen her sister's boobs before, and yet she had never really taken note of them. Should she have? Or would that have been weird? Instead she looked at the page-three models, the topless women on Twitter, flicking through photos in incognito mode on her phone, comparing herself, always comparing herself. Never good enough.

She should never have sent that photo. She'd known it even as she took it, her thumb hesitating over the message before hitting send and throwing her phone on the bed, knowing, *knowing*, that she was making a mistake. She'd washed her hair, fluffing out the curls so they sat nicely for once. She'd put on make-up, filling in her brows and coating her lashes with mascara, her lips painted a cherry red. She looked again in the mirror, wondered if she would fit in now, if she would be good enough. Now, she wishes she had faded into the background like she usually does.

Her phone screen lights up from its place on the hard chair beside the bed, too bright for the small dark room. Is it a room without a door? It feels more like an enclosure, a place to keep her while they decide what to do with her. Could they lock her up for this? She is no danger to others, and she isn't sure if she truly wants to die. She just wants it all to stop.

A wave of exhaustion passes over her and she sighs, squeezing her eyes tight. She wants to sleep. She wants to sleep and dream and wake up a different person, someone new and without the thoughts and memories that plague her. The fears that threaten to drag her down, tendrils reaching up to grab her ankle like icy fingers in the dark.

Her phone lights up again, bright even with her eyes closed, and she opens them, reaching out and picking up the phone. She presses her thumb against the scanner and squints against the glare of the screen. Eight messages from Seb, all unread. Three from Alicia, one a meme that Izzy would probably find funny under normal circumstances. One from her mum, telling her to rest and that she'll be back in the morning. And another which makes her stomach lurch, her breath quickening as she reads the words.

I'm so sorry, Izzy.

6

LIV

I'm at work, having my afternoon cigarette break round the back when my phone rings. *Davenport School* flashes up on the screen and I frown.

'Hello?'

'Hello, is that Ms Taylor?'

'Yes, speaking.'

'Ms Taylor, it's Mrs Harris from Davenport. The headteacher's secretary.'

'Hello,' I say cautiously.

'Could you come down to the school please? There's something we need to discuss.'

'Is it about Seb? Is he all right?'

A pause. 'You'd better come down, Ms Taylor. As soon as possible.'

Sean, my manager, makes a face when I tell him I have to leave. He is twenty-four and never fails to sneer at people, women in particular, who have to balance childcare with working. I suppose his parents expected more from their son than managing a petrol station, and he is taking his frustrations out on the rest of us, but today I don't have time to worry about it. I grab my bag and leave, walking as fast as I can towards the school. I only learned to drive when Paige moved into Brad's flat a year into their relationship. His flat was a few towns away and a long walk from the train station, so I finally learned to drive and bought an old banger out of the newspaper which is, miraculously, still going. These days I don't often need to use the car, but I suddenly feel a desperation to get to the school as quickly as possible and curse myself for leaving the car at home. The walk will take at least twenty-five minutes, and I'm sweating by the time I reach the first set of traffic lights. I tap my foot as I wait for the lights to change, tutting as a cyclist shoots through the red light as I'm crossing. It's almost one straight road to the school, along the dual carriageway, past the Ford garage and what will be the new Aldi. I turn down the road and begin to puff my way up the hill, swearing under my breath and promising to give up smoking, as I always do whenever I make this journey on foot.

When I arrive in reception, I feel hot and unkempt, and pause to smooth down my hair before approaching the receptionist. 'I'm Liv, erm, Olivia Taylor,' I say, trying to smile through my anxiety. 'Seb Taylor's grandmother. I was asked to come in?'

The receptionist is already tapping away at her keyboard, her long acrylic nails making a racket against the keys. I'm wondering how she does anything with those talons when she looks up at me. 'Please go straight through,' she says, indicating a door behind me. Her expression is neutral, but I feel a flash of fear as I turn towards the door and knock.

A woman opens it, her short hair neatly coiffed, her lips coated in a pale-pink lipstick. 'Ms Taylor,' she says, and I notice she has lipstick on her teeth. 'I'm Mrs Harris, we spoke on the phone. Come in.'

I step inside and find myself in a small corridor, with a desk at one end and a door marked STAFF ONLY at the other. Another door is set in the middle, with MR LOACH, HEADTEACHER emblazoned across the front. I suddenly feel as if I am the one in trouble, as if I have gone back thirty-odd years. *Buck up*, I tell myself as she knocks on the door. *You're an adult now.*

A voice calls out and Mrs Harris opens the door to reveal a man who can't be older than twenty-eight, thirty at a push. He rises from his chair as I enter, his hand held out for me to shake.

'Please, take a seat, Mrs Taylor.'

I don't correct him. I haven't been Mrs since my husband died. 'Is Seb okay?' I ask, sitting on the uncomfortable seat and placing my bag on my lap. 'Where is he? Is he in trouble?'

'Tea?' Mrs Harris asks from her place in the doorway. 'Coffee? Water?'

I glance at her and shake my head. 'No, thank you.' I see Mr Loach give her a nod and she leaves, shutting the door behind her. I swallow, suddenly wishing I'd taken her up on her offer. My throat is dry, my tongue too large for my mouth. My heart pounds as I wait for Mr Loach to speak.

'There's been an... incident,' he says, pursing his lips.

'Is he hurt? Was there a fight? I know it's happened before, but it was nothing serious, just boys being boys, you know. But he's assured me that–' The headteacher raises a hand and I stutter to a stop.

'No, no. Nothing like that. This is rather more delicate.' He pauses, lifting a sheet of paper from his desk as if checking his notes before continuing. 'An allegation has been made that your son–'

'Grandson,' I interject automatically.

He clears his throat. 'Your grandson, Sebastian, has been involved in the sharing of a graphic image.'

I stare at him, my mind trying to understand the words. 'A

graphic image?' I pause, a hand rising to my throat. 'Not *porn*?' I whisper, feeling my cheeks flush. I know Seb is a teenaged boy, and teenagers have their needs, but porn at school? I can't believe he'd be so stupid.

'It was an indecent image of a young girl. A student here.' The words stun me, snatching my breath away. 'It was apparently sent around a few group chats and on social media,' Mr Loach continues, consulting the paper again. 'Lots of students have now seen it, but it appears your grandson was involved in distributing it.'

Distributing. I swallow, my cheeks burning. 'So you're saying that Seb has... shared this image around? Sent it to his friends?'

'That is the allegation, yes,' Mr Loach says, laying the sheet of paper down and placing a hand over it. 'Now this is, of course, a serious matter, which is why we have had to inform the police.'

I stare at him. 'The police? Will he... Is he going to be *arrested*?' The words of Seb's other grandmother, Evelyn, flash into my mind. *Don't ever get yourself caught up with the law. They won't see past the colour of your skin.* I shake myself.

'The police are investigating,' Mr Loach says carefully. 'And will be in touch with you in due course.'

'What happens next?' I manage to ask.

'Seb and the other boys are being suspended for the rest of the week.'

'Suspended? But how can you... How do you even know he's involved?'

He frowns as if he is disappointed in me. 'We take such allegations very seriously, Mrs Taylor. We have a zero-tolerance policy towards bullying. You can take him home with you today.'

He stands, and I realise the meeting is at an end. I follow suit, my legs so weak I grab hold of the desk to stop myself falling to the floor. My mind is racing, the revelation sending waves of nausea through me. Indecent. Suspended. Police.

I make it as far as the door before the question bubbles up inside me, forcing its way past my lips. 'And the girl? How is she?'

Mr Loach purses his lips into a thin line. 'Isabelle tried to take her own life a few days ago. She's lucky to be alive.'

7

SEB

He is waiting for his nan in reception. When she exits the headteacher's office, her back ramrod straight, her bag clutched against her side, anxiety prickles up his spine. His premonitions have come true, and suddenly he feels as if he is standing on the edge of a cliff, the wind buffeting him from behind, as if the slightest misstep will send him hurtling over the edge.

'Let's go,' Liv says shortly, nodding at the receptionist before turning towards the double doors. He follows, sheepishly, his heart pounding.

'Nan,' he says when they're outside, but she shakes her head.

'Not here. We need to have a private conversation.'

If Seb had to pick his nan's three favourite sayings, they would be: *have you eaten? rise and shine!* and *don't make a scene.* Her 'not here' means she is likely to make a scene if forced to discuss this outside of the privacy of their home. The thought sends another stab of unease through him.

She marches down the road, her back still stiff, and Seb trails along behind her, worry gnawing at him. Liv rarely shouts, and she has never raised a hand to him, not once, but he cannot shake the intrinsic fear of disappointing her. Of throwing everything she has done for him back in her face. He knows without being told that she has sacrificed a lot for him, sees it in the holes in her socks, the teabags used twice, the extra hours at the petrol station. Money has always been tight, but never has Seb gone to bed hungry or to school in a dirty uniform, and that is all down to her.

As they approach the hill past the train station, Seb suppresses a groan. He *hates* walking up this hill. It feels never-ending, a long, arduous climb that makes his calves and lungs burn. But his nan strides ahead and he follows without complaint. He should stop smoking, he thinks, while he's still young enough to reverse the damage.

When the front door has closed behind them, and Liv has kicked off her shoes, Seb heads for the stairs, hoping against hope that he can slip away unnoticed.

'Oh no you don't,' she says, her hands on her hips. 'Kitchen, now.'

He follows her into the kitchen, sliding into a chair as she fills the kettle and flicks it on. Her solution for everything: a cup of tea. But that won't solve this situation. Seb stares at the wall beside him, the paint faded to a pale yellow that reminds him of the time he vomited after eating the gelatinous mashed potato from the school canteen. *I could paint it*, he thinks. *Make it look nicer for her.* But when Liv turns to him, two steaming mugs of tea in her hands, he knows it will take a lot more than a bit of paint to get out of this one.

'Nan,' he says, but she holds up a hand and he falls silent.

'I know you,' she says, sitting down opposite him. 'I know what kind of boy you are. What kind of person you are. You have always been so kind to Izzy, and she's a lovely girl.' She lifts her mug, takes a sip. 'Tell me what happened.'

'I honestly don't know,' Seb says, relief flooding through him.

27

'I got sent a photo on Snapchat that Izzy seemed to have taken herself. She was... half-naked, in her room.'

'She took it herself?' Liv asks, bewildered. 'But why?' Seb shrugs. He has no idea either. 'Who did she send it to?'

'I don't know. She's not answering my messages. All I know is that it got sent to me, and I didn't share it, I swear.' He looks down, the reality of the situation hitting him again. 'Am I going to be in trouble?' he asks, and his nan reaches out, taking his hand in hers.

'No,' she says firmly. 'You didn't do anything. It'll be fine.'

He nods, tries to believe her, but he can't stop the anxiety building inside him, or the frustration. Why did Izzy take that picture? Who did she send it to? Why isn't she answering him?

Liv squeezes his hand. 'It's not your fault,' she says, pinning him with her gaze. 'But you need to show me the photo.' Seb opens his mouth to argue, but Liv speaks first. 'I need to see what we're dealing with here. I need to know all the facts. The police are involved, love. This is serious.'

Seb nods again, reaching into his pocket and pulling out his phone. 'It's just a group chat,' he says, opening the app. 'We mostly share memes,' he says, and her brow creases. 'Funny pictures, you know.' He feels his cheeks heat up. 'Not... *that*. It's not for *that*.'

'Who sent the photo to the group?'

'Ben, from the year below. He said he got it from someone else.'

She sighs, wrapping her hands around her mug while Seb stares down at the table between them. 'I know being a teenager is hard, love, but this kind of thing... You just can't be getting involved with it.'

'I'm not,' Seb protests. 'I mean, I'm just in the group, that's all. I'd never do that, not to Izzy.'

'And you didn't send it on?'

'No,' he says, meeting her gaze. 'No, I didn't. I wouldn't.' He suddenly remembers being five or six, running around Izzy's garden with water pistols. He remembers a birthday party when he was sick after eating a wedge of cake. He remembers her small pale hand in his and not noticing, not caring about their differences. He remembers the way she would look at him, all the words they could not say out loud passing between them in that one look, one brow slightly arched, her lips twitching with the ghost of a smile.

Liv holds out her hand and Seb passes her his phone. He knows she is young to be a grandmother, is barely older than some of his friend's mums, but she has always had a certain amount of fear when it comes to technology. She didn't even have Facebook until last year.

She starts scrolling through the messages, her lips pursed as she reads. Seb suddenly feels uncomfortable, knowing that she will see the memes he's sent to his friends, the side of his sense of humour he wouldn't usually share with her.

'I'm gonna get on with my homework,' he says, standing up, then stops. 'Nan.' Liv looks up, the phone in her hand. 'You know I wouldn't do anything to hurt Izzy, don't you?'

She nods. 'Of course I do, love.'

He turns then, half-runs up the stairs, desperate to hide away in his bedroom. He collapses onto his bed, his hands over his eyes as he replays the day in his mind. Izzy hadn't met him before school like she usually did, and he hasn't heard from her since last week. It was during afternoon registration that the secretary had come to get him, after whispering to his form tutor for several minutes. He waited outside the science block while she went to other forms, and was surprised to see so many boys trailing after her. Josh gave him a look, and Seb went cold. He knew, suddenly, that it was about the photo. He thought about it still sitting on his phone and mentally kicked himself. Why hadn't he deleted it?

The secretary led them to the main hall, where Mr Loach and a uniformed police officer were waiting, a plastic cup of water in his hand. Chairs were set out in front of the stage, where the boys were directed to sit. There were six of them in total, four from Seb's year, and two from the year below.

'Right, chaps,' Mr Loach said, his face grim. 'We need to have a little chat.'

8

CAITLYN

In the end, it is Alicia who gets to the bottom of it.

I call my eldest daughter on my way home that night, so close to tears from fear and exhaustion, that it only takes her chirpy 'Hi, Mum' to make my eyes spill over. I tell her everything, minus the gory details, and she listens in shocked silence. I picture Alicia's mouth open as she digests my words, her hand at her throat, the topaz ring we got her for Christmas last year glistening on her index finger.

'Oh, Mum,' she says, and I have to choke back a sob at the tenderness in her voice. 'You haven't seen it, have you?'

'Seen what? The photo?' I feel my chest tighten. 'Have you? Alicia, how have you seen it?'

Alicia takes a deep breath. 'I'm coming home.'

'No,' I say quickly, brushing the tears away as I drive on autopilot. 'No, you can't. You have lectures, assignments.'

'And a sister who needs me,' she says softly, and I start crying so hard I have to pull over.

She turns up that night, an overnight bag slung over her shoulder, her battered Corsa parked at an angle behind my car on the driveway. Her key is barely in the lock before I rip the door open, throwing my arms around her neck and crying into her hair. Suddenly, she is the mother and I the child, the one who needs comfort and reassurance, and for all her adventurous ways, my eldest daughter has always been my rock. She always knows the right thing to do.

She leads me into the open-plan kitchen, switching on the under-cupboard lights with an 'Alexa, turn on the stars'. The smart lights were a gift last year, and Alicia and Isabelle delighted in giving them all bizarre names. Alicia's bedroom is 'the disco', while Isabelle's is 'the cave', and the decorative bulbs hanging over the dining table are named 'the great hall'.

'Why can't we give them proper names?' Michael complained while the girls told Alexa to turn the lights different colours.

'Because that would be *boring*,' Alicia said, turning round and sticking out her tongue.

'God forbid, not *boring*,' Michael said, rolling his eyes. 'A fate worse than death.' But a smile was playing around his lips. He is good with them, has always been kind and warm towards them since we got together, but lately I have sensed a pulling back, a distance growing between my partner and my daughters. Is it because of Izzy? I know Michael struggles to understand her, is of the 'sticks and stones' persuasion, but he still cares about her, doesn't he?

Alicia helps me onto a stool at the island and makes her way over to the kettle. She makes a face when she opens the fridge door, and I realise we don't have any of the oat milk she prefers. She catches me looking and smiles. 'Never mind,' she says, 'I've grown used to drinking black tea. Milk is the number-one thing that goes missing in student flats.'

She busies herself making the tea, pulling out a plate and arranging chocolate digestives that neither of us will touch. I sit slumped against the counter, my head in my hands, only lifting my gaze when I feel her hand touch my wrist. In her other hand is her phone.

'I don't want to show you this,' she says quietly, 'but you need to know what's going on.' She unlocks the phone and places it down on the counter before me, tapping the screen to bring up a picture. It is dark, but my eyes quickly adjust and I feel a sense of horror wash over me as I realise what I am looking at.

'Isabelle?' I whisper, my hand fluttering over the screen as if it would scald if touched. I notice the way her body is positioned, awkward almost, one leg forward, toes pointed like she is practising ballet. Her hair is down, dark curls cascading over her shoulder like a waterfall, and her face is half-hidden by her phone. But it is my daughter, breasts and stomach bared, vulnerable.

'She took this herself?' I ask, but it isn't really a question. I recognise her bedroom behind her, the bedroom she has slept in since she was a child, the dusky pink walls now fading and covered in posters. 'Why? Who did she send it to?'

Alicia shrugs. 'That's what we need to find out.'

'Was it a dare? A game?' A memory comes back to me, an article I read online about teenagers hurting themselves on social media as part of a game, and I tell Alicia about it.

'I don't know, Mum. I don't think Izzy would do something like that.' She frowns. 'But maybe someone forced her to take it. What about her boyfriend?'

'Seb?' I shake my head. 'I don't think so. He's not like that.' Without looking at her, I know she is rolling her eyes, but she doesn't say anything. 'What am I going to do, Alicia?' I moan, feeling my eyes burn with tears again as she puts her phone away and grips my hands in hers. 'How can I help her? She won't talk to me. She won't talk to anyone.'

'She'll talk to me,' Alicia says, her eyes wet with tears. 'Leave it with me, Mum.'

9

LIV

I call into work first thing, and after waiting almost five minutes for Sean to get to the phone, I tell him that I won't be in today.

'It's a family emergency,' I say, remembering with a jolt the last time I used that phrase, though Sean had still been in nappies back then. Well, not quite.

Sean sighs. 'All right, Olivia,' he says, drawing out my name, even though he knows everyone calls me Liv. It's even written on my name badge. 'I'll get Tina to cover you.'

'Twat,' I mutter as I hang up.

I go upstairs and tap on Seb's door, and I'm surprised to see he's awake, sitting against the headboard with his old, clunky laptop on his knees.

'Morning, love,' I say, going in to sit on the end of his bed. 'How are you?'

I take him in, this kind, honest, beautiful boy who I loved as soon as Paige placed him in my arms. 'Hello, Nan,' she whispered to me, and I felt something shift inside me, my heart growing bigger to make room for this new addition. My grandson, with his lopsided grin and deep-brown eyes that have always twinkled with mischief. His unmistakable teenage-boy smell which is hidden beneath a haze of Lynx or whatever they use these days. The row of size-ten shoes in the hallway, neatly lined up on the row above my size fours. The cartoon boxers I bought him for Christmas one year which he still wears. The detritus I find in every pocket; old chewing-gum wrappers and tangled earphones and suspicious-looking tissues. The thought that he could be taken away from me takes my breath away, and I feel my eyes burn with unshed tears. The tears I have been holding back since I was called into his school yesterday.

'What's up, Nan?' he asks. He looks worried and withdrawn.

I try to smile. 'Nothing, love. Just thinking.'

'Don't strain yourself,' he jokes, and I tut before smiling for real this time. His face turns serious again. 'What's going to happen now?'

The smile falls from my face. I think of the messages I read last night, hundreds of them, the 'banter' between the boys that made me cringe, the memes I didn't understand, until I got to the photo of Izzy. That poor girl. My heart aches when I think of what she's going through, how upsetting the whole thing must have been for her. How desperate she must have felt, to try to take her own life.

And now the police are involved. Will they need to speak to Seb? Will he be arrested? I have a sudden vision of him in handcuffs, looking tiny in the back seat of a police car, and I shudder. No, I think decisively. That won't happen. As awful as the whole thing is, Seb didn't do anything wrong. He can't control what others send him.

'Have you heard from Izzy yet?' I ask. He shakes his head. 'Maybe we should go round there, see how she's doing.' I reach out and pat his knee. 'Don't worry,' I say, trying to sound confident. 'It'll all come out in the wash, you mark my words.'

~

I leave the house at eleven o'clock, telling Seb to heat up a tin of tomato soup for lunch. 'There's gluten-free bread in the freezer,' I call, swinging my bag over my shoulder and pulling on my shoes. I hear a grunt that could constitute a response, and try to push away the anxiety that's needling at me. He'll be okay. He'll speak to Izzy and everything will be fine.

With a glance at the darkening sky, I unlock the car and slide behind the wheel, my nerves jangling as they always do when I'm about to drive. I've never been confident on the road, probably due to having learned to drive later in life. I inhale deeply and turn on the engine, easing carefully out of the space and onto the road that will take me to my mother's house.

This is the house I grew up in, which my paternal grandfather bought for my parents when they married. The house my mother and I continued to live in after my dad left. Now she rattles around in the four-bedroom, semi-detached house, alone but for the ghosts. It has high ceilings and large windows, and a long, wild garden which I used to spend hours in as a child, searching for fairies amongst the brambles. Even in the depths of winter, it was preferable to being inside the house, which was often no warmer as Mum hadn't paid the gas bill. These days she gets help with such things, because forgetting to pay the bills carries less judgement if you have dementia instead of just being drunk.

I park behind her rusted BMW that hasn't been moved in two years, and get out just as the first raindrops begin to fall. Fishing for the house key in my bag, I hurry up the steps and duck under the cover of the porch.

'Hiya, Mum,' I call, shutting the door behind me with a firm shove. The latch is temperamental, and several times I've come over to find the door wide open, Mum none the wiser.

'Why don't you downsize?' I asked her once when I was cooking her lunch. Something simple, scrambled eggs or chicken soup or, if she was feeling really adventurous, ham, egg and chips. 'This place is much too big for you.'

'This is the only thing your father ever gave me,' she said, lighting a cigarette and blowing the smoke into the air, forgetting or ignoring the fact that I, too, was something he gave her. 'It'll be yours one day. Don't wish away your inheritance.' But although my mother is sixty-eight and has dementia, I suspect she'll stick around for many years to come. My mum has always been... difficult. I suppose these days you would call her a hoarder, rooms full of junk she will never use, doors kept closed for years, the dust and spiders taking over. I drop my bag on the bottom step, the only one without something sitting on it and call out to her again.

'I'm in here!' Her voice comes from the back of the house. I follow it, poking my head around the kitchen door and sighing when I see the mess. She looks up as I enter. 'This sodding machine,' she says, waving her hands at the dishwasher. 'Three times I've put my whites through, and they're still filthy.'

'Let's have a look,' I say, opening the door and seeing that, yes, my mother has been trying to wash her clothes in the dishwasher instead of the washing machine. 'Leave that to me, Mum. You know I'll do it.'

She tuts. 'I'm quite capable, Olivia. I'm not an invalid.'

Only she – and Sean, the twat – calls me Olivia. When she remembers my name, that is. Last week I was Samantha.

'I know that, Mum,' I say, keeping my voice even. 'Why don't you put your feet up? I'll bring you a nice cup of tea.'

Putting her feet up has always been one of Mum's favourite pastimes, alongside drinking her way through three bottles of vodka in a night and telling me I'm a disappointment. Though she doesn't do the latter anymore; I don't buy her any alcohol when I do her weekly shop. She shuffles out of the room, muttering under her breath, while I load the soggy clothes into the correct machine and turn it on.

'Have you had breakfast?' I ask when I take her tea through to the sitting room. She has always insisted on calling it a sitting room, probably because she takes it at its word and does nothing but sit in there, her legs up on the pouffe that is older than I am, her hands clasped over her stomach. There isn't even a TV in here, just shelves of books and stacks of newspapers on the large coffee table, the legs groaning with the weight. I spot a box for a smoothie maker which I know she has never used, perched precariously on top of an open box with clothes hangers sticking out the top. I suppress a sigh and call her name when she doesn't answer.

She tuts again, and I add another line to my mental tally. So far her record has been seventeen tuts in one visit. 'Yes, thank you,' she replies curtly. 'I had a Jammy Dodger.'

I place her tea on the table beside her chair and perch on the edge of the sofa. 'What do you fancy for lunch today? I saw there's some fish fingers in the freezer.'

Mum shakes her head. 'Those are for Harold.'

I stare at her. This is a new one on me. 'Who's Harold?'

She tuts – three – and fixes me with a steely gaze. 'Harold!' she says, as if repeating his name will jog my memory. 'From the post office. He comes by on a Wednesday to help me.'

Harold from the post office. I've never heard of him. 'What does he help you with?'

'Oh, this and that. Last week he pulled up all the weeds in the front garden. Doesn't it look nice out there now?'

I nod automatically, though I hadn't noticed any difference to the small patch of grass out the front. 'You're not cooking for him, are you? You know that's what I'm here for, Mum.'

'You can't be here every second of the day, Olivia,' she snaps.

'I am allowed my own life.' I open my mouth to respond, but she continues. 'He cooks them himself, if you must know. Always makes me a fish-finger butty.'

I'm beginning to suspect that Harold is in fact a figment of Mum's imagination, but I change the subject. My head is too full for her dramatics right now. 'I was destined for the stage, Liv,' my mother would say when I was younger, with a faraway look in her eye. And when she'd look back at me, the only thing I saw there was yet more disappointment.

'How's that boy of yours?' she asks now, surprising me. She doesn't often remember Seb's existence.

'Oh, he's all right,' I lie. 'Studying hard for his exams.'

'And Paige? Is she still working at that cinema?'

I freeze. I know people with dementia often forget deaths, but this is the first time Mum has forgotten that her granddaughter is no longer alive. That her boyfriend, the father of her child, beat her to death eleven years ago.

'Yeah,' I say, swallowing the lump in my throat. 'Yeah, she is.'

10

CAITLYN

I'm back at the hospital by eight o'clock the next morning, Alicia in the car beside me. She squeezes my hand as I park up.

'It'll be all right, Mum,' she says. 'One step at a time.'

I count the steps from the car park to the front entrance – thirty-eight – and then again to the lift – fourteen – focusing on placing one foot in front of the other, and not on the daughter lying in a hospital bed, her wrists bandaged, her throat and stomach sore. Alicia gives me a small smile as we approach Isabelle's cubicle, a smile that says *relax, your anxiety is contagious,* and I pull the mask over my face, smiling broadly at the figure in the bed.

'Morning,' I say, bending down to kiss Isabelle's forehead. It is slightly clammy; is she too hot? Are they taking care of her in here? I take a deep breath and say, 'Look who I've brought.'

Alicia steps up beside me, perching on the edge of the bed and grinning at her sister. 'Anything to get me away from my mock exam,' she says, winking.

I sit down on the chair, exhaustion suddenly sweeping through me. Alicia and I had stayed up late the night before, moving from tea to wine, drifting from the kitchen to the living room, Alicia sitting on the chair behind me, braiding my hair as we talked about everything except the photo. Alicia and I talk most days, texts flying between us with *have you eaten enough greens?* and *can you lend me twenty quid?*, but I have missed having my eldest daughter around. My two girls are like night and day. Isabelle has always been serious and quiet, slipping silently up the stairs and into her room, the door shut tight, music playing until she goes to bed, or until she falls asleep and I turn it off, tiptoeing into her room and watching her for a moment, marvelling at how it feels as if she was a toddler only yesterday. You can sometimes forget Isabelle is there, but you know whenever Alicia is home. Her shoes are kicked off in the hallway, her jacket and bag thrown onto the bottom step. She sings along to her music or listens to podcasts about the history of abortion or racism in the United States while she cooks, pans crashing, drawers slamming. She leaves huge piles of washing-up in the sink, which Michael frowns at but doesn't think to clean himself. She stretches out on the sofa, munching on Haribo or Maltesers, packets discarded on the floor, and then she is gone as quickly as she arrived, with a peck on the cheek and a waft of strawberry conditioner. She is a whirlwind, my daughter.

Is it my imagination, or does Isabelle look brighter today? There's something in her eyes that wasn't there before. Is she happy to have her sister with her? Though they are four years apart in age, Isabelle has always been wiser than her years. 'You should've been the older sister,' Alicia likes to say, nudging her, and it's true. Isabelle is sensible, steady. When she isn't hurting herself, that is.

'How are you today?' I ask gently, and try not to notice the flicker of annoyance crossing Isabelle's face as she turns to me. As if I am unwelcome here. As if I am at fault. 'Are you feeling any better?' I consider the term. Better than what, exactly? Better than on the brink of suicide? It's not as if this can be marked by any reliable timepoints, not like a broken leg or a cold. *I can put weight on the leg now* would be better. *I didn't wake up with a stuffy nose* would be better. How do you measure *better* when it comes to mental health? *I didn't try to kill myself today.*

I shake myself, realising that Isabelle is no longer looking at me but at Alicia, who is babbling on about the cake she will make when Isabelle comes home.

'I'm thinking chocolate. What do you think, Siz?' Her pet name for her sister. Siz for Isabelle, Sis for Alicia. 'Ooh! Or coffee and walnut?'

Isabelle smiles then, a ghost of a smile that I latch onto, clinging to it like a drowning woman clings to a piece of driftwood. *She's smiling, so she must be okay. Everything is going to be okay.* But I know there is so much more to this. So much I am in the dark about.

The curtain behind us opens to reveal a nurse, plump in her bright-blue uniform and smiling widely. 'Morning, duck,' she says to Isabelle in a thick northern accent. Yorkshire maybe? 'Are you ready to go home?'

'Home?' I repeat, feeling my eyes widen. 'But she's... I mean, there's not–'

'Isabelle is feeling better today,' the nurse says, smiling at me in a way that makes me feel like a small child throwing a tantrum because another kid has stolen my toy. 'She's ready to go home.' She hands me a sheaf of leaflets I hadn't noticed she was holding. 'These are to take with you.'

I glance down at them, my mind struggling to process the words. *Anxiety & Panic Attacks. Sleep Problems & How to Manage Them. Self-Harm.* My brain stutters over the last one. Self-harm. Is that what my daughter has been doing?

I look back at the nurse, but she is already retreating. Is that it? I want to shout. A few bits of paper and a pat on the shoulder? *Off you go, duck, try not to do it again. We're short of beds in here.*

I try to compose myself as I turn back to face my daughters. Alicia is silent for once, and I can tell her own thoughts are echoing mine. Isabelle's eyes look tired, as if she has been awake for several days in a row, and I suddenly feel as if I am far, far out of my depth.

11

SEB

Josh: Can u believe this??

Ben: My dad went mental when he found out I sent it to the group

Liam: I know. It's proper mad

Lew: I didn't even see it before I got dragged out of form! It was hot though, am I right?

Josh: 😩

Liam: Don't be gross, dude

Lew: What?? What did I say?

Seb turns his phone to do not disturb before throwing it down on the bed beside him. He hasn't been into the main group chat since he gave his phone to his nan, but his friends have created a separate one and spend most of their time complaining about how unfair it all is. *We didn't take the photo.*

44

We didn't share it. Why are we being blamed? And Seb agrees, feels frustrated that he has been suspended from school and is waiting for the police to knock at the door, but he cannot rid his mind of Izzy and how she must be feeling. Where is she? Why hasn't she been replying to his messages? The thoughts whirl around and around in his head. Why? Who? The frustration that she will not speak to him. His messages are becoming more and more frantic, and yet they remain unread, not received. He is shouting into a void.

It isn't until he checks Snapchat that he discovers what has happened. Abby has put up a story, a filter turning her face into a cat, her voice high-pitched. 'Wondering where Frizzy Izzy has been lately?' she says into the camera, before glancing over her shoulder as if checking for eavesdroppers. 'Rumour has it she's in hospital. Tried to top herself.' She taps the side of her head, widening her eyes. 'Mental.'

Seb feels as if a bucket of cold water has been thrown over him. Izzy is in hospital? Izzy has tried to kill herself? His arm falls down on the bed, his phone thumping to the floor. He does not retrieve it. He cannot move. He is frozen, stupefied by shock. No. It can't be true. And yet somehow, he knows that it is. Because Izzy has done this before.

He remembers hearing about the last time, just before the summer holidays last year. The rumours flew around the school – Izzy has cut herself, Izzy has taken some pills, Izzy, Izzy, Izzy – and he saw her in town a few days later, long sleeves covering her hands, her eyes sunken and red-rimmed. They went to the park, takeaway coffee cups on the bench between them, Izzy's eyes on the water as it flowed slowly past. Seb understands not feeling comfortable in your own skin, and so they talked, or rather, he talked and she listened, their childhood friendship opening up again like a flower in sunlight.

Seb closes his eyes, feeling anxiety wash over him again. He knows that however he is feeling, Izzy will be feeling even worse. He suddenly feels desperate to speak to his dad. He scrolls through his apps until he finds the Prison Voicemail app, his thumb hovering over it for a second before tapping it. He sees a new voicemail from his dad, sent the day before, and clicks on it.

'Hi son, it's your dad.' Brad's voice is loud and comforting through the speaker, and Seb instantly feels a little better. 'Hope you're studying hard and being good for your nan. Did you get the mark back for that coursework yet? I read that book you told me about, *Of Mice and Men*. It's good, innit?' Seb smiles at this. Only his dad could describe a book like that in so few words. 'I've been seeing the priest more lately. He keeps telling me he's not called that, and he's not got the collar and everything, but he's the priest to me. Anyway, we've started doing what he calls 'group therapy', and it's actually quite good. It's just me and three other lads so far. One of them's got a tattoo of an upside-down cross on his leg, which he tries to hide when we're with the priest.' He laughs, and it's like honey in Seb's ears, like hearing music for the first time. 'Anyway, how are you, son? How's school? Have you got a girlfriend yet? Hope you're getting on all right and not giving your nan any gip. Shout me back when you're free. Love you.'

Seb replays the message again, one hand pressed against his chest as he feels his heart begin to slow. His dad's voice is soothing, the north London accent both familiar and foreign to his ears. He has sketchy memories of his dad, none of which are wholly reliable, but his other nan, Evelyn, always shows him photos when he visits her, getting out the huge albums and laying them out on the table, a sad smile on her face. She misses him, Seb knows, is proud of how Brad has turned his life around in prison, but she is also ashamed of him, and of what he did. Would she be ashamed of Seb too? Would his dad?

He takes a deep breath, clears his throat, and records his

response. 'Hi, Dad. Yeah, yeah, everything's fine. I got a C for that one, but I reckon it deserved a B, not gonna lie. What's the priest like? Does he wear brown cardigans and have a moustache? That's how I picture him. Have you been christened yet? Will they have to dunk you in the bath? Or just chuck a bucket of water over you? I wish I could see it.' He laughs, picturing it, allowing his rambling to distract him from everything else. 'Nanny Evelyn says hi. She still can't work this voice-note thing out, she says, but I'll try to set it up for her when I next see her. Auntie Rosa is pregnant again, did she tell you? Four kids, that's mad. I don't reckon I want any – and I know what you're gonna say. "Not yet, my boy, get your education behind you first."' He deepens his voice, mimicking his father. 'So no worries there. And don't ask me about girlfriends, Dad. I've got nothing to tell you.'

I don't know why I do it, but something possesses me to buy two bouquets of flowers instead of one. I'm going to Paige's grave today, as I do once a week, and I use my measly ten per cent staff discount to buy her fresh flowers from the petrol station. But here I am, walking in the opposite direction to the graveyard, two bunches of flowers in my hand.

As I approach Izzy's house, I remember arriving here for a birthday party when Seb was small. There were balloons and a bouncy castle and even a magician. Seb and Izzy were part of the small group of children who moved up to the same secondary school together, while others went to neighbouring towns and some even to the private school a few miles away. They were good friends back then, I remember, though they drifted a bit as time went on. I'm glad they found each other again. It was always those two on the periphery, talking and playing quietly, though Seb was a popular child, well-liked. I can still see Seb taking Izzy's hand and bringing her closer to the other children, passing her a ball or a paintbrush, encouraging her to join in. Is he still doing that? Did he lead her into danger this time?

This street is very nice, full of large, detached houses with long driveways and porches and clean windows glistening in the sun. I stand at the edge of the driveway, the bunch of flowers suddenly looking cheap and wilted next to the vibrant rosebush in the front garden. I'll just leave it on the doorstep, I decide, marching up the drive and putting the bouquet down before turning and walking quickly away. A noise behind me makes me look back to find a woman in the doorway, an empty milk bottle in her hand. She has short, straight hair that looks like it's been professionally styled, but her skin is pale with purple marks beneath her eyes. Izzy's mum.

'Oh,' Caitlyn says, finding me standing like a lemon on her property. 'Hello?'

I curse inwardly. 'I, uh, I just brought some flowers.' I gesture at the bouquet on the step beneath her. 'For Izzy. I was so sorry to hear that, you know...' I trail off, awkward.

The woman frowns slightly. 'Thank you. And you are?'

I swallow. 'Olivia. Liv. I'm–'

'Seb's nan,' she says, recognition dawning. 'Hi. I haven't seen you since...' She thinks for a moment. 'Isabelle's seventh birthday. He threw up after the cake.'

I'm surprised she remembers. 'That's right. He has coeliac disease, though we didn't know it at the time. Gluten,' I add when her face clouds over. 'He can't eat gluten.'

'Yes, I remember now. He told me a few weeks ago, when he was here for dinner.' I nod, remembering Seb worrying about being able to eat safely at her house. I wonder suddenly why I haven't reached out to Caitlyn before now. Seb and Izzy have been together for a few months, should I have made contact with Izzy's mother? Should we have communicated, gotten to know each other better over coffee? It had never crossed my mind to get involved in Seb's relationship, but now I wonder if I should have.

'He kept apologising,' Caitlyn says, tilting her head as if remembering. 'As if he can help it. And he brought dessert. Gluten-free profiteroles. They were delicious.'

'That sounds like Seb,' I say, lifting the second bouquet and turning to go. 'Anyway, I must–'

'How is he? Seb?'

'Fine, he's fine. I'd really better be off, I'm–'

'Has he said anything? About the photo?' Her question stops me in my tracks.

I turn back slowly, my mind racing. I shake my head. 'He doesn't know anything about it.'

'But she must have taken it for him.' It isn't a question. Caitlyn takes a step towards me, her eyes hardening.

I feel a flush of indignation. 'She didn't. He would never... He had nothing to do with it, honestly. It's awful, and I'm sorry, but–'

'Why would you be sorry?' she demands. 'If Seb had nothing to do with it?' I can see the mother rising up in her, a lioness roaring to protect her young.

'I've really got to go,' I say, panic washing over me. This was a stupid idea, coming here. What was I thinking? 'I'm expected. Give Izzy my best!' And I walk away, almost jogging until I reach the end of the street and turn the corner, out of view, before I slow down.

'You, Liv, are an idiot,' I mutter to myself as I walk towards the church and Paige's grave. I wonder if I've made things worse now. *Shit. What have I done?*

The flowers on Paige's grave are brown and wilted, the plastic wrapping covered in water. I throw the old ones into the bin and rest the new bouquet gently against the gravestone. 'Hello, love,' I whisper, crouching and ignoring the ache in my back. I'm getting too old, I think, then remember that my daughter will never get any older. No matter how much time passes, this realisation never gets any easier. As I've watched her son grow, from small, cheeky toddler to bigger, even cheekier teenager, I'm often hit with the realisation that she isn't here to see it. I don't believe in the afterlife, can't bring myself to believe in any god who would have stolen my daughter from me in such a horrific way, but a tiny part of me still hopes she's looking down from somewhere, watching her son make his way through the world.

'You'd be so proud of him,' I say, brushing some dirt from the headstone. 'He's working so hard for his exams. He'll be off to university before we know it, perhaps even to Cambridge. Wouldn't that be something?' I smile to myself. Seb will be the first person in our family to make it to university. I'd always wanted that for Paige, had looked forward to seeing her settled in her student halls, coming back for the long summer and Christmas breaks full of stories and new things she'd learned. Still, she'd managed to sit her A-levels before she gave birth, so she achieved more than I did.

'Things aren't all a bed of roses, mind,' I say, unable to stop myself. I realise that I haven't spoken to anyone about the situation with Izzy, or my fears about what will happen to Seb. Who could I talk to about it? 'I'm a bit out of my depth to be honest. Nothing compared to what that poor girl is going through, though, I suppose.' I see Izzy's mother again, the raw desperation in her face as she realised who I was, what she thought I could give her. 'I do hope she pulls through all right. Teenage years can be so difficult, but things get better as you get older. More life experience, I suppose.'

I remember Paige as a teenager, fourteen or fifteen, slamming her bedroom door when I said she couldn't go out unless she tidied her bedroom. 'You could be a right little madam,' I say, smiling. 'Your tantrums as a teenager far outweighed your tantrums as a toddler. Seb is an angel in comparison.' And he is, an angel. He's helpful, kind, thoughtful. He works hard at school, rarely gives me any lip, always pulls his weight around the house. He went through a phase of 'keeping up with the Joneses', as I called it, always wanting the latest gadgets and trainers, but the thing with Seb is that he will listen when you take the time to explain things to him. One day I sat him down and wrote out our finances, showing how our outgoings compared with my piddly earnings at the petrol station and the child benefit I receive for him.

'So you see, love,' I said gently, as he did the calculations in his head, 'there just isn't enough money left over for new trainers this month.' He'd nodded, his face serious as understanding dawned.

'I'll help,' he said, brightening suddenly. And he did. He spent that summer, and every summer since, washing cars, feeding the neighbour's cats and one particularly vicious hamster, mowing lawns, painting fence panels. He made himself little posters and dropped them through letterboxes, and I put one up in the petrol station, ignoring Sean's frown of disapproval. He made enough money that first summer to buy himself the trainers he wanted and then some, but, instead, he dropped it into an old jar and handed it to me.

'For you, Nan,' he said, smiling sheepishly, 'for looking after me. I did the sums, and by my calculation you've spent hundreds on me over the years. I reckon I should start contributing.'

My eyes glisten with tears as I remember his face as I hugged him, taking the money out of the jar and counting out the money for his trainers. 'I'll keep the rest for you,' I said, placing it on a shelf in the kitchen. 'For university. It'll be your takeaway fund. For when it's your round at the student union.'

I've been adding to it ever since, a few pounds here and there. Seb knows where it is, but as far as I'm aware he's never taken from it, not even when his friends got brand-new phones and headphones and god knows whatever else. I've managed to take on more shifts at the petrol station as he's got older and can be left to fend for himself a bit more, and though money is tight, it's no longer a struggle. No, money is the least of my worries now, what with my cantankerous mother and the police investigation looming over us.

'Oh, Paige,' I say, sighing. 'What am I going to do?'

13

CAITLYN

S he is home.

    I hold on to Isabelle's arm as Alicia unlocks the front door and helps her inside, but it is me who needs support really. Me who is struggling to put one foot in front of the other. Six steps from the car, up two steps, then we are inside, the door closed behind us, shutting the world out.

Isabelle heads straight for the stairs, and I open my mouth to call out, to tell her no, she cannot go upstairs, I want her where I can see her, but Alicia silences me with a look. She follows her sister up the stairs while I make hot chocolate, squirting cream on top and digging out a packet of marshmallows that have seen better days. I glance at the flowers Seb's grandmother left, still in their plastic wrapping, the petals squashed against the side of the sink, and feel a flash of regret for having a go at her. It isn't her fault. I must dig out a vase for the flowers, maybe take them up to Isabelle. It will do her good to know people are thinking of her.

I carry the mugs up, knocking on Isabelle's door with my foot and pushing it open. 'Here we are,' I say brightly, crossing the room and setting the mugs down on the desk. Her laptop is closed, and I'm suddenly seized by the desire to grab it, to take it downstairs and comb through every file, every photo, every message, to see who has been harassing her. Why didn't it occur to me while Isabelle was in hospital? I realise just how useless I have been, how utterly I am failing as a mother.

'Thanks, Mum,' Alicia says from her place on the floor, her back against the bed. Isabelle is sitting cross-legged on top of the bed, the duvet bunched around her like a fort. 'We're going to watch some films.' This is code for *leave us alone*. But I hover in the doorway, words bubbling up inside me, clogging my throat, fighting to get out. I stare at Isabelle, but she is looking down at her lap, fingers playing with a loose thread on one of her bandages.

'All right,' I say finally, shoving the words down. 'I'll go and make something for lunch.'

I stand in the middle of the kitchen, the floor cold beneath my socked feet, my mind buzzing. My eyes settle on the leaflets we brought home from the hospital, and I am suddenly soaked in rage. It flares through me, flames lighting up my skin as I march over to the island and grab them, screwing them up and throwing them across the room with a silent scream. Is this it? Is this all the help Isabelle is going to get?

I dig my phone out of my back pocket and find the number for the therapist we used to see. I remember dragging Isabelle to the first appointment, a few weeks after her first suicide attempt last year. She sat there mute the entire time, letting me fill the fifty minutes with inane chatter, my hands trembling in my lap. After a while, she started going on her own, and she seemed to be making progress. Evenings and weekends were calmer, with fewer arguments and markedly less tension. We even went out a few times, for coffee or to the cinema or for lunch in Isabelle's favourite Italian restaurant, Alicia driving back from Cambridge to join us. And now it has happened again.

I close my eyes, rubbing at them with the heels of my hands. How did we get here? What must have been going through Isabelle's mind to make her take that photo? And now what? A police investigation, the whole school knowing what has happened. So many eyes on my daughter's body, seeing her at her most vulnerable.

I had no intention of involving the police, but by the time I thought to inform the school of Isabelle's absence on Monday, they had already known about the photo.

'The police have been informed,' the headteacher told me. 'A student reported the image to her form tutor. Since it involved a minor, our hands were tied.' He cleared his throat. 'We were not aware of Isabelle's, uh, actions, of course. We wish her the best.'

Actions. Incident. Attention. Such everyday words, so simple, yet so foreign. How I long for words from the before time. Breakfast in bed. Long weekends. *Have you brought an umbrella?* and *What do you want to watch?* and *Have you done your homework?* October evenings on the sofa wrapped in blankets, pizza eaten straight from the box, ice-cream tubs with two spoons. And even further back, the girls dressed in yellow wellies and blue raincoats, their hair in pigtails, jeans splashed in mud. Paint all over the dining table, sticky handprints on the windows, an empty biscuit wrapper lying on the floor. The days when it was just me and the girls, after their father, Anthony, left and before Michael came. The sleepless nights worrying about money, the mad dash in the mornings to get them to school and arrive at the office by nine o'clock. The after-school clubs, the missed nativity plays and unironed school uniforms. I was always tired, my limbs aching, weighed down by an extreme fatigue that I know now was due to fibromyalgia, the chronic illness I have had to learn to live with.

And then, a couple of years after Anthony left, my parents died, suddenly, one after the other, leaving behind enough money to pay off the rest of the mortgage and finish the extension we'd started, and I could work part-time instead. My parents had moved to Australia when I was twenty and had only been back to visit a handful of times in the years since, making do with photos of their grandchildren and the occasional, often stilted phone call. We were not close, had very little in common, and I'd escaped my childhood as soon as I could, moving away for university and sending the odd letter back, returning only for a few days at Christmas.

I wonder if it is my fault Isabelle has found herself on this dark path. With no grandparents, an absent father, no cousins or aunts or family friends. A mother who couldn't get out of bed some days. Our life has become so insular, just us three until Michael appeared, when things started to get brighter, my illness carefully controlled by medication. And then Alicia left for university. Was that the catalyst? Losing her sister? I think back, trying to remember if Isabelle has ever talked about missing Alicia, beyond what would be expected, but my mind is blank, the events of the past few days too heavy, too overwhelming.

I stare at my phone, thumb hovering over the therapist's number when it rings. *Private number* flashes up on the screen.

'Hello?'

'Hello, Mrs Bennett?'

I swallow, knowing that this could only be about one thing. 'Speaking.'

'Hi, it's PC Willis here from Hertfordshire Constabulary. Is now a good time to talk?'

14

IZZY

She doesn't sleep.

She lies awake long after Alicia falls asleep, one arm flung across her face. She relishes the feeling of someone in bed beside her, the warmth of her sister's body, her slow, steady breaths. She has felt so alone recently, cast adrift in the middle of a storm, her life raft shrinking bit by bit.

Alicia will be gone tomorrow, back to Cambridge and lectures and nights out. She will be back, Izzy knows, at some point in the coming months, but there is rarely a plan when it comes to her sister. She will simply turn up one day, a grin on her face, a bottle of wine hidden in her bag or a huge bag of sweets, full of Izzy's favourites. And in the meantime they make do with voice notes and video calls and sharing memes on Facebook, and Izzy will pretend that it is enough.

She misses having friends, misses having more in her life than her mother and sister. She thinks back to last summer, before everything started to go wrong. A soft pillow beneath her head, blonde hair tangled up with hers, the taste of mint on her lips. A gasp, a giggle. And then she was cast out, cast in a role she wasn't sure how to play.

Izzy stares up at the ceiling, watching the headlights from cars on the road below cast shadows across the room. She hasn't spoken yet, not even to Alicia. She feels as if she may never speak again. If she doesn't talk about it, then it won't be real. If she doesn't mention the photo, and the utter humiliation she felt when she saw it had been shared around the school, she can pretend that none of it happened. But her wrists itch beneath the bandages, and her throat is still sore, and she knows that she cannot pretend for much longer. It is bubbling away inside her, toxic fumes almost enough to choke her.

She will tell Alicia tomorrow, she thinks. When they wake up in the soft morning light, limbs entwined, Alicia's hair and her strawberry shampoo tickling Izzy's nose. She will pretend they are children again, hiding beneath the duvet, the air full of whispered secrets and giggles. Nothing bad ever happened to that little girl, when Alicia still called her Siz and she believed in Father Christmas. Even when their dad left, walking out with one suitcase and without a backward glance at his two daughters, even when their mother fell into a deep depression, her illness taking over, Izzy still had her sister. She felt safe. Loved. Happy. Now she can't remember the last time she felt any of those things.

Alicia shifts in her sleep, rolling over onto her side. She has always been a fidgeter, flinging her arms and legs out, forcing Izzy to the very edge of the bed. But she doesn't mind. She is glad of the company, glad even of the elbow pressing into her side. It means she isn't alone.

'Tell me,' Alicia says the next morning, and Izzy does, just as she had promised herself last night. She opens her mouth and, for the first time in days, words tumble out, her voice quiet and unsteady. She tells her sister about a boy, because, of course, it is always a boy, who she thought liked her.

'Seb?' Alicia asks, her face screwed up.

Izzy shakes her head. Not Seb. Seb isn't that kind of boy, has never been like the rest of them. Staring, wanting, demanding. No, Seb had nothing to do with this. This was all Izzy, and her desperate need to be liked. Included. Validated.

Alicia is silent while she speaks, the story spilling out like it has been rehearsed. Because it has. Izzy spent those days in the hospital thinking about what she would tell people, the story that would be the most palatable. Stupid Izzy, making stupid decisions again. It is easy for everyone to believe.

'Have you spoken to Seb?' Alicia asks.

Izzy shakes her head again. She doesn't want to speak to him, doesn't want to see the pain and pity in his eyes.

Alicia sighs. 'You should. The police are involved now, Iz. This is serious.'

She feels her stomach tighten at the word *police*. She doesn't want them involved, wonders if it was her mother who called them. She realises that, in order to find out, she would have to talk about it, and nibbles at her lower lip, torn.

'Mum didn't call them,' Alicia says, as if reading her mind. 'It was the school. Someone reported the photo to a teacher apparently.'

Izzy stares at her sister, shock hitting her like a wave of cold water. Who would report something like that to a teacher? Or is that what you're supposed to do? Tell an adult. Tell someone you trust. Don't suffer in silence. *But it is my suffering*, she thinks, *my silence.*

'You need to speak to her. Mum. Tell her everything. She'll sort it all out.' Alicia places a hand on Izzy's knee, squeezes gently. 'We're here for you, both of us. Forever.' The front door slams, making them both jump. They hear Michael's voice in the hall and pull a face, forever in sync. 'Come on,' Alicia says, leaping out of bed. 'I'm gasping for a cuppa.' She holds out a hand and Izzy takes it, trying to absorb her sister's strength as she follows her downstairs.

'I just don't get it, Cait,' Michael is saying as the girls enter the kitchen. 'I thought it was all over. I–'

'Morning!' Her mother's voice is too loud, her smile too bright. Izzy cringes from it, tries to hide behind her sister, but they are almost the same height now and Alicia is slimmer, showing no signs of her poor student diet of cheesy chips and oven pizzas. 'How are we?' Caitlyn asks. 'Tea? Coffee? I can make some porridge if you like.'

'Tea!' Alicia says, heading for the kettle, leaving Izzy trying to blend into the wallpaper. It is a dark blue with a gold metallic coat, glistening in the morning sunlight flooding through the skylights. She makes her way to the island, sliding onto a stool and hiding her hands in her lap. She wishes she'd worn long sleeves.

'Nice flowers,' Alicia says, fingering a petal. 'Who are they from?'

'Seb,' Caitlyn says brightly. 'His nan dropped them off yesterday. Wasn't that nice of her?' The question is directed at Izzy, but she does not respond. 'Did you sleep okay, darling?' her mum asks when the silence stretches too long, sitting down beside her, a mug of coffee clasped between her fingers. Michael is leaning against the cooker, hiding behind the newspaper.

Izzy nods, swallows. 'Fine,' she says. She watches her mother's eyes light up, realising that this is the first word she has said to her since they were in the ambulance together, Izzy's brain hazy and scared, so very scared. She can't remember the things she said, has only a few memories between the razor slicing her skin and waking up in a hospital bed, the sheets beneath her white and scratchy. She clears her throat. 'Mum, I–'

'Izzy,' Caitlyn says at the same time, then stops, smiles. 'Sorry, you go.'

But the moment has passed. Izzy shakes her head, gratefully accepting the cup of tea from Alicia and sipping it, the liquid warming her throat.

Caitlyn takes a deep breath. 'There's some news, sweetheart. From the police.' She glances at Michael, who is watching them now, his expression carefully blank. 'They want to come over tomorrow, to speak to you. Would that be okay?'

Izzy feels panic begin to rise up inside her. 'T-tomorrow?' she stammers. 'But I don't... I can't...' Her chest begins to tighten, her breath coming in short gasps.

'It's okay, Iz,' Alicia says, putting an arm around her shoulders. 'We'll be here, won't we, Mum? It'll be okay.'

Izzy tries to absorb the words, tries, fails, to control her breathing. The world begins to spin around her and she leaps up, knocking Alicia's arm away and running, running, running.

15

LIV

After visiting Paige, I check on Mum, hanging another load of washing up on the rickety airer and cooking her a batch of soup which she can reheat without blowing the house up. Hopefully. I get home in the early evening to find Seb washing up, his headphones covering his ears. He jumps when I place a hand on his back.

'All right, Nan?' he asks, knocking one earphone off with his elbow. 'How's Granny?'

I make a face. 'She's... herself. Seven tuts today.'

'Seven.' Seb smiles. 'What did you do wrong?'

'Oh, everything and nothing. The usual.' I slide onto a chair, my lower back hurting after hoovering the upstairs landing and Mum's bedroom, around the piles of crap. I'll do downstairs next week. 'How was your day?'

Seb turns back to the sink, lifts a shoulder. 'All right. Did some studying. Left Dad a message.'

I feel myself bristle at his words. I know he does this, leaving voice-note thingies for his dad, listening to Brad's responses. I'm not quite sure how it all works, and I'd rather not know if I'm honest. If I knew how to leave that man a message, well, I couldn't be held responsible for the things I'd say. Eleven years ago, my daughter died at the hands of the man who was supposed to love her. He'd strangled her, his large hands circling her neck, leaving vivid purple bruises. Bruises I'd seen before on her body; fingermarks on her arms, a yellowing bruise on her hip, all accidents, or so she claimed. But I knew. I'd seen it before. I'd lived it.

I shake myself back into the present. 'Do you want a cup of tea?' I ask, bracing myself to get up. Seb puts out a hand.

'You sit down, I'll make it,' he says, and I smile at how the roles have reversed, the young taking care of the old.

'Thanks, love,' I say, remembering my mother's icy responses to my offers of help. Was she always so bitter? Yes, I think. Yes, she was.

We sit together in the living room, Seb tapping away at his phone. My phone rings just as *EastEnders* is starting. PC Willis introduces herself, and I feel a stab of fear. Seb is quiet while I speak to her.

'They want to come tomorrow,' I tell him when I hang up. He doesn't say a word, his eyes flicking away from mine, unease pouring from him. I should speak to him, I know, but the words won't seem to come. All I can think about is the way Caitlyn looked at me, asking me what my grandson knew. As if he is at fault.

I would be lying if I said I've never worried about it. The sins of the father and all that. Seb was four when Brad killed my Paige. He saw it happen, watched from his hiding place in the dark wardrobe as his father strangled his mother.

It wasn't the first time Brad had hurt her. I'd known something was going on behind closed doors. But they lived a few towns away, in a one-bedroom flat Brad had lived in since he was sixteen, and I couldn't be there every second of the day. They'd met at a pub in town, vaguely knew one another from nights out, and soon Paige was spending all her time at that flat, slowly moving her stuff over; a toothbrush, some spare underwear, the blanket I'd knitted for her one Christmas. She was seventeen and in love with this twenty-two-year-old man who had no job and no prospects.

'You're going to university next year,' I said, one day I'd caught her at home. I was seeing less and less of her by that point, the house empty and silent. 'Are you sure you want to get mixed up in something now?'

Paige rolled her eyes in that way only teenagers can. 'What difference does it make?'

'You should be focusing on your exams, Paige. Studying. Not wasting your time on someone like *him*.'

She glared at me then, a mixture of anger and indignation. 'Someone like him,' she repeated. 'Black, you mean? I didn't have you down as a racist, Mum.'

Her words had stunned me. No matter how much I tried to tell her that I wasn't racist, that the colour of his skin had nothing to do with how I felt about him, that it was her future I was concerned about, she wouldn't listen. And then, six months before she was due to leave for university, she found out she was pregnant.

The violence started soon after Seb was born. Or had it always been going on, and Brad no longer cared about hiding it? He had her then, trapped and isolated in that tiny flat, her days and nights full of cooking and cleaning and taking care of Seb, while he drank the child benefit away down the pub. I watched my daughter turn from confident young woman to a haggard, unkempt version I barely recognised. I saw her going down the same path as I did, throwing her future away, the future I'd worked so hard to secure, and there was nothing I could do about it.

But I loved Seb the moment I saw him. He was large, bigger than Paige had been when she was born, with a head of dark curls. He grabbed my finger in his tiny fist as I held him for the first time, as if telling me that I'd better make room for him. That I was his as much as he was mine.

Brad missed the birth, of course. He didn't see his son until Paige was discharged from hospital two days later. I drove them to the flat, keeping well below the speed limit, my knuckles white as I gripped the steering wheel, a new, nervous driver. Paige held Seb in her arms, her eyes trained on his face the whole way. The flat was a mess. Empty cans and pizza boxes littered the floor, dirty dishes piled up in the sink. Brad was sprawled across the sofa, one big toe poking through a hole in his sock, the scent of weed in the air.

'I can't leave you here,' I hissed to Paige when Brad didn't stir. 'Come back home, love, your room's still the same. The cot will fit on the back seat.'

But Paige had fixed me with her gaze, those bottomless blue eyes of hers, and shook her head once. And I had left her there, to four more years of neglect, hunger, abuse. If anyone is at fault, it's me.

'Nan,' Seb says, and I jump, startled out of my memories. 'You do believe me, don't you?'

I stare at him, noting the same ski-slope nose as Paige, the same arched brows. He has so much of her in him; his laughter when you catch him unawares, a high giggle that bursts between his lips; the sparkle in his eyes when he's being cheeky, or has been caught with his hands in the biscuit tin; the way he stirs a cup of tea three times, then taps the spoon on the side twice, just like she used to. But when I look into his eyes, I can't ignore the shadow of his father. Did he see too much when he was a child? Was he irrevocably scarred? Is he destined to follow the same path? No. I can't let that happen. I won't.

'Of course I do, love,' I say, reaching out to place a hand on his cheek. 'Don't ever doubt it.'

16

SEB

He tries not to worry about the radio silence from Izzy, or the impending police visit. He cooks dinner for his nan, chopping carrots and onion for a stew. He helps her with the dishes, puts on a load of washing, mops the floors. He makes her a cup of tea when she gets home from work, and goes to feed next door's cat. He spends the days in his room, reading the same page of his textbook over and over, unable to focus. He is consumed by anxiety, by guilt. Because he does feel guilty for what has happened. Izzy didn't have to take that photo, but his friends have been sharing it, laughing about it in the group chat, and he hasn't said a word. He is complicit.

By night he dreams of his mother, memories interwoven with fiction to paint a picture he knows doesn't reflect the truth. By day he thinks of his father and his upcoming parole hearing, and wonders if someone can change from murderer to model citizen. Vile to virtuous. Evil to good.

His dad has told him everything, given his side of the story in lengthy voice notes, played and replayed until Seb felt as if his father's memories match his own. But he is still just a child, and try as he might, he cannot understand the complexities of his parents' relationship.

'I killed her,' Brad told him, not without shame but without hesitation. 'I hold my hands up to it. I was in a bad place, a really, really bad place. The kind of dark that no light can penetrate. I had no boundaries, kept pushing my limits. Just one more shot, another zoot, try a pill. I was trying to chase the darkness away, but instead I was plunging deeper into it.'

His father sometimes tells him about his mother, his voice softening every time he mentions her. He tells him about her hair, how he loved to run his fingers through it. He tells him about her smile, the way she would laugh when tickled. And he tells him the truth, the side Seb is afraid of, the half-remembered shouts and the tears running down his mother's face. He is afraid of those memories, wants to tell himself that they aren't real, but his father does not flinch in the face of them.

'There was love,' he says, 'but it wasn't enough. I should have done more, but nothing was going to pull me out of that hole.'

Nothing except prison, and, more recently, Jesus. His father found God a couple of years ago, back when they only wrote letters to one another a few times a year. Christmas, birthdays, Father's Day. Before the voice notes, which are so easy they almost feel natural. Normal. Seb hated writing letters, would sit at his desk with a sheet of paper before him, his mind blank. The words wouldn't come. But with the voice notes, he feels as if he is having a real conversation with his father, hearing his words in his own voice, instead of the memory of it.

'I should have done more.' His dad's words echo inside his head, exploding like fireworks in his brain. Seb is suddenly galvanised, seized by the knowledge that he could, should, be doing more to help. To be there for Izzy.

He goes upstairs to get dressed, pulling up Snapchat and tapping on Izzy's name as he pulls on his jeans.

Are you free today?

To his surprise, she reads his message straight away.

Yeah, why?

Let's do something. I need to get out of the house.

He waits, expecting her to go silent again, but then she responds.

OK. Come to mine in an hour?

It takes him half an hour to walk to Izzy's. He stops by the shop and picks up two cans of Coke and chocolate bars – Snickers for him, Boost for her. He realises that he has gone about this the wrong way. He should have stood up for her, should have called his friends out. He should have tried harder to reach her, should have gone to her house when she wasn't answering his messages. He should have protected her.

And so he arrives at her house full of purpose, a renewed sense of the way forward. The police will realise that he had nothing to do with what happened when he speaks to them, and Izzy will be okay. Everything will be okay.

Seb rings the doorbell and waits, already grinning when the door opens. But it is not Izzy who opens it. It is her stepdad, Michael, who Seb has always got on with, but there is no sign of that man now. He is frowning, his lips twisted as if he has just bitten into a lemon.

'You. What are you doing here?'

'Is Izzy here?' Seb asks, his smile faltering at the venom in Michael's words.

'No she bloody isn't,' he says, stepping out of the house and bringing the door closed behind him. 'And even if she was, she wouldn't want to see you.'

Seb swallows hard, his mouth flooding with saliva. 'But she asked me to come,' he begins, but Michael waves a hand, cutting him off.

'I suggest you leave. Before I call the police.' And then he slams the door in his face.

17

CAITLYN

I sabelle sits at the far end of the sofa, picking at the skin beside her thumbnail. I fight the urge to grab her hands, to force her to keep still. She is still furious with Michael for telling Seb to leave earlier, and I have to admit that I am too. *But he was only trying to protect her*, I try to tell myself as we sit opposite two police officers, untouched cups of coffee on the table between us. Michael comes in and sits beside me, squeezing my hand in his as he addresses the officers, and suddenly I am grateful for his presence.

'What happens next?' he asks, his voice all clipped and professional, and I picture him talking to his subordinates at work in this way. 'Have you made an arrest yet?'

The officers exchange a glance before the woman, PC Willis, speaks. 'We need to talk to Isabelle now, to get her side of the story, before we decide how to proceed.'

'Story?' I interject, glancing at my daughter. 'There is no *story*, no *sides*. It's pretty clear what happened.'

'There are always sides,' PC Willis says calmly, flashing a small smile which she probably hopes will be disarming, but actually only serves to make her look smug. 'Now, Isabelle,' she says, turning her upper body away from me and towards my daughter. 'Or is it Izzy?'

'Izzy,' she mumbles, her sleeve half-covering her mouth.

PC Willis smiles at her. 'Izzy, can you tell me what happened, in your own words?' Isabelle is silent, the clock ticking too loud above the fireplace.

'I've explained everything already,' I begin, but PC Willis silences me with a look.

'We need to hear it from Izzy, Mrs Bennett,' she says, and I feel myself bristle. But I stay quiet, watching Isabelle's face for signs of distress. She is clearly uncomfortable, chewing on the end of her sleeve. Alicia takes her sister's hand, moving it away from her mouth and gripping it tightly in her lap. Isabelle takes a deep breath, blowing it out slowly before speaking.

'I took a photo. I sent it to someone. They shared it around. End of story.'

'Who did you send it to?'

'No comment.'

Michael makes a noise of frustration and I lean forward, touching Isabelle's wrist, once more surprised by the rough bandages beneath my fingers. 'That isn't helpful, Isabelle,' I say gently.

'You're not under arrest,' PC Willis says. 'You're not in trouble.'

'Though it is illegal to possess and share indecent images of a minor,' PC Singh adds.

Isabelle snorts, but I feel my breath quicken as the words sink in. 'Even though the image was of herself?' I ask, an article I half-remember reading a while ago floating into my mind.

PC Willis nods. 'Yes. You're fifteen, Izzy.'

'I know,' Isabelle mumbles, her bravado vanishing into the air like smoke.

'Can you tell me why you took the photo?' Isabelle is silent, staring at her hands. 'Did someone pressure you to do it?'

'No. I just took it.' Isabelle glances up at me. 'I know it was stupid, all right? But everyone does it. It's no big deal.'

PC Willis purses her lips, and the look on her face tells me that it is a big deal to her, as it is to me. 'So you took a photo and sent it to someone you trusted. Do you know why they shared it?'

Isabelle shakes her head. 'I didn't know they were going to.'

'If you tell us who it was you sent the photo to,' PC Willis says, leaning forward, 'we can find out what happened. It would really help us.'

'But I don't want to know what happened,' Isabelle says. 'I don't want you involved. I just want to forget about it.'

'Was it your boyfriend?' PC Singh asks, glancing at his notes. 'Sebastian Taylor?'

Isabelle's eyes widen. 'No. No. He had nothing to do with it.'

'So he didn't ask you to send a photo of yourself to him?' Isabelle shakes her head, her cheeks colouring. 'Peer pressure can be difficult to ignore,' he continues. 'Especially from boyfriends.'

'I told you,' Isabelle says, her voice rising, 'it wasn't Seb. He had nothing to do with it.'

'All right,' PC Willis says, smiling at Isabelle. 'So it wasn't Sebastian. Was it one of his friends? Someone from school?'

Isabelle is silent again, staring resolutely at the wall.

'Are you part of this Snapchat group, Izzy?' PC Willis asks, holding up a phone. I crane my neck to see the screen but nothing looks familiar. 'Do you recognise any of the names here?'

'Shouldn't you know that already?' Michael interjects. 'Shouldn't you be investigating who is in that group?' He sits forward, releasing my hand. 'Have you spoken to that boy yet? I know Izzy says he had nothing to do with it, but you need to investigate him properly. He came here earlier, probably to intimidate her or something. I told him to clear off.'

PC Willis gives him a look. 'That's what I'm doing, Mr Bennett,' she says coolly.

'Pearson,' I say quickly. 'We're not married. He's not...'

'He's not my dad,' Isabelle says bluntly. 'He's not even my *step*dad.'

'All right. We'll leave it there for now.' The police stand to leave, and I see them out while Isabelle scurries up to her room, Alicia on her heels, and Michael stomps off to the kitchen.

'We'll be in touch,' PC Willis says, her eyes meeting mine as I take her proffered card, and I think I see something else there now, a softness I hadn't noticed before. 'But call me if you need to. Anytime.'

For once I am glad Isabelle is in her room, because Michael starts ranting about this whole thing being 'a waste of time' and just 'more of Isabelle's attention-seeking behaviour' as soon as I enter the kitchen.

'Have you called the therapist?' he demands when I start pulling things out of the fridge to make dinner. 'She needs to go back, urgently. Maybe even a spell in hospital. That'd do it, shock her out of all this. I mean, really. How could she be so stupid.'

I put the pack of peppers down slowly, my hands trembling as I fight to control my voice. What I want to do is scream at him, pick up the peppers and onion and chopping board and throw them at his head. Instead I turn, slowly, fingers gripping the counter behind me.

'No, Michael,' I say quietly. 'She will not be going into hospital or anywhere else for that matter.'

'But, Cait,' he splutters, and I hold up a hand.

'She will be going back to counselling. She clearly needs

someone to speak to, perhaps a specialist in this area, but I will not be having my daughter committed. Do you understand me?'

He opens his mouth as if to protest, and I think, *go on, say it again. I dare you.* As if reading my thoughts, he closes his mouth again without speaking. I know this reaction is coming from a place of fear, of concern that he cannot help her, but it is the wrong path to take. He stomps out of the kitchen, and I breathe out when I hear the study door close behind him.

I nod once to myself, then turn back to the counter, selecting a knife from the rack and carefully chopping the vegetables into cubes. I've decided to make a curry, one of Isabelle's favourites, with naan bread covered in cheese and soft, fluffy rice. She can even have a shandy if she wants.

I try to focus on the cooking, but Michael's words keep coming back to me. Because, despite the insensitive way he has, he's right. Isabelle needs help. And, right now, I don't know how to give it to her.

18

LIV

I dream of Paige. I dream of the day I turned up at her flat, after almost two days of radio silence. The prickling of anxiety as I went up the stone steps, the lift forever broken. My footsteps echoed around me, the smell of urine strong and unmistakable, and I grimaced at dark patches on the walls. I dream of my fist rapping against the door, then my open palm slamming against the wood, my daughter's name on my lips.

The police took two hours to arrive. My legs were numb from standing on the balcony outside, ducking down every so often to shout through the letterbox. I could see a pair of shoes discarded in the small hallway, a pile of junk mail on the bottom stair, but I could hear nothing but the sound of traffic rushing by behind me, the occasional dog barking or child shouting. I knew something was wrong. Paige hadn't been answering my calls, and when I rang her mobile again, my ear pressed against the letterbox, I could hear it ringing inside the flat.

They broke down the door, the police officer's heavy boot slamming against the wood once, twice, three times. It sprang open, smashing against the wall and bouncing back. I rushed forward but they stopped me, an arm blocking my way. 'Let us have a look around first,' another officer said, her voice gentle, and I felt nausea rise.

They found her in the bedroom. Her eyes were open, staring sightlessly at the ceiling. Her arms were by her sides, one leg sticking out at an unnatural angle. And Seb, four-year-old Seb with wide eyes full of fear, was with her, playing quietly with his toy cars beside the body of his dead mother. Brad was nowhere to be seen.

I rang Evelyn that evening, crouched on the bathroom floor while Seb splashed around in the bath. She broke down, her voice thick with emotion as she apologised over and over again. 'He's not well,' she sobbed, 'he hasn't been well for a long time. But I haven't been able to help him. And now...'

And now, my daughter was dead. And I had no more tears left to cry.

It took five days for them to find him. He was holed up at a friend's house, off his head on heroin, and he tried to throw himself out of the seventh-floor window when the police forced their way in. I dream of this often, this scene I did not witness but have imagined so many times in the years since. I had seen Brad's wild eyes before, the way his head jerked around as if hearing a voice. He was not well, had been diagnosed with mental health issues when he was fifteen, given his own flat after he attacked his sister and, unable to cope any longer, Evelyn threw him out, but instead of taking the medication prescribed by the doctor, he opted for weed and ecstasy and, later, heroin. Paige had tried to help him. She had hoped that having a child would change things, but anyone could see that Brad was not ready to be a father. Anyone except Paige. She paid the price for her naivety.

I find myself in the kitchen in the early hours, a cup of tea clutched between my fingers. That was the last time I had anything to do with the police, and now they are coming here today to interview my grandson. I have to remember who he is, the boy I have watched grow from toddler to teenager, who has always been kind and thoughtful and *good*. He is good. He is innocent. He is not his father.

Seb is eating a bowl of cereal when the doorbell rings. I get up to answer it, anxiety gnawing in my stomach. A man and a woman stand on the doorstep, the marked police car parked on the road beyond.

'Hello, Ms Taylor?' the woman says. I nod. 'I'm PC Willis and this is PC Singh. Can we come in?'

My blood runs cold as I step back, opening the door to let them in. What else can I do but let them in? I wonder if I should have called a solicitor, but no. Only guilty people do that. And besides, I can't afford one.

I glance at Seb as he places his cereal bowl into the sink, leading the police into the living room and offering them a cup of tea. Both shake their heads. I step out of the room, wringing my hands in front of me, as Seb is making his way down the hall.

'Nothing to worry about,' I tell him, placing a hand on his shoulder that I hope will be reassuring. 'It'll be all right.'

The officers are sitting together on the couch. They look squashed, as if this is a miniature house and they are giants. I perch on the footstool while Seb sits in the armchair.

'How can we help you?' I say, pressing my hands between my knees. I try to smile but neither of the officers return it.

'It's just an informal chat, Sebastian,' PC Willis says, looking at Seb. 'You're not under arrest at this present time.' I bristle at the words, at the inference that he *will* be arrested at some point. That it is inevitable.

Seb nods, then shakes his head. 'It's okay, I'd just like to get it over with really.' His leg begins to bounce up and down, and I wonder if the officers can tell how nervous he is. Surely everyone is nervous in front of the police? It doesn't mean he has anything to hide. Does it?

PC Willis gives a small smile. 'We'll try to keep this as brief as possible.' She glances down at her notes. 'It is our understanding that you received a photo on Monday 6 March at approximately 1500 hours. Can you tell us about that?'

Seb shifts under her gaze. 'Erm, yeah, well, not really. It just got sent to the group chat.'

'And who is in this group chat?'

'Loads of us. Lads from school. Girls too. There's like fifty people.'

'Surely you already know who is in it?' I cut in, trying to control the tremble in my voice.

PC Willis ignores me, and I suddenly see why she has chosen a career in the police. She has something inside her, a tenacity to do her job right. To see things through. But will she know the truth when she sees it? Or will she be blinded by her own ideas and prejudices, as so many of us are?

'How many of the people in your group would you say you're friends with?' she asks Seb. 'Can you give us their names?'

He glances at me, panic suddenly in his eyes. 'Does he have to?' I ask. 'He doesn't – I mean, we don't want any trouble.'

'I just want to help,' Seb adds. 'If I can. But I don't know much. All I know is that that photo was sent to the group chat the other day.'

'Which number did it come from?'

Seb frowns. 'Erm, it came from Ben. I don't know his surname. Jenkins maybe?'

'Ben Jenkins maybe.' PC Willis writes it down, and I feel myself bristle again. 'Okay.' She sets her pen down, locking eyes with Seb again. 'How well do you know Isabelle, Sebastian?'

He glances at me before answering. 'Quite well. We've known each other since primary school.'

'And you have been in a relationship since December last year?' Seb nods. 'Have you and Isabelle Bennett ever engaged in sexual intercourse?'

Seb sits back in his chair as if he has been punched. His mouth opens, closes, opens again. 'No,' he says eventually, shaking his head. 'No, never.'

'He's not long turned sixteen,' I protest. 'He hasn't had sex yet.' PC Willis glances at me as if to say, *well, he wouldn't say so in front of you, would he?* I suddenly want to wipe the smug look off her face. Why is she speaking to him like this? As if he is a suspect. But, I realise suddenly, he *is* a suspect. He, or any other boy in that group, could have requested that photo, could have forwarded it on. Could have been, what word did Mr Loach use? *Distributing it.* And he is her boyfriend. It's always the boyfriend, isn't it?

'Do you know if any of your friends have ever slept with Isabelle?'

Seb shakes his head again. 'No, not that I know of.'

'Would you be angry to discover that she had slept with one of your friends?'

'What? No. Why would I?'

'Have you ever accused Isabelle of cheating on you?'

'What has that got to do with anything?' I interject before Seb can respond. 'Why are you asking him this?'

PC Willis raises an eyebrow. 'I'd like Sebastian to answer the question please.'

'No,' Seb says. 'We haven't even been together that long.'

'Do you often drink underage, Sebastian?' She changes gear so quickly, I feel as if I've been left behind. I suddenly regret not having a solicitor with us. Should Seb stop answering their questions? Is he digging himself an even deeper hole?

Seb lifts a shoulder. 'Sometimes. Everyone does it.' He sounds sullen, even to my ears, and I cringe inwardly.

'Did Isabelle often join you on nights out?'

'Yeah, sometimes,' he repeats. 'Most of the time.'

'Your social media tells a different story. You don't often tag her in posts, do you?'

Seb glances at me, confusion on his face. I give a shake of my head. She is trying to lead him with her questions, and I know there will be a trap somewhere along the way.

'Did she go to the New Year's party with you last year?' PC Willis asks, holding up a phone to show a photo of Seb and his friends, party hats on their heads. 'Or this one, in February?' Another photo, this time taken in a field somewhere, a bonfire crackling in the background. 'Or–'

'Sorry,' I cut in, frustration turning my voice into a whip. 'Can you please explain what this has to do with that photo?' I look at both the officers, trying to read their faces, but their expressions are carefully blank. 'If you're trying to insinuate that my grandson somehow forced Izzy to send him a photo, then you couldn't be further from the truth. He has always been kind to Izzy, always tried to include her.'

'Nan,' Seb says, his voice low, and I stop talking. I suddenly feel so far out of my depth, as if I have plunged into the middle of the ocean, with no land in sight.

'We are not trying to insinuate anything, Mrs Taylor,' PC Singh says. 'Just trying to gather all the facts.'

'Then stick to the facts,' I snap. 'What Seb may or may not have done in the past has no relevance here.'

'Oh, but it does,' PC Willis says. 'It helps us to understand what led up to the moment Isabelle tried to kill herself.' Her words are intended to shock, and I see them hit Seb with a physical force. She tilts her head, staring at him as if trying to read him. 'Has Isabelle ever mentioned hurting herself before?'

'No.'

'But she has done it before, hasn't she?' Seb shrugs, avoiding her gaze. 'You don't know? I would've thought she would speak to her boyfriend about such things. But, wait,' she says, snapping her fingers. 'That's right. She's been ignoring you, hasn't she? Avoiding you? Her stepfather didn't let you in the house, isn't that right? Why do you think that is?'

'She's been having a hard time,' Seb mumbles, his eyes hardening. 'And he's never liked me. Michael.'

Seb drops his gaze, and I feel a shiver run through me. I'd assumed he had been speaking to Izzy about everything, supporting her. Has she been avoiding him? And I thought he got on with Michael, I remember Seb telling me that they sometimes watched the football together. Has he suddenly turned against him?

'Do you know why that is?' The question is innocent, the police officer's voice light, but the underlying meaning is bold and unmistakable.

'Probably something to do with the colour of my skin?' Seb says angrily, and I wince internally. *Calm down. Don't get angry. It's what they want.*

'Perhaps,' PC Willis says, with something like triumph, and again I wonder what her game is. 'Though that's quite an accusation. Perhaps there's another reason why he doesn't want you going out with Isabelle? Perhaps he has seen something he doesn't like?'

Before I realise what I'm doing, I am on my feet, one arm raised to point towards the door. 'I think you'd better leave,' I say, trying and failing to keep my voice steady.

The police officers glance at one another before PC Willis speaks. 'You do realise how serious this is, Sebastian?'

'Seb has answered your questions,' I say evenly, though my body is trembling with rage. 'He has nothing else to add.'

They stand, filing out of the room without a word. I open the front door, watching PC Singh head towards the car. PC Willis pauses on the threshold, turning back to face me. 'I thought you'd be more concerned about this,' she says, her voice quiet. 'After what happened to your daughter.' The breath leaves my body, her words slamming into me like a blow. She shrugs, stepping out of the front door, and I can almost hear her thoughts trailing behind her. *Like father, like son.*

19

IZZY

She cannot stop thinking about the police, the way the male officer looked at her. *Stupid girl. Stupid, stupid, stupid girl.*

He isn't wrong. She thinks about the girl who took that photo, who sent it to someone she thought liked her. It is so out of character for her, so *not Izzy* that she cannot understand why she did it. But she could have a good guess.

'Why don't you wear your hair like Abby?' her mum would say, twirling a strand of Izzy's wild hair around her fingers. 'Or at least put a brush through it. It's so tangled, Isabelle.'

'Would you like your brows waxed? You could come with me to the salon next time.'

'How about a walk? Work off those brownies!'

'Why don't you go out with Sian/Jess/Abby/insert name here anymore? Have you had a falling out?'

Microaggressions, Alicia calls them. Their mother is the queen of nitpicking. And although Alicia rarely acknowledges it anymore, Izzy remembers comforting her sister when she still lived at home, her eyes red from crying.

'She means well,' Alicia said after getting it off her chest. 'I know she just wants what's best for us.'

'But how does she know what's best?' Izzy said. 'What's best for her isn't going to be what's best for you, or for me.'

Alicia smiled then, wrapping her sister in her arms. 'We just need to figure it out for ourselves,' she said.

But Izzy hasn't managed to figure it out yet, whatever *it* is. When she straightened her hair for school one day, she managed to fry the ends and had to trim them off. When she wore lipstick, a teacher sent her to the toilets to scrub it off because 'you're here for an education, Isabelle, not a night out'. When she wore shorts to the cinema with a group of friends, one of the boys called her Chub Rub for the rest of the day. Even when she started going out with Seb, the girls laughed at her, whispering behind her back about it not being real, how he was only with her out of pity or desperation. As if they knew the truth.

She doesn't want to be like *them*, those girls who call her names and laugh at her, but she wants to be liked *by* them. She just wants to be seen. At home, she blends into the background of everyday life, against the backdrop of washing and dinner and homework. At school, she feels like a ghost, haunting the corridors between lessons, sitting mute at her desk, getting average grades and average parents' evening reports. Once, her science teacher mixed her up with another student, another girl who blends in so easily, she almost disappears entirely.

Now she longs for the days of blending in, when she was just someone who hung around on the edge of the group, never speaking up, never putting herself forward. *It was easier then*, she thinks now, *when I was invisible.*

Izzy lies on her bed, staring up at the ceiling. Michael has gone into the study, she heard his footsteps stomping along the hall after the police left. She thinks of when she had let Michael answer the door to Seb, when she had known who it would be, and how Michael would react. But despite telling him to come, she could not face him after all, the boy she has betrayed. The friend she has hurt.

She wonders if they are ashamed of her, if they would ever admit to it. Michael might, but Izzy knows her mother truly does mean well. She thinks of the days when it was just the three of them, when Caitlyn was more stressed and had less energy, but somehow the days seemed brighter, happier. Perhaps it was because anything was better than those months when she didn't have a mother, when Caitlyn locked herself in her bedroom, consumed by sadness and alcohol. She was just glad to have her mum back, glad she wasn't saying those horrible things anymore.

How sad, she thinks. *How pathetic.* Those are the words she heard in the school toilets, the day she tried to end her life. Some of the girls were huddled in front of the mirror, swapping lip gloss and drawing on their eyebrows in a way Izzy has never managed to master. She was hiding in one of the cubicles, feet drawn up, reading the writing on the back of the door. *I was here* scrawled in red pen. *Who?* she thought. *Not me. I'm not here.*

'She's so pathetic,' she heard Abby say. 'How desperate do you have to get?'

'I know,' Jess piped up. 'Who does that?'

Ghosts, Izzy thought. *Ghosts who want to be seen.*

'It's all for attention,' Abby said. 'It's sooo obvious. Desperate for people to like her.'

'Who would?' Sian said. 'She's so weird.'

Weird. Pathetic. Desperate. Is that all they think of me? Tears slipped down her face as she listened to her classmates. She tried not to remember when she and Abby were at primary school together, how Izzy had helped her learn to read. She tried not to remember the birthday parties and trips to the park or the zoo, before they drifted apart. She tried not to remember that sleepover from the summer before, the gentleness of Sian's fingers as she spread the mask over Izzy's face, dabbing a blob of bright green on her nose with a grin.

She tried not to wonder if they had actually seen the photo, but by the end of the school day, her fears were confirmed. *Everyone* had seen it. She heard whispers everywhere she turned, was convinced that every laugh she heard was directed at her. She remembers running home, desperate to escape, desperate for it all to *just stop*.

She tries not to remember taking the pills, or the feel of the razor in her hand. She tries to block it all out, wonders if she really had wanted to die, or if she'd just wanted it all to stop. What was the difference anyway? If she was dead it would stop, and it would stop if she was dead. And at that moment, the snide comments and muffled giggles ringing in her ears, she had wanted it to end, one way or another.

Izzy closes her eyes, her fists clenched by her sides. She thinks of the police officer, PC Willis, and how she had looked when Izzy refused to name the person she sent the photo to. Disappointed, annoyed. But Izzy hadn't wanted the police to get involved. She hadn't wanted any of it. She had only wanted to go to sleep and never wake up. But now she isn't just the girl who sent *indecent images* of herself. She is also the girl who'd tried to kill herself, and that is a stain she thinks will be hard to wash out.

20

───────

CAITLYN

The next day, I book an appointment with the therapist, managing to get a cancellation slot at short notice. Alicia has extended her trip home for a few days, brushing aside my worries about her falling behind with her course with a smile.

'I'm top of my class,' she said with a wink, which I know is a lie, but I also know that Alicia can breeze through almost anything in life, and besides, I need her now more than ever.

I do not tell Isabelle about the appointment until we need to leave. She glares at me as I stand in the hall with my coat on, my handbag held before me like a shield.

'Come on, Isabelle,' I say, trying to keep my voice light. 'After what... After everything, you need to talk to someone.'

Alicia comes down the stairs behind her sister, placing a hand on her shoulder as she passes. 'We'll all go,' she says, smiling. 'Together.'

And so we go, Isabelle in the front beside me, her head turned towards the window, away from me. Even Alicia is quiet as we drive to the therapist's office then sit for a moment, the engine off, the afternoon sun bright through the windscreen. I lead the way into the building, up three flights of stairs that smell of polish and into a small waiting room, where I get us all a cup of water and we sit clutching them, muscles clenched, silent, until we are called in.

The therapist, Libby, gives us a smile as we sit opposite her on the lumpy couch. 'Nice to see you all again,' she says. 'Though I wish it were under different circumstances, of course.' She crosses one ankle over the other, seemingly relaxed. 'Caitlyn, would you like to begin?'

I take a deep breath, but to my surprise, Isabelle speaks first.

'We're here because of me,' she says, 'again.'

Libby looks at her. 'Do you want to tell me what happened, Izzy?'

She picks at the side of her thumbnail. 'I took a nude photo of myself and it got shared around the school, and now everyone thinks I'm a hoe. A slut.'

I recoil at the word, the hard *t* at the end. 'Now, Isabelle,' I begin, but Libby gives a shake of her head that says *let her finish.*

Isabelle sighs. 'That's it really.'

Libby is frowning slightly. 'Someone shared a photo of you without your consent. Would you like to tell me why you took it?' Isabelle shrugs. 'I'm not the police, Izzy,' Libby urges gently when Isabelle doesn't speak. 'I'm not here to gather evidence. I'm here to help you work through this trauma.'

Trauma. Damage that occurs as a result of a distressing event. An 'after' word.

'I understand you hurt yourself?' Libby asks. 'What made you do that?'

'I just wanted it to stop.' Isabelle's voice wobbles as she speaks, and I see Alicia slip an arm around her, knowing that if I tried to comfort my daughter I would be pushed away. When did this happen? When did we drift so far apart? 'I didn't see another way out.'

'Out of what?' Libby asks.

'This. Everything. Everyone has seen the photo. *Everyone.*' Tears slip down her cheeks now and I feel my own eyes burn. 'They all hate me. I heard some girls talking about it at school, that day, and I just couldn't take it anymore.'

'Are people bullying you again, Izzy?'

Isabelle wipes her nose on her sleeve, nods. 'Still. It's the same people, just a different theme. *Izzy is a weirdo* has turned into *Izzy is a slag.*' She laughs then, a humourless bark of laughter. 'And I still have no friends, no matter what I do.'

'What do you mean by that?'

I glance at my daughter, trying to read her expression, her body language, but she is just radiating pain. I reach out and take her hand, and she lets me hold it, my thumb pressing against her knuckles.

'I mean that it doesn't matter what I do, how I dress, whether I wear make-up or not, whether I go out drinking or not, whether I *try* or not, it's always the same. Nobody likes me. I'm alone.' My heart tears in two at her words, and I reach for a tissue to blot away her tears. She moves her face away, her fiery gaze locking onto mine. 'You've always told me to be more like the others,' she says with such venom I flinch away, but her fingers grip onto mine. 'You've always tried to pressure me into being someone I'm not.'

'Isabelle, no, come on. I–'

'See? It's Izzy. Izzy. Not Isabelle. You're the only one who calls me that.'

I blink as if stunned. 'But I gave you that name,' I say, 'after my grandmother. It's a beautiful name.' Alicia is staring down at her feet. I turn to Libby as if seeking support. 'I don't mean anything by it.'

'Perhaps Izzy is trying to tell you who she is,' Libby says gently.

'It's because you wanted an abortion,' Izzy says, so softly I almost miss it. 'It's because you didn't want me.'

I stare at her, my youngest daughter, with her tear-soaked face and fingers gripping mine. As if realising she is still holding them, she lets go, brushing my hand away like a bug on a dinner plate. Alicia still won't meet my gaze.

'Who told you that?' I whisper, my heart pounding loudly in my ears.

'You did,' she says, her eyes flashing with rage. 'Did you think I had forgotten? Did you think I wouldn't remember something like that?'

Alicia leads her sister down the stairs, while I stand in the waiting room, my heart pounding in my ears. *It's because you didn't want me.*

It's not true! I want to scream. But the memory is coming back to me, flooding my vision. An empty vodka bottle, a dark, musty room. Two small faces peering at me from the end of the bed. Shame heats my cheeks as my own voice rings in my ears. *I should never have had you. I was never meant to be a mother.*

Libby comes up beside me, a warm hand on my back. 'While family therapy is of great importance,' she says, tucking a strand of hair behind her ear, 'I would like to suggest a session with Izzy alone, if she would consent to it. I suspect she may benefit from it. And I think you should come again, too, by yourself. There's a lot to work through.'

I walk away without answering, my muscles trembling, bile rising in my throat. I caused this. I am the reason Isabelle doesn't want to live. *I am a bad mother.*

21

SEB

Lew: Has anyone seen Crooks lately??

Liam: I don't think you should call him that

Lew: Why? He doesn't mind

Liam: Racist doesn't know when he's being racist

Lew: Shut up man, how can I be racist?

Josh: Oh here we go

Liam: "I'm not racist, I have black friends"

Lew: Fuck off. He's not even black

Liam: 🙂

Despite the casual racism, Seb smiles as he reads the messages. Liam and Lew always seem to be butting heads about something, but he appreciates Liam sticking up for him now. He feels a pang of regret for not sticking up for Izzy in the same way, pushes it away.

Seb: Bunch of dickheads. Who's up for some *FIFA* later?

Lew: Yes!!!

'There he is!' Lew says when Josh leads him into the snug. 'Sorry about the Crooks thing, mate. I didn't realise you were so sensitive.' He elbows him playfully.

'Dorito?' Liam says, offering him the blue pack.

Seb shakes his head. 'May contain.'

'Oh, shit.' He snatches the packet back as if just smelling them would make Seb keel over. 'Hang on, I brought some chocolate too.' He rifles through his bag and pulls out a share pack of Minstrels. 'These are all right, aren't they?' Josh snatches them from Liam's hand. 'Oi!' he protests. 'Those are for Seb, you twat. You can have these.' He throws a pack of Doritos at Josh. The Minstrels sail into Seb's lap and he grins.

'Cheers.'

'Are we playing or what?' Lew says, holding up the controller. 'You're like a bunch of old hens. Cluck-cluck-cluck!'

'Shut up,' Josh shouts, throwing a crisp at his head. It bounces off Lew's knee and lands on the floor.

'Five-second rule!' He laughs, snatching it up and putting it in his mouth.

'Animal,' Liam says, shaking his head.

Seb lets the banter wash over him, finding solace in the laughs and groans as they play. He is rusty compared to the others, who play online together most evenings, but he doesn't have an Xbox or even a TV in his room. At least he has Netflix, which he can watch on his phone.

'Have you heard from Izzy?' Liam asks while Lew is in the toilet and Josh goes to get more drinks from the kitchen.

Seb shakes his head. 'Not really. She asked me to go round the other day but her stepdad told me to clear off.'

Liam frowns. 'Why? I thought he was all right.'

'Yeah, he used to be.' Seb lifts a shoulder. 'Maybe he blames me for what happened.'

'Do you think? It's mad though. I can't believe she did that.' Liam rests his head against the sofa behind them. 'Who do you think shared it? The first time?'

Seb shifts uncomfortably. 'Dunno.'

'Honestly, mate,' Lew says, coming back into the room, 'I thought it was you. You're her boyfriend, you're gonna ask her for nudes.' He laughs. 'I've got a whole folder on my phone.'

'Of naked pictures?' Liam asks.

'Yep. Don't get excited, I'm not showing you. Oh wait, I forgot.' Lew taps the side of his nose. 'You bat for the other team. Have you got your own folder then? Men with their pecs out?' He rubs his own chest, smirking.

Liam shakes his head. 'Don't be so childish.'

'Izzy's picture went straight into the wank bank.' Lew grins. 'She's actually pretty hot, Seb. You lucky boy.'

Seb feels himself bristle as Lew claps him on the shoulder. 'Leave it, yeah?' he says, shrugging away from him.

'Not cool,' Liam mutters. 'She's obviously upset about it.'

'Shouldn't have taken it then.' Lew shrugs. 'She *obviously* wanted it to be seen.'

Seb is suddenly on his feet, bustling past Josh in the doorway.

'Where you going?' he shouts after him. 'I've just ordered pizza. Gluten-free too.'

'Sorry,' Seb says without stopping, opening the front door and stepping out into the afternoon sun. The air is warm; he gulps it down, trying to calm his racing heart. Were his friends always so insensitive? Has Seb always been too weak to stand up to them?

Pussy, he berates himself as he walks. *What's the matter with you?*

22

LIV

The front door slams and I jump, hurriedly stuffing the photo album I'd been looking through down the side of the chair.

'Hello, love,' I call as he kicks off his shoes in the hallway. 'Did you have a nice time?'

'Fine,' he grunts, then stomps up the stairs without looking at me. His bedroom door closes with a loud click and I sigh. He's just rattled by the police interview, I tell myself, and he's worried about going back to school. It'll blow over.

I pick up the photo album, finding the page I'd been staring at. Seb as a baby, his dark curls like a halo around his head. He is laughing, his eyes closed, one chubby arm raised in front of him as his face turned towards the person holding him. Brad. Though his face is cut out of the picture, you can see his hands holding Seb around the waist, one leg propped up to keep his son steady. These moments were so few and far between, but Paige always made sure she caught them, as if to prove to Brad that he could be better. To prove it to herself.

I think of the suspicion and judgement in the police officer's raised eyebrow, the eyes blazing as they looked at my grandson.

My grandson, the child I have raised since he was four years old, the child I watched being born, his dark curls cupped beneath my daughter's palm as she glowed with pride. He has never been in trouble before, never. He's had a few fallings out, but he has never bullied anyone, never pushed another child at school or stolen their pencils. He was always the kind child, the helper. He helped tidy the toys away at nursery, or handed out worksheets to his classmates. 'We can always rely on Seb,' one of his teachers told me once, smiling warmly, 'to do the right thing.'

Has he done the right thing now? I cannot believe he would have shared that photo, or have asked Izzy to send it in the first place, but I can't shake the feeling that there's more to this situation, more revelations to come. And so, as soon as he left earlier, I called Evelyn.

Her warm, West Indies accent came over the phone after three rings. 'Hello?'

'Evelyn,' I said, swallowing, 'it's Liv.'

'Liv,' she said, her voice like honey. Despite everything, I have always liked Evelyn. The first time I met her, she struck me as a no-nonsense woman, firm but loving, and to her credit, she denounced her son as soon as he was arrested. But she couldn't turn off her love for him, and if I'm being honest with myself, I can't help but understand that. 'Is everything all right? How's our boy?'

I smiled. Our boy. 'He's fine,' I said automatically, then paused. 'Actually, there's a situation I wanted to talk to you about.'

'I cannot believe it,' she said when I finished telling her about the photo and the group chat. 'Not Seb. He is such a sweet boy. He has always respected women.'

'I know. He's only been questioned about possibly sharing the photo, but he says he hasn't.'

'Is it because he is her boyfriend?' she asked. 'Someone close to her?'

'Maybe. I'm just... I'm worried that there's more to it, something related that he doesn't want to tell me.'

Evelyn was silent for a moment. 'I have a suggestion,' she said, and I held my breath, waiting, knowing what was coming. 'I think he should see his dad.'

It was the first time she had ever suggested it. Seb had mentioned it a few times over the years, but I'd always told him that he can make up his own mind when he's old enough. But now he is old enough, I realise with a jolt. He's sixteen, and can start to make his own decisions. But I just want to protect him, to shield him from the world for a little bit longer.

'Seb reckons his dad has turned his life around,' I told my friend Jackie over a rare pub lunch last year. 'Found god.'

She sighed, reaching out to pat my hand. 'I suppose what you've got to ask yourself is whether you believe in the criminal justice system.'

I stared at her, my mind working over the question. Did I believe in the criminal justice system? Did I believe in rehabilitation and second chances? I couldn't answer her then, and I still can't now. How can you ever make up for taking an innocent life?

'I can take him,' Evelyn continued. 'It's about time I faced my son.' And I felt pity wash over me, a kind of deep sympathy for this woman who is the mother of a killer, who lost half her body weight during the build-up to the trial, and started covering her thinning hair with bright scarves. The woman who clutched my hands between hers, her eyes full of tears, and whispered an apology over and over again. The woman who has sent me money for Seb's school trips and lunches over the years, who bought him new shoes for school and the smartphone I couldn't afford. Seb lost both of his parents that day eleven years ago, and both of his grandmothers stepped in. Stepped up.

And though I was relieved to be sharing another burden with this woman, relieved to have her on my side, I couldn't give her the answer she wanted. Not yet. Not ever.

I arrive ten minutes early for my shift at the petrol station, plastering a smile on my face as I head for Sean's office. He lifts an eyebrow as I enter.

'The wanderer returns,' he says sardonically.

Twat, I think. 'Good morning,' I say.

'Are you back now?'

I glance down at myself. 'I'm here, aren't I?' I try to laugh, but it sounds forced even to my ears. 'Thanks for being so understanding.' The word is unpleasant in my mouth, the untruth leaving a bad taste.

'All sorted then?' I nod, and he waves a hand, dismissing me.

Twat, I think again. *Complete and utter twat.*

I'm refilling the drinks cabinet when a man enters the shop, car keys jingling in his hand. I move behind the counter and it isn't until he says, 'Number four, please,' that I recognise him. I remember him picking Isabelle and Alicia up from nursery one day, dressed in paint-splashed jeans and a white T-shirt, wearing sandals no matter the time of year. He was an artist, I remember Caitlyn telling me once when she invited me in for a cup of tea while the children played in the garden. He'd had a big break, a famous exhibition that had brought in the critics and the money alike, allowing them to buy their beautiful house. And then he left, when Izzy was about four or five, and he hasn't been back. Until now.

Anthony glances at my name badge before his eyes find my face. 'Liv,' he says, smiling. 'Seb's nan. Nice to see you again.'

I smile back, cautiously, surprised he remembers me. 'Ready for you,' I say, indicating the card machine. He taps his card against the side before slipping it back into his wallet. He waits for his receipt, the machine printing excruciatingly slowly.

'How's things?' he asks. 'How's that boy of yours?'

His question surprises me. 'Fine, he's fine. How's Izzy?' I feel my cheeks heat up as he stares at me. 'I'm so sorry for what happened, really. It was awful. Seb is just so upset. We all are.' I snap my mouth shut, cutting off the babble as confusion enters his eyes.

'Why?' Anthony asks, his smile faltering. 'What's wrong with her? What's happened to Izzy?'

23

IZZY

She does not know the man standing in front of her. There is something familiar about him, the way his short hair sticks up slightly at the back of his head, the small scar on the left side of his jaw, half-hidden by stubble. And yet she cannot place him, cannot give him a name, until he holds out his hand and says, 'Izzy, it's me, Anthony. Your dad.' And the world tilts again.

Her mother is coming up behind her, hands firmly clamped to Izzy's shoulders, moving her aside, putting her body between her daughter and this man, this self-proclaimed father who has been a mystery for so many years. More than half her life, she thinks, has been spent without him, and she has forgotten him.

'What are you doing here?' Caitlyn hisses. The man, who she cannot yet think of as *Dad*, holds up his hands as if he is warding off an attack.

'I was in the area,' he says, and Izzy recognises the faint smile on his lips, the tug upwards that reminds her of Alicia. *But where am I?* she thinks. *Can I find myself in him?*

Caitlyn glances back at her, eyes wide, mouth slightly open, then looks back at Anthony. 'You'd better come in.' And then he is inside, wiping his feet on the mat, gazing around the hallway.

'I like what you've done with the place,' he says, and Caitlyn shoots him a look as if he has insulted her. Izzy follows them into the kitchen, these people who made her, who brought her into this world, and wonders if he, too, has seen it. The photo. It must be why he is here.

Is this what she will think whenever she meets someone new or sees someone from her past? *Have you seen it? Have you seen the photo of me?* She fears this is her life now, the constant anxiety gnawing at her stomach.

Caitlyn flicks on the kettle, taking three mugs down from the cupboard. 'Still two sugars?' she asks without turning round.

'None for me,' Anthony says, winking at Izzy. 'Sweet enough.'

A noise comes from her mother's nose, like a snort cut short, and she does not turn until she has finished making the tea, clattering the spoon noisily against the cups. She places them down on the island where Izzy and her father sit opposite one another, then leans against the counter, her own tea clasped in her hands as if she cannot trust herself to keep her hands free.

'What are you doing here?' she asks again, her voice sharp. 'Why have you come?'

He takes a sip, then another, looking at Izzy over the edge of the mug, and she feels something shift inside her. A memory of his hands holding her ankles, how she felt as if she could touch the stars when she was on his shoulders. She shakes it away, remembers instead that morning she woke up, late for school, and padded into her mother's room to find her hidden beneath the duvet, the room musty and dark, an empty bottle lying on its side on the floor.

'I'm here to see my girls,' he says after a moment, and Izzy sees fury flash in Caitlyn's eyes.

'You haven't seen your *girl*s,' she hisses the word, 'in over twelve years. Why now?'

Anthony sets his mug down on the counter and stares into it, as if the answer is floating on top of the tea. 'Because it's been twelve years,' he says, solemn now. 'I've missed them.'

'You heard, didn't you?' Izzy says, and her parents look at her in surprise, as if they had forgotten she was there. 'About the photo.'

He shakes his head.

'Am I supposed to believe that you've turned up here out of the blue?' Caitlyn sneers. 'Now, of all times?'

Anthony throws up his hands. 'Why am I being attacked here? I've just come to see the girls. It's been a long time.'

'Too long,' Caitlyn mutters, and Izzy is reminded of how her mother used to sound, not long after her father left and it was just the three of them, when there was no money for days out or ice creams, and no cuddles or stories at bedtime. When her mother was drinking, blurry eyed and cold. *I should never have had you.*

She feels her eyes burn with tears and she stands, pushing the stool back so it scrapes along the tiles, something Michael always tells her off for, and walks out of the kitchen.

She sits on the top step, listening to her parents – her *parents*, a term she hasn't used in years – argue.

'I have a right to know.'

'You gave up your rights when you walked out on us.'

'Alicia told me–'

'Alicia? What? When did she–'

'Tell me what's happened. I want to help.'

Her mother's voice drops then, and Izzy knows she is telling him everything. About the photo, about the razor. Hot tears spill down her cheeks, shame burning through her like wildfire. How can she ever show her face anywhere again? How can she go back to school, or go into town, and face the people who have seen her half-naked? They have seen the scar on her left knee from falling off her bike, the plain black knickers a size too big. They have seen her vulnerable, and they have shared it, giggling as they send the photo on and on and on, forwarded and posted and devoured, until there is nothing left of her.

Later, Caitlyn pushes open her bedroom door, a slice of lemon cheesecake on a plate held out like a peace offering. Izzy takes it but does not eat. She watches her mother's face, noticing how the shadows fall across it, making her appear older. Ancient. Tired.

'Your dad wants to help,' she says, a hand on Izzy's knee. 'I told him what happened.' She sighs then, her shoulders slumped, her body deflating like all the air has gone out of her. 'He wants to talk to you.' Izzy starts to shake her head, opens her mouth to say *no, no, I don't want to talk to him, not about this*, but Caitlyn continues. 'He said... He said you could live with him, if you wanted. In Plymouth. Move schools. It could... I don't know. It could be a good thing. A fresh start.'

Izzy blinks once, twice, trying to absorb this information. She could move away, start again, where nobody knows her and what she's done. A way out.

'When?' she asks, and her mother closes her eyes as if in pain.

24

CAITLYN

Two weeks pass. Two weeks since Anthony turned up again. Two weeks since I had a shouting match with Alicia, when I discovered she had been speaking to him in secret.

'He's my *dad*,' she said, indignant at first, then increasingly angry. 'He's our dad. We have the right to know him.'

'But why didn't you tell me?' My own anger had quickly turned to tears, hot and humiliating as they ran down my face. 'Why did you have to go behind my back?'

'Not everything is about you, Mum!' she shouted. She has always had a quick temper. 'Why do you always make things about you?'

She turned then, running up to her bedroom and slamming the door. Fifteen minutes later she was down the stairs and out the front door, storming down the driveway towards her car, Izzy on her heels.

'I can't stay here anymore,' she told her sister loud enough for me to hear. 'She just drives me mad!'

And then she was gone, Izzy suddenly looking five years old again as she watched Alicia's car disappear down the road.

Now I stand in the doorway to my daughter's room, watching as she sorts her clothes into three piles: stay, take, charity. She will keep some of her clothes here, and I can't help but picture her wardrobe half-empty, just like my heart.

But it is the right thing to do, for her to move away, to have a fresh start. It is, it is, it is. I repeat the words in my mind, in time with my heartbeat. I have failed at being a mother, have failed to keep her safe, and now she must go, learn to be someone new in a new place. Learn how to be Isabelle – Izzy, I remind myself. Izzy, Izzy, Izzy.

She packs slowly, methodically, thinking carefully about what she will need at her dad's. She will come back every fortnight, travelling the five hours on the train from Plymouth, changing only at London Paddington and then getting the Tube to Hertford, where I will pick her up. I try to make myself look forward to those weekends as quality time with my daughter, but there is a rock forming in my stomach, the fear that she will hate coming back, that she will stay in Devon forever.

She looks up at me then, her head tilted slightly to one side as if she can hear my thoughts. 'I'm taking my Portal,' she says, nodding towards the small rectangular screen. 'We can video call all the time.'

I nod, smile, but deep down I know that the video calls and texts will dry up within weeks. That she will be too busy with her new school and new friends to remember her mum. *You should be glad about that*, I scold myself. Alicia keeps in touch, when we haven't fallen out that is, but it is minimal and sometimes days go past without hearing from her, and that should be what I want for Izzy too. And I do, but I am afraid that she will need me, that something will happen and I won't be there to comfort her. And I am afraid that she won't need me at all, that she will forget all about the almost sixteen years spent in this house, the majority of which were happy and full of love and laughter. That she will forget about me.

I shake myself, turning away from my daughter packing up her life and going downstairs – thirteen steps, unlucky for some – where Michael sits on the sofa, his bare feet resting on the coffee table, the football blaring out of the TV. I grimace as I pass. In the kitchen, I open the fridge and stand there, feeling the cold air send goosebumps rippling across my skin. I take out a red cabbage and onion, find a carrot in the drawer, and dig out the jar of mayonnaise. I move the chicken breasts from the fridge to the chopping board and begin to dice them, throwing the cubes into a frying pan.

'What's cooking?' Michael asks when he crosses the room to take another beer from the fridge.

'Fajitas with coleslaw and salad,' I say without looking at him, adding spice to the browned chicken. This is what I do, in the absence of a career and children who need me. I cook. I bake. I clean. I make iced coffees instead of going to Starbucks, make my own Yorkshire puddings on Sundays, even stuff seashell moulds with my own sodding toilet cleaner recipe. I have too much energy to do nothing, and not enough energy to do something full-time. At least here I can break when I need to, switch off when the brain fog is too heavy. I can't imagine going back to an office now.

The smell brings Izzy from her room, and I ignore the flicker I feel when I notice how calm she looks. Relieved.

'Can I help?' she asks, and I hand her the iceberg lettuce to rip into shreds while I slice peppers. We work in tandem, throwing the salad into the large bowl before Izzy starts setting the table. We often eat at the island, but I prefer the table in front of the bay window, with its stylish dove-grey chairs and runner that names all the different kinds of pasta. She gets cutlery from the drawer and sets out wine glasses for each of us.

'This one?' She lifts a bottle of wine from the fridge door, and I nod.

'One glass, with lemonade,' I say half-heartedly, knowing that her father will let her drink, knowing that she does it anyway. Knowing that I cannot stop her. I think of Anthony as I microwave the wraps, his smooth, tanned skin that screams *south of France*, the ring on his wedding finger. The way he spoke of her, Miranda, his new wife. *His only wife*, I remind myself. *We were never married.* And I remember the way he laughed at marriage and children and mortgages back when we were students, as if he were above such desires, as if it was pathetic to want those things. And now he has them, and I am not a part of any of it.

'Do you want water, Mum?' Isabelle – *Izzy* – asks, breaking into my reverie.

'Hmm? Oh, yes please.' I watch her take the filter jug from the fridge and fill three tall glasses with water. 'Thank you, darling.' I reach for her as she passes on her way to the table, pressing my lips against her hair. 'For helping.' She gives me a small smile, and it warms me like the sun on a spring day.

'Michael,' I call, placing the bowls of chicken and salad on the table. 'Dinner.' I realise with a flash of annoyance that he has not moved to help once, has only got up to get himself another beer – the third, judging by the empties lined up on the table – and he grunts as he turns off the TV. I may be losing one teenager, I think, but I still have one here.

We sit at the table, Michael and I at opposite ends, Izzy in the middle. She tops her wine glass off with a tiny bit of lemonade and I hide a smile. She is growing up, I think, with a mixture of sadness and pride. She will get past this. She will.

'Have you spoken to Seb?' I ask, sipping my wine. 'Have you told him about the move?'

Izzy takes a bite of coleslaw and chews. 'Yeah. We're... I mean, it's quite a long way.'

I frown. 'What does that mean? He's not broken up with you?'

Something flashes across her face, too fast for me to identify. 'No, Mum. I broke up with him.'

I consider her words, wanting to ask so many questions, knowing I shouldn't push it. *It's her choice*, I tell myself, spooning some chicken into the middle of my tortilla. *Don't interrogate her.*

'Good idea. You're too young for a long-distance relationship,' Michael says through a mouthful of fajita, breaking the silence. 'All packed?'

'Yep,' she says after a beat. 'Almost.'

'When's Anthony coming to collect you?'

'Saturday,' I say, spooning some coleslaw onto my plate. Two days. In just two days, my daughter will be leaving home. I pick up my glass and take a large gulp of wine.

'When do you start at the new school?' Michael asks.

'Not for a week,' Izzy says.

'She's taking some time to settle in. She'll start a week on Monday.'

'A week off, eh?' Michael grins. 'Go and enjoy the city. Plymouth is great. Cheap drinks too. I can tell you where all the best pubs are.' I glare at him as Izzy stares down at her plate. 'Ah, yes, on second thoughts,' he says, picking up another tortilla and loading it with chicken. 'Not far from Cornwall though. Some lovely beaches just across the bridge.'

'I'm sure Anthony will have things planned,' I say coolly. 'They've been living there for a while now.'

'Sure,' Michael says, eating his fajita in two bites and downing his wine. 'Right, better crack on.'

There used to be times when I would look at the clock and say, *now? But we've not finished eating. You spent all day lounging in front of the TV, why are you working now?* but now I say nothing. I listen to his footsteps as he leaves the room, the soft click of the study door closing behind him, and drink my wine.

'He can't wait for me to leave, can he?' Izzy says softly. 'He wants me gone.'

I look up sharply. 'I don't give a fuck,' I say, and the air crackles between us. And then Izzy smiles, a real, I-can't-believe-you-just-said-that-Mum smile, and we begin to laugh, giggling at first, then louder, heads tipped back, eyes wet with mirth instead of sorrow for the first time in forever.

25

SEB

Seb is lying in bed, staring up at the ceiling. He hasn't slept, Izzy's words echoing through his mind as the minutes turned to hours, dusk to dawn. *I can't do this anymore. I'm sorry. I'm going away.*

He ignores the messages from the group chat, turning off notifications and putting his phone on do not disturb, his mind too chaotic to focus on anything but the pain of what has happened. *I can't do this anymore.* Do this. Do what? He feels anger building up inside him at the unfairness of it all. It was *Izzy* who sent the photo, *Izzy* who started it all. Now he is being questioned by the police, whispered about at school. And, now, he has been dumped.

His phone rings, and he lifts it to see Rosa flashing up on the screen. When he answers, her accent is so similar to his dad's that it takes his breath away.

'Your nan rang,' she says. He closes his eyes, shame flooding through him at the thought of his two grandmothers talking about it all. 'We're coming over.'

His eyes snap open in surprise. 'When?'

'Now. We're about ten minutes away. Get dressed and put the kettle on. I'm parched.'

Seb throws on some clothes and quickly brushes his teeth before running down to the kitchen. His nan is already at work, will no doubt have orchestrated this visit so she wouldn't have to be here. Though she doesn't object to his father's family involvement, and she has always got along well with Evelyn, he knows she finds it too painful to spend time with the family of the boy who killed her daughter. And though Evelyn has always condemned his father's actions, he knows she understands Liv's pain.

The kettle clicks and the doorbell rings at the same moment, and Seb jogs down the hallway to open the door. Immediately he is engulfed in his aunt's arms, her sweet perfume filling his nostrils, her stomach firm where it presses against him. She takes a step back and holds him at arm's length. 'Look at you,' she says, smiling. 'You look more like Brad every day.'

This is the kind of thing Liv cannot bear to hear, and he is glad she isn't at home.

'What's up with your hair?' he asks, reaching out and flicking one of the twists. His aunt smacks his hand away.

'Haven't you ever been taught not to touch a black woman's hair?'

He grins. 'I thought that didn't apply to me.'

She tuts. 'You and men everywhere.' She places a hand on her rounded stomach and breathes out. 'I must be mad, going through this again.'

'When are you due?'

'September.' She grimaces. 'Another sweltering summer spent looking and feeling like a whale.' Rosa hears a sound behind her and turns. 'Ah, there you are, Mum,' she says, reaching out to take her mother's arm. 'You got what you needed?'

Evelyn holds out a stack of paper, folded in half, which Seb takes, a question on his lips. She pats his cheek. 'I always come bearing gifts, you know this. And it's a special occasion.'

'Is it?'

'Is it?' Rosa mimics and laughs. 'Let's stop hanging about on the doorstep and go inside. My feet are killing me.'

'The kettle just boiled,' Seb says as he leads them into the house. They move into the living room while Seb goes into the kitchen to make the tea.

'Ah, at last! A girl could die of thirst here,' Rosa says when he enters the living room, three mugs balanced precariously in his hands. 'Any biccies then?'

'Just some gluten-free chocolate digestives. They taste a bit like dust,' he says.

'Gluten-free?' Rosa looks appalled.

'He's got celeriac disease, remember,' Evelyn says, frowning.

'Is that right? Celeriac?'

'Coeliac.' Seb laughs. 'Close enough.'

Rosa tuts. 'I'd have stopped to pick some up on the way if I'd known. Some hospitality.' Seb sits on the sofa beside his aunt, clutching the papers in his hands. 'Oh, for God's sake,' she says, rolling her eyes. 'Have a look then. I'm on the edge of my seat here.'

He unfolds the paper and reads the words. Application for provisional driving licence. He looks up at his nan, a grin forming on his face. 'Really?'

'It's hardly a round-the-world trip,' Rosa says, but she's smiling too.

'A belated birthday present,' Evelyn says, smiling. 'A boy needs a way of getting around in a place like this.'

'She still calls it "the countryside".' Rosa snorts. 'Thinks you don't have buses out here. Or trains.'

'We have both,' Seb says, laughing. 'But a car would make

life so much easier.' His face falls then, as he considers what will come next. 'But the lessons, they'll be too much. And I could never afford a car or the insurance.'

Evelyn reaches out to pat his knee. 'It'll all be taken care of, don't you worry.'

Seb knows not to pry; both of his grandmothers are very proud, particularly where money is concerned, but he can't help but worry. 'Are you sure?' he asks. 'I could get a proper job in the summer now I'm sixteen, I think the supermarket is hiring.'

But Evelyn is shaking her head. 'You need to be focusing on your studies,' she says. 'Not stacking shelves and worrying about money. You leave that to us.' He grins then, getting up to wrap his nan in a hug. She pats his back affectionately. 'You know you can always count on us,' she says when he releases her. 'To back you, one hundred per cent.'

'Yeah,' Rosa chimes in, 'even if you are a little git.' She pinches his arm and winks, and he wonders suddenly what his aunt was like as a child, whether she treated his dad the same way she treats him. She is five years older than Brad, and was already married with two kids by the time he met Seb's mother.

'Did you like my mum?' Seb asks suddenly. The room is silent for a moment, the strangeness of the question echoing in their ears. They rarely speak of her, he realises, even less than they speak of his dad, and he wants to know what they thought of her, wants to hear their memories of her.

'Of course,' Evelyn says after a moment. 'She was a lovely girl. A slip of a thing, with beautiful dark hair.'

'Like yours,' Rosa says. 'The reddish bits are from her.'

Seb touches his hair without thinking, picturing the tight curls he knows are from his dad. But there is some of his mother there too, and this makes him feel warm inside.

'She was very bright,' Evelyn says, 'quiet, not shy exactly but thoughtful, I suppose. She only spoke when she had something to say.'

'Did you get on? What did she like?' he asks Rosa. 'Did you like the same music and stuff?'

Rosa laughs. 'Oh, no. She had awful taste in music.' Evelyn gives her a look and Rosa winks at Seb. 'Your mum preferred reading over anything else. Always had her nose in a book.'

'We used to swap books sometimes,' Evelyn says, smiling now. 'She'd leave little notes inside the front cover. *Thought you'd like this one* or *Saw this and thought of you.* She was lovely like that.'

Seb feels himself smiling as he pictures it, this woman he barely had time to get to know. And then something changes in Evelyn's face, and he feels his stomach clench.

'Sorry,' he says quickly. 'I shouldn't have... It was insensitive.'

'Don't you dare,' Evelyn says, her eyes flashing. 'Don't you ever apologise for asking about your mother.'

'It's our fault,' Rosa says, 'for not speaking of her. We just thought... It's hard for us, I guess.' Her face is serious for once, her eyes clouded. 'It's not our place.'

'But you didn't kill her.' The words are out of his mouth before he can consider them, consider the impact they will have. They seem to hit Evelyn like a blow and she sits back, a hand to her chest.

'We didn't,' Rosa murmurs, 'but we didn't stop him either.'

A noise from the hallway shatters the silence that follows. Seb stands as Liv enters the hallway, a bag for life hanging off one wrist. She stops when she sees Evelyn in the armchair, her eyes widening.

'Liv,' Evelyn says, making as if to rise, 'we just dropped by to see Seb. We brought–'

'No,' Liv hisses, and Seb is taken aback. 'I explicitly told you *no.*'

'It's not what you think,' Rosa cuts in, standing. 'We just brought Seb another birthday present. Look, show her, Seb. Show your nan.'

He unfolds the paper still clutched in his hand, holds it up so she can see. Her expression changes, her eyes clearing as she reads the words. 'Oh,' she says.

'What did you think it would be?' he asks, bewildered. He has never heard Liv speak to Evelyn in that way, not once. 'What did you say no to?'

'Nothing,' Evelyn says quickly, waving a hand. 'It's nothing for you to worry about.'

Seb looks between them, taking in Evelyn's carefully calm expression, Liv's forced smile as she drops the shopping bag and takes his arm.

'Driving! Well. I can't believe you're old enough.' He sees her exchange a look with Evelyn and wonders what they are hiding from him.

I watch Evelyn's car disappear down the road and feel something tear inside me. Am I cruel to stop Seb from seeing his father? Does he deserve to know him, no matter what he has done? Eleven years is a long time, and part of me hopes that the criminal justice system does work, that Brad has paid for his crime, but it is me who will continue to pay, my grief no less now than it was the day I found my daughter's body. No, time does not mean you forget about those who have gone, who have been taken from you, it only gives you the opportunity to make room for the grief, to let the ghosts make your heart their home.

Seb goes upstairs and I drink my tea, the house quiet around me until it is too much to bear, the silence too loud. I decide to walk to my mother's today. I call goodbye to Seb before grabbing my bag and stepping outside. The sun is warm on my face, the sky above vast and cloudless. I try to imagine what it will be like when Brad is released. Evelyn told me that he will soon be eligible for parole. I try to picture him at the tiny table in my kitchen, eating a Sunday roast with me and Seb, but I cannot imagine him there without Paige. My daughter will never eat a meal with us again. She will never see her son pass his exams or learn to drive or fall in love.

'Oh, Paige,' I murmur, pressing a hand against my chest. 'What would you do?' But I know the answer. I know what Paige would want, and it is exactly what I cannot bring myself to do.

As I walk past the shops, a bike goes whizzing by me and I jump. Two more follow, teenagers whooping and laughing as they pull up by the benches where a small group sits. When Harry and I moved in, this was a new council estate, with lovely greenery all around. But they've kept building over the years, trying to keep up with demand, I suppose, and recently I've noticed more kids hanging around, smoking and drinking and causing trouble. I walk past quickly, keeping my head down.

To my surprise, Mum opens the door before I can get my key in the lock. 'I've told you before,' she says, pointing a bony finger in my direction. 'No cold callers. Push off, go on!'

'Mum,' I say with a sigh. 'It's me. Olivia.'

'Olivia?' She peers at me, her eyes like slits. 'I don't know anyone called Olivia.'

'Well, you named me,' I say, trying to keep my voice pleasant.

'Paige?' The name takes my breath away. I stare at her, my heart pounding. 'Is it you, Paige?' She reaches out a hand to touch my shoulder, and I try not to flinch away. 'I thought you were dead,' she whispers. 'Are you a ghost?'

I fight to control myself, my pulse beating in my ears like the ocean, and take my mother's hand. 'Let's get you inside, Mum.'

I settle her down with a cup of tea and a plate of ginger nut biscuits, and go upstairs to change her bed. The duvet is out of its cover, screwed into a ball and flung across the room, and I picture her wrestling with it, sixty-eight-year-old mother with dementia and COPD roaring with fury as she ripped the sheets away. I find a butter knife under one of the pillows, clean at least, and the incentive spirometer she brought home from her last trip to hospital cracked down one side. I sigh, knowing she has no patience for the treatments prescribed to her, knowing it will impact her health irreparably.

I tuck the fresh sheets in at the corners and run my hand over the faded pattern. A lavender scent tickles my nose, and I stifle a sneeze. As I open my eyes, my gaze falls on a photo frame on her bedside table. It is of Seb as a child, two years old and walking on unsteady legs towards the camera. Paige's feet are just visible in the background; she's wearing the white pumps that she insisted on buying even though they used to wear out within a month. I touch a finger to her feet, then to Seb's face. He is still my rainbow child, the one good thing to come out of all the pain and darkness. I need to remember who he really is, rather than the portrait the police have tried to paint of him.

I hear a loud rapping from downstairs and jump, my mind having wandered too far again. This is happening more often lately, and a seed of concern is growing inside me. Early-onset dementia is hereditary, after all.

I shake myself and hurry down the stairs to find Mum opening the front door. A woman stands on the porch, a bunch of flowers in her hand.

'Hello, Jean,' the woman says, offering the flowers to my mother. 'How are we today? Oh.' Noticing me on the bottom step, she flashes me a smile. 'Hello, I'm Maggie. I live over the road.'

'Hi. I'm Liv, Jean's daughter.'

Maggie's eyes widen slightly. 'Oh!' she says again. 'I didn't realise you had a daughter, Jean. How lovely.'

I try not to let the words sting. 'Do you know my mum well?' I ask, moving towards the door.

'We met last week,' Maggie says. 'Under... unusual circumstances.' She glances at Mum before continuing. 'I don't wish to speak out of turn, but–'

'Maggie helped me when Ken was unwell,' Mum says, and I frown at her.

'Ken?'

She flaps a hand at me. 'Yes, Ken. My husband. He had a fall and couldn't get up.'

I look at Maggie and note the sympathy in her eyes. 'I see,' I say slowly. 'Well, thanks Maggie. For helping. Would you like a cup of tea?'

'That would be smashing,' she says, and Mum moves aside to let her in.

'Don't listen to this one,' she stage-whispers to Maggie as they follow me into the kitchen. 'She's the one who's been stealing my crockery.'

I bite back a response as I fill the kettle. Who the hell is Ken? My father's name was Roger. A secret lover? My mum and I have never been close, but surely I'd have known if she'd remarried?

Maggie's laugh is high and tinkling. 'I'm sure she isn't, Jean.' She winks at me before placing a hand on Mum's arm. 'Why don't you go and sit down? We'll bring the tea through.'

'And a Cherry Bakewell,' Mum demands as she turns back towards the living room. 'I know she's hidden them somewhere.'

'I suppose that *she* is me,' I say, making a face to lighten the words. 'Does she have any Bakewells in?'

'I brought her some a few days ago,' Maggie says, opening the cupboard next to the fridge. 'Aha! Here we are.' She brings out an unopened box and lays it on the counter before turning back to me. 'I'm glad to have met you, Liv,' she says, smiling. 'I was concerned that your mum didn't have anyone taking care of her.'

'I'm here as often as I can be,' I say, too sharply. 'I work, and I have a grandson who lives with me.'

'Oh, how lovely!' Maggie exclaims. I wonder how old she is, and realise that she's probably around my age. 'My son recently had a baby, they called him Oscar. He'll be one in September. How old is your little one?'

'Sixteen,' I say, and watch the confusion flicker over her face for a moment before explaining. 'I was a young mum, and so was my daughter. She... passed away, when her boy was four. I've been looking after him ever since.'

'Oh, you poor thing,' Maggie says, placing a hand on my arm. 'How awful. I'm so sorry.'

I turn away to make the tea, not wanting this woman's sympathy. I have never done well in the face of pity, the baleful glances and *oh, you poor thing*. Sympathy doesn't get me up in the morning; sympathy doesn't pay the gas bill or fill the fridge or keep Seb on the straight and narrow.

'So, this Ken,' Maggie says after a moment. 'Does he exist?'

'I don't think so. I've never heard of him.'

She purses her lips. 'It was quite a to-do, I have to say. She came screeching out of the house in just a nightie, no shoes or slippers on. It was around three o'clock in the morning, she scared the living daylights out of me. Woke half the street up.'

I pause in stirring the tea, concern bubbling through me. This is a new development, something else to keep me up at night. Not only do I have to worry about her setting the house on fire or falling down those sodding stairs, but now she's taken to running around the streets in her pyjamas.

'She said Ken had fallen over,' Maggie continues. 'Paul, that's my husband, ran upstairs to the bathroom, but there was nobody there.' She shakes her head. 'Poor love. Dementia, is it?'

I nod. 'My dad had it too. Nasty illness. Have you thought about sending her to a nice home? There are some lovely ones in the area, or even by the sea. My dad went down to Kent, he loved it there. They did everything for him – cooked, cleaned, even personal care. Nothing for me to worry about at all.'

I bite my tongue to keep from biting her head off and pick up two mugs of tea to take into the lounge. Maggie rests a hand on my arm again and I try not to flinch. I don't know what it is about this woman, but she is rubbing me up the wrong way.

'Looking after an ageing parent is hard,' she murmurs, 'especially when a teenager's at home as well. What about your husband, does he help?'

'He's dead,' I say, and she must see something in my eyes for she takes a step back. If only she knew the truth. As my mother said one day when I turned up with a screaming Paige and a black eye: 'You've made your bed. Now you have to lie in it.'

27

CAITLYN

'Have you got everything, darling?' I ask for the fifth or sixth time, my hands on Izzy's shoulders. She rolls her eyes, but she is still smiling.

'Yes, Mum. Anyway, I'll be back in a few weeks.'

'I know, I know,' I say, though it will be closer to four weeks by the time she comes back. She is staying longer this time, to get settled in. I pull her in for another hug then release her, and instantly feel the lack of her. Michael stands behind me, hands in his pockets, one shoulder leaning against the door frame. I look up at Anthony, who is leaning against his car in a similar fashion, and I think, *if you don't look after her, I will bloody kill you.*

'We'd better be off,' he says, avoiding my gaze as if he has read my mind. 'Beat the traffic on the M5. It can be hellish.'

'Bye, Mum,' Izzy says, leaning in to peck me on the cheek. I breathe her in.

'Bye, darling. Safe journey. Text me when you get there!'

And then she is gone, strapped into the passenger seat beside a man she hasn't seen in so many years, but who is her father and is offering her a way out. I wave until the car disappears around the corner, my arm dropping to my side like lead.

I suddenly wish Alicia were still here, that *someone* was here to throw their arms around me and tell me that everything is going to be okay. Michael has always taken a back seat where the girls are concerned, and I know he thinks I am silly for wanting to hang on to them. 'She's growing up,' he said when I told him what Anthony had offered. 'Maybe some space will do her good. Do you both good.'

But Izzy has not grown up. She is not an adult. She is still a child, still so young and vulnerable and in need of a mother's protection. And yet I have failed her. Time and time again, I have failed to be there for her in the way she needs. When Anthony left and I fell into a pit of vodka and despair; when the bullying started and Izzy cut herself for the first time; when she tried to take her own life, once and then again. Now she is gone, and I have no one to blame but myself. *I am a bad mother, and bad mothers lose their children.*

I go back inside to find Michael in the kitchen making a pot of coffee. He puts his hands on my shoulders and squeezes. 'She'll be fine,' he says, rubbing his hands up and down my arms. 'It might be the making of her. A fresh start.'

I nod, because I want this to be true. I want Izzy to have a fresh start, to find herself and the path she is meant to take. I clutch the coffee Michael makes me in both hands and sit down on the sofa, curling my legs beneath me. I can hear him tapping away at his keyboard in the study, and wonder when this distance between us began to grow. We got together when Izzy was just about to start secondary school, and Alicia was almost a teenager and already rarely in the house, always out shopping or at the cinema or, later, drinking with friends. I am not some clueless mother who has no idea what her children are up to, but they have managed to pull the wool over my eyes a few times over the years. Or have I just been so wrapped up in myself that I've missed the things going on in their lives? When Izzy was struggling to make friends at school, I was busy worrying about shaving my legs for dates with Michael. When Alicia moved away to university, Michael was moving in, his pants taking up space in my underwear drawer, his razor stowed in the caddy in the bathroom. The razor Izzy used to...

I flinch away from these thoughts, burrowing down deeper into the sofa, my head resting on the arm. When the dental practice I worked at as a receptionist went bust three years ago, I took my redundancy pay and decided not to get another job. My health was at its worst then, and although I am better now, we get by with Michael's salary, plus there was enough left over from the sale of my parents' house to keep us going, even after the renovation. I remember the dreams I had when I was a student, of graduating with a first and going on to a master's degree. I'd wanted to do a PhD, to be *Dr*, not *Mrs*. But then I met Anthony, and my life changed forever.

I flush with guilt as I remember those dark days, after he left. He had tricked me into motherhood, I raged as I drank bottle after bottle, holed up in my room like an angry teenager. I had never wanted children, or at least, they had not been on my radar. And yet I'd found myself pregnant at twenty-one, just after I graduated from university, and he had convinced me not to have an abortion, to move into his studio flat and be a family.

'Our greatest adventure,' he said, and I, stupid and young and flushed with love, had gone along with it.

I do not regret my children now. I suppose that is what I'm meant to say: *I wouldn't change them for the world.* But does it make me a bad mother to want to change the timing? To want to change how things played out?

~

I make myself wait a full five hours before texting Izzy. According to Google Maps, it takes about four-and-a-half hours to get to Plymouth from here, coffee breaks and crashes notwithstanding. Her reply comes back immediately.

Just got here, Mum, my room is huge!! x

I smile as I'm flooded with relief, ignoring the pang of loss that hits me in the stomach. Send me a picture x I type back.

A photo comes through within seconds, followed by three more. I see a large bed against one wall, a window beside it, and then the room opens up to what looks like a living space, with a large bay window on one side and two doors on the other.

It's basically a studio flat! I type. Wow! Is that an en suite? x

Yep! My own bathroom and walk-in wardrobe. Miranda said I can decorate it however I like xx

How lovely! What are you going to go for? x

Not sure yet, Dad said he'll take me to B&Q one day x

Dad. Already he is Dad to her again, not the man who left when she was four and never again showed his face, never sent a birthday or Christmas card. I am amazed at how he has waltzed in and saved the day, able to give Izzy exactly what she wants – what she needs – at this moment in time. I wonder again whether Alicia had told him all about the photo, but no, she said she hadn't. Had he come across the photo online then? I cringe as I picture it being shared wide across the internet, retweeted and reposted again and again and again, until everyone in the world has seen my little girl at her most vulnerable.

Viral, another 'after' word.

28

SEB

Going back to school is worse than Seb had feared. He tries to pay attention in lessons, keeping his head down as he doodles in his exercise book, but all he can hear are the whispers, the burn of eyes staring at his back. He hears her name everywhere – *Izzy* – and tries to ignore the shame coursing through him. They are all laughing at him, the boy who got dumped by the most unpopular girl at school, and it needles at him, sending prickles along his skin. His head is pounding by the time the bell rings at the end of the day, his mouth dry and fuzzy, and he packs up his bag quickly, rushing out of the classroom without stopping.

He is almost at the bus stop when he hears his name being called. He turns to see Liam and Josh jogging down the path, bags bouncing on their backs.

'Where you been?' Liam asks breathlessly. 'Haven't you seen our messages?'

'We heard about Izzy moving away,' Josh says. 'Are you okay?'

Seb lifts a shoulder. 'I need to catch my bus.'

Josh glances at Liam before speaking. 'You busy tonight?'

'We're going out,' Liam says. 'You should come. It's been ages since we had a night out.'

Seb thinks for a moment, trying to remember the last time he went out with his friends. He remembers trying to persuade Izzy to go, the way she bit her lip as she shook her head. *Come on, it'll be fun.* And it was, until the night was cut short by Izzy feeling unwell.

It was a party at Sian's house, the lights turned pink and purple, pulsating in time with the music. She had recently moved in, the house a new build on the edge of town, and her parents were away for the weekend. She held court in the kitchen, mixing drinks and putting out bowls of crisps and nuts, laughing loudly. Abby made Izzy a drink, pressing it into her hands with a grin, and before long Izzy was so drunk, she could hardly hold her head up. Seb remembers the way Sian and Abby had giggled as she staggered to her feet and disappeared out the front door to throw up in the bushes.

'They spiked me,' she told him the next day, after he had taken her home and put her to bed with a glass of water, leaving quietly so her mother didn't hear. 'They put something in my drink.'

'You just drank too much,' he said. 'Something didn't agree with you.' And she had stared at him, her eyes full of hurt that he didn't believe her. That he had, once again, failed to stick up for her.

'All right,' he says now, banishing Izzy from his thoughts. 'I'll be there.'

At home, he kicks off his shoes and goes into the kitchen to check the fridge. His nan writes everything down; her work shifts, when she's looking after her mum, and he sees that today she is working until eight.

Bolognese in the fridge she has written beneath on the whiteboard. *Garlic bread in the freezer xx*

But Seb isn't hungry. He goes upstairs, shrugging out of his uniform and pulling on a pair of jeans. He lifts his mattress and takes out a pouch of tobacco which he stuffs into his pocket. He checks his phone before he leaves, tapping on the Instagram app and watching Izzy's story for the third time today. It is a video taken from a moving car, a huge river glistening beneath the sun as the car drives past. The location tag says Plymouth. Seb feels as if she is moving further and further away from him, until she is nothing but a speck on the horizon.

Liam and Josh are sitting on a bench opposite the water, watching the swans huddling by the edge. Seb counts four cygnets as he approaches them, their grey feathers fuzzy and damp from the river.

'Take your time,' Liam says with a grin. 'We almost started without you.'

They walk along the path, towards the bridge and over it, then through the long grass until they come to a quiet spot beside the river, where the grass is flattened and littered with old cigarette butts. They sit with their feet dangling off the edge, the water rushing past beneath them.

'I saw Izzy's stories earlier,' Josh says. 'Have you spoken to her?'

Seb feels his stomach tighten at the mention of her name. He shakes his head. 'Not since she dumped me.'

'Who's she living with?' Liam asks.

'Her dad.'

'I thought he wasn't in the picture.'

'Why are you asking me?' His words come out stronger than he intended and he winces inwardly.

'All right,' Liam says, holding up his hands. 'Just asking.'

'Sucks though,' Josh says, lighting a cigarette. 'Her just dumping you like that.'

'Yeah,' Liam says. 'Especially after, you know.'

Seb does know. He feels his cheeks heat up as he realises that even if he is not blamed for what happened, he is still viewed differently now. Judged. Pitied. He doesn't know what's worse.

'She's always been a bit funny,' Liam says thoughtfully. 'Even as a kid.'

'Was she?' Josh asks. 'I didn't know you were close.'

'Since we were ickle babies.' Liam laughs, looking at Seb. 'All three of us, remember?'

Seb nods, a memory flashing into his mind. The three of them in assembly, singing 'All Things Bright and Beautiful' at the top of their lungs. They were in the same class, seated at the same table. And then at break time, when Liam refused to let Izzy play It, telling her that girls couldn't play, even though Alex was a girl and *she* was playing.

'Alex is cool,' Liam sneered, and Seb can see it again now, the way he curled his lip as he spoke. He is different now, Liam, softer, and Seb is surprised at the memory. How cruel children can be. How easily they can hurt each other. How strong the echoes are, reaching through the years to haunt you.

'Anyway,' Liam says now. 'Have you heard from the police lately?'

Josh sighs. 'No. My dad went mental when they came to interview me. I think they're too scared to come back.'

'I wonder who else they spoke to,' Liam says. 'They can't have interviewed the whole school. Have you heard from them, Seb?'

'They've only been round once. I think they blamed me though.'

'Why?'

Seb shrugs. 'Because I'm her boyfriend. Was,' he adds quickly. 'I think they thought I'd pressured her into taking it.'

'But she didn't send it to you, did she?' Josh asks.

Seb shakes his head.

'I wonder who she did send it to in the first place,' Liam says. 'And why.'

'It's not cool, is it,' Josh says. 'When she had a boyfriend.'

Seb feels his stomach tighten, frustration building up inside him. 'Can we stop talking about the fucking picture?' he says, reaching out and grabbing a can of cider from Liam's bag. 'I'm sick of hearing about it.'

'What picture?' Seb turns to see Abby behind him, Sian and Jess flanking her. He suppresses a groan. 'Silly me,' Abby says, sitting down beside him. 'There can only be *one* picture we're still talking about.'

'Can I have some?' Sian asks, sitting beside Liam and taking the cider from his hand before he can answer.

'Oi!' He snatches it back before she can take a sip. 'Get your own.'

She flashes him a grin as Jess sits on his other side and takes it from him again. 'Too easy.' Jess laughs.

Abby sits beside Seb, her bare knee grazing his. He resists the urge to shuffle away. 'So,' she says, opening her bag and bringing out a bottle of vodka. 'The picture.'

'We weren't talking about that picture,' Seb snaps. 'Just leave it, yeah?'

Abby rolls her eyes. 'How typical of a *man* to not want to discuss a girl being violated.' He feels himself burn with indignation, and opens his mouth to retort before she bursts into laughter. 'Kidding! Izzy was totally up for it.'

He stares at her, shock rendering him speechless. Up for it?

'What does that mean?' Josh demands.

'Well,' Abby says, flicking her hair over her shoulder. 'I have it on good authority that Izzy knew exactly what she was doing.'

'Yeah, okay then,' Seb says, turning away from her.

She ignores him. 'She knew it was going to get shared around. We tried to warn her, didn't we, girls?'

Jess nods. 'What are friends for?'

'You weren't friends,' Seb snaps. 'She hated you.'

'Ouch,' Sian murmurs.

'Hate is such a strong word,' Abby says. 'We tried our best with her, we really did. It's not our fault Izzy never fit in.'

'Or annoyed *every*one,' Jess adds.

'So that's why you spiked her drink that time?' The words are out before Seb realises what he's doing, before he even realises that the pieces are slotting together. 'That's why you shared that picture all over social media?' His lips twist in disgust. 'You were never her friend.'

Sian looks shocked. Abby looks at him with wide eyes, cocking her head to one side. 'We all know she's an attention-seeker.' She smiles then, a slow smile that looks almost like a grimace. 'Who says she didn't share it herself?'

Seb walks home, hands stuffed into his pockets, a black cloud hanging over him despite the bright sun beating down from a clear blue sky. He thinks of Abby's words. *Izzy was totally up for it.* Up for what? It was all drama, wasn't it? Izzy was a drama queen, everyone said so. An attention-seeker. That's why she took that photo, he thinks. That's why she broadcast herself to the world, without a thought about how Seb would feel about it. Had she ever cared about him at all?

They have known each other for so long, their formative years mingled with memories of one another. He thought they had a connection, something primal that recognised itself, two halves of a whole. And now she is gone.

His phone buzzes in his pocket, but he ignores it. He knows it will be one of the boys, asking if he's all right after he left so abruptly. But he couldn't handle Abby's smug grin, the way they were still laughing about Izzy. He wonders if they will ever stop talking about her, ever stop looking at him with barely concealed pity and disdain.

As he rounds the corner, he almost bumps into someone coming out of the shop, pulls up just in time.

'Sorry,' he says, taking a step to the right as if to pass, but the figure reaches out a hand.

'Seb?'

He looks up, recognition dawning as he takes in the face before him. 'Jodie? Bloody hell, I haven't seen you in forever.' He tries to remember the last time he saw her, and a memory pops into his mind, of when they were ten or eleven, still young and innocent, sharing sweets on a bench on the park before their paths separated.

'Still a posh boy then,' Jodie says, whacking his arm with her hand. Seb feels his cheeks flush, denial on his lips, until she laughs. 'I'm fucking with you. How's things?'

'All right,' he says, unable and unwilling to say anything else. 'You?'

Jodie shrugs. 'Yeah, all right.'

'You still live round here? I haven't seen you in ages, I thought you'd moved.'

'Nah.' She grins, showing white, even teeth. 'Well, I went to live with my dad in Enfield a few years ago.'

'Oh. How is he?'

'Dead.' Seb blinks at her, trying to align her grin with her words. 'Yeah. He was a dickhead. Heroin.'

'Oh,' Seb says again. 'So you're back?'

Jodie sighs. 'Yeah, for the time being. Till she chucks me out again.'

'Your mum?' Seb is taken aback. He'd always thought Jodie's mum was nice, with their small, tidy flat and cat with the silky black fur.

'Yeah. She got a new bloke, innit. He took a liking to me, shall we say.' She fumbles in her pockets, comes up with a roll-up and lighter. 'She didn't believe me. Bitch.'

'Is he still there? At your mum's?'

'Nah. He ran off with some younger bird last year, left her in a shitload of debt.' Jodie blows a smoke ring and grins. 'Suppose she deserves it.' Seb doesn't say anything. 'Where you off to anyway?' she asks.

'Nowhere. Home.'

'Nowhere. Home,' she mimics, deepening her voice. She finishes her roll-up and flicks it to the floor, sparks connecting with the pavement. 'You should come out tonight, in town. Unless you've got big plans.' She whacks his arm lightly.

'I've just come from there,' he says. 'I need to get home.'

'Come on. It'll be fun. We've got loads to catch up on.'

'All right. When?'

'Now?'

29

IZZY

In the bathroom – *her* bathroom, she reminds herself – Izzy turns on the shower, steam filling the air as she takes off her clothes and steps under the water. Miranda has left out toiletries for her: a bar of fruity body wash on a wire shelf, bottles of shampoo and conditioner that have words like 97% *natural* and *for curly hair.* She closes her eyes and inhales the scent of the shampoo, her fingers scrubbing her scalp.

'Your hair is beautiful,' Miranda said when she arrived, engulfing her in a hug. 'Your dad showed me a photo. I hope I've bought you the right stuff.' She smiled warmly. 'Curls are so *in* right now.'

Izzy has never been *in*, not ever. But maybe she can be, here, now. Maybe she can be someone else entirely.

She rinses and conditions her hair before opening the shower door, the mat soft beneath her toes, the towel fluffy and warm from the rail on the wall. She looks around the small room, admiring Miranda's taste. The white metro tiles have been laid in a zigzag formation, the wall on the far side painted a light teal. The sink is a wide bowl, and the cupboard below contains everything you could ever need; bamboo toothbrushes, spare tubes of toothpaste, mouthwash tablets. A pack of razors.

Izzy closes the cupboard door and wipes the condensation from the mirror. She uses the microfibre towel to squeeze the water from her hair and rakes through the curl cream Miranda pointed out when she gave her the tour. She vows to learn how to take care of her curls properly, instead of trying to tame them. Maybe she should stop trying to tame herself.

In the bedroom – *her* bedroom – she opens the wardrobe and looks through the clothes hanging on the rail. She hasn't unpacked yet, but Miranda has thought of everything, it seems, and Izzy looks through the rows of new leggings, jeans, pyjamas. She sees a maxi skirt and a few T-shirts, and a drawer full of underwear. She blushes, wondering how Miranda knew her size, before selecting a pair of leggings and a T-shirt with David Bowie's face on and moving to the dressing table. She opens a tub of moisturiser and spreads it along her legs and arms, enjoying the mango scent and the soft, slippery feel of her skin. She feels pampered, relaxed.

Dressed, she checks her phone for the time. Seven o'clock. She pads down the three steps separating her room from the rest of the first floor, then heads down to the kitchen. She can hear music drifting out of the open door, and the low hum of voices which stop when she enters.

'Hey, Iz,' Anthony says, turning from his place at the sink. 'Dinner's almost ready.'

'Smells good,' Izzy says. 'Can I help?'

'No, no,' Miranda says, waving a hand as she stirs something on the hob. 'You sit down. Would you like a drink?'

'Sure. Is there any Coke?'

'In the fridge. Help yourself.'

'I'll have one too, please,' Anthony says. 'Diet,' he adds when Miranda glares at him. 'Trying to reduce the sugar.'

'You know sweeteners are just as bad for you,' Izzy says as she takes the cans from the fridge. 'Our bodies can't process them.'

'See?' Anthony grins as Miranda tuts. 'I knew you'd come in handy. Grab me a normal one, will you? We're celebrating, after all.'

Izzy smiles as she sits at the table. *Celebrating.* A word usually reserved for birthdays and holidays and anything other than her just being there, just existing.

'We'll go to B&Q tomorrow if you want,' Anthony says, drying his hands on a tea towel and coming over to sit opposite Izzy. 'We can just have a browse if you haven't decided yet.'

'I think I found a grey I like,' she replies. 'Or maybe a dusky pink.'

'Good choice,' Miranda says. 'I love a light pink. Have you texted your mother yet?'

'Yeah. I sent her pictures of the room too. She said it's the size of a studio flat.'

'A bedsit in my language,' Anthony says with a chuckle.

'Oh, good,' Miranda says. 'I'm sure she'll be missing you.'

I'm not, Izzy thinks but doesn't say.

'What's for dinner?' she asks.

'Harissa cauliflower with potato wedges and salad,' Miranda says.

'We don't eat meat,' Anthony adds. 'Sorry, I should've said before.'

'We don't mind if you do though,' Miranda says quickly. 'It's not a problem.'

Izzy shakes her head. 'I don't mind. That sounds really nice.'

'Set the table, will you, Ant?' Miranda says as she opens the oven door.

'Oh, let me.' Izzy jumps up, wondering when she was last

this helpful at home, pushing the thought away. 'Where are the plates?'

Miranda points at a cupboard and Izzy takes three grey-rimmed plates down, setting them out on the table before going back for cutlery and napkins. The bi-fold doors are open and a cool breeze flutters through. It is colder down here, Izzy thinks, but pleasant. The weather has been unseasonably warm, and she hopes it holds for her first trip to the sea. She can't wait to explore the city.

Miranda sets out plates of food and sits down, pouring herself a glass of water. 'Help yourself,' she says, holding the bowl of cauliflower out to Izzy. She spoons out a portion before handing it to her father.

They eat in companionable silence for a while, the food new and delicious to Izzy. She thinks of the effort her mother goes to cooking for them all and feels a pang of regret for not appreciating it more. For not appreciating *her* more. She will call her later, she thinks. She will make an effort.

'I thought we could go out for brunch on Monday,' Miranda says, laying down her cutlery and picking up her water. 'While your father is at work. I've got a few days off.'

'Where do you work?' Izzy asks, stopping short of using the word *Dad*. 'Mum said you used to be an artist.'

Anthony laughs. 'Used to be, yes. Now I run a gallery on the Barbican, showcasing other, more talented people than myself.'

Miranda lays a hand on his arm. 'Hush. You're still talented. He painted that, you know.' She indicates a painting hanging above them on the wall. Izzy looks at it, cocking her head to take in the scene. A large ruin stands on top of a cliff, the sea sparkling beyond.

'What is it?'

'It's an old tin mine,' Anthony says. 'Over in St Agnes. Lovely place. We'll visit sometime.'

'I work in finance,' Miranda says, making a face. 'Not quite as glamorous. It's mostly from home, though, so I can't complain.'

Izzy sips her drink. 'How long have you lived here?' she asks. 'This house is amazing.'

'We moved in properly about two years ago,' Miranda replies, smiling. 'After the main renovating was done. We still lived in a bit of a building site for a while, but it was worth it.'

'How do you like your room?' Anthony asks. 'Do you have everything you need?'

Izzy nods. She tries to imagine the father she knew when she was younger, but fails to conjure up an image. How could she have forgotten him so easily? Then she remembers: her mother. When she finally emerged from her depression, for Izzy recognises now that Caitlyn had been depressed, she had refused to speak of him again, taking down all photos and reminders of him. He had been erased, scrubbed from their lives and their minds for good.

'It's great,' she says, trying to push away the guilt she feels. 'It's perfect.'

30

CAITLYN

My feet pound against the floor, my ponytail swinging as I run. I listen to the story of a foundling hospital in the eighteenth century, losing myself in the mesmerising voice of the narrator. Michael is going away again tonight, and the house is empty, the silence too loud, and so I am running, breathing hard but steady as I navigate around the families picnicking on the grass, the dogs chasing balls thrown high into the air.

I have kept tabs on Izzy's social media since she left, watched with an ache in my heart as she explores Plymouth, double-tapped the photos of her bedroom and the kitchen in her new home, the beautiful fireplace in the living room. Miranda has good taste. I have checked her social media too, found her on LinkedIn and ran through her professional life. On paper – or rather, on screen – she appears to be a kind, intelligent woman with a good career. Pity she has such bad taste in men, but I can't really judge her on that. Anthony was always charming, with his bright smile and eyes full of mischief, and who am I to say that he hasn't changed, that he is no longer the man who walked out on his family because it wasn't living up to his expectations. Because we were tying him down, too heavy for him to carry.

I am not bitter. Things worked out, after the depression and the constant worrying about money and my health failing. I suppose it would make me a bad daughter if I said I was glad when my parents died and I inherited enough to silence those worries, but it's true. Though glad is probably too powerful a word; it implies an emotional connection, something that tethered me to them. Relieved is probably the better word. After their funeral in Melbourne, which I did not attend, I've rarely thought about them. There had been so much distance between us throughout my life, their disappointment that I was not a boy to replace the son they'd loved and lost before I was born so great, it overshadowed everything else. I spent a lot of my childhood with my grandmother, a tiny woman with a fierce personality who I named Izzy after, and who she reminds me of more and more as she gets older. Isabelle the elder was a true matriarch, with very clear ideas on what she expected from people, and that is probably why her daughter, my mother, rarely spent any time with her, but she was also loving and kind. I enjoyed spending time with her. My parents were the kind of people who didn't seem to like children, though I know from the stories and the amount of photographs they had of my brother that they had loved him. So perhaps it was just me they didn't like, me who was the disappointment.

If someone were to ask what my childhood was like, I would have to say it was quiet. Awkward. Disjointed. Laughter was scarce, love even scarcer. So it's no surprise then that I escaped as soon as I could. My grandmother died when I was seventeen, and then I moved across the country for university, visiting a few times a year, then twice, then only at Christmas. And then I was pregnant, and the path I had so carefully crafted for myself was ripped up from beneath my feet.

I slow down as I cross over the bridge, taking out my earphones and pausing at the end to watch a family of swans navigate the water below. The cygnets are grey and fluffy, tiny beside their majestic parents. A moorhen squawks from the bank and I start off again, walking this time, following the river as it bends around the perimeter of the field. It is quiet here, only the rushing of the water and the sounds of the cars flying over the A10 in the distance. My breath slows as I walk, my muscles tingling as they cool down. I perch on the end of a bench, popping open my water bottle and gulping the liquid down. I close my eyes and breathe in, inhaling the scent of the muddy riverbank beneath me, the freshly cut grass on the field. And then I smell it, the unmistakable scent of weed drifting towards me.

I open my eyes. This area is popular with teenagers, hidden away from small children and inquisitive dogs. I wonder suddenly if Izzy used to come here, if she ever laid in the tall grass with friends, watching the clouds move across the sky. I haven't always paid her the attention she deserves, haven't always taken her sadness seriously. And then the bullying started, and I foolishly believed that it would blow over, that it was normal teenage behaviour and everything would work out. But then she started to hurt herself, small cuts on the insides of her thighs to begin with, hidden beneath her clothes. Clumps of hair in the bin, tucked beneath a wad of tissue. Packets of crisps and biscuits going missing from the kitchen, the sound of her throwing up in the middle of the night.

I remember the first time I found her hastily trying to cover the gash on her wrist with a plaster. That was when I realised the true depth of what was going on. How much it was hurting her. She started going to counselling, and although she was still withdrawn, spending most evenings alone in her room, I thought things were getting better. I thought *she* was getting better.

At first, she refused to show me the messages she was

getting. She told me she'd deleted her social media accounts, and then she started to stay off school, claiming she had a migraine. It all seemed to happen so fast, and yet, looking back, I can see so many opportunities for me to have stepped in. To change the course of events. And then maybe none of this would have happened. The photo, the suicide attempts. Izzy moving over two hundred miles away and leaving me feeling as if a part of me has been ripped out.

Voices drift over to me, the words too muffled to make out. I decide to follow the river all the way around and cut through past the church. I pick up the pace, jogging along the path, narrowly avoiding a cyclist too focused on his phone to notice me. As I go through a gate and past another field, the voices get louder, mingled with music and laughter. Through the trees, on what I thought was private land, I see several figures lying on the ground, and a few seated on what looks like a bench beside a small brick building. Is it a public way after all? There are some cows in the field beyond, staring mournfully at the group, tails flicking. I hear the smashing of glass and slow down, peering through the growth. They are throwing bottles at the building, their laughter loud and raucous. Are they drunk? At this time on a weekday?

I frown. I'm certain that this stretch of grass belongs to the farm across town, where I sometimes buy eggs and meat. They're going to be very annoyed that a group of teenagers are smashing bottles on their property. I take out my phone, pausing as I think of Izzy, of what I would do if I found out she had been part of something like this, and decide that the parents of these teenagers, for they are surely teenagers, should know what their children are up to.

31

SEB

By the time they reach town, Seb is howling with laughter. He remembers how funny Jodie used to be, how observant she was. She still arches one eyebrow when she cracks a joke, still tips her head back to laugh. He suddenly realises that he has missed her, this friend who was only a friend outside of school, away from the Izzys and the Joshs and the Liams. Someone who lived two streets away, whose mum told him to make himself at home, and *just go up, Seb, no need to stand on ceremony*. He had let this friendship drop, focused instead on the people his nan thought he should be spending time with, doing the things his nan told him to do, and he realises his error now.

'So what are we doing anyway?' he asks as they walk through the supermarket car park. It is early evening, the air still warm, and the park is full of children, playing and screaming at the top of their lungs.

Jodie glances at him out of the corner of her eye, mischief in her gaze. 'You'll see.' She leads him across the road and onto the field, then over a small bridge. The path is lined with trees, the sky blocked out by heavy leaves, and the river trickles past, moorhens drifting by along the water.

They turn down a smaller path, cutting through the trees, clothes snagging on branches like outstretched fingers. It is colder here, away from the late spring sun, and Seb realises he can no longer hear the sounds of the young families in the main park. Jodie pushes open a low gate, and as Seb follows, he sees that they are in an enclosed space, with high barbed wire fencing them in.

'What is this?' he asks, looking around.

Jodie grins. 'Just a little place we found.' As she speaks, Seb notices a small brick structure at the far end. The door swings open and a girl steps out, both arms raised above her head.

'Jode!' she calls. 'Who's the boy?'

'An old mate,' Jodie says as they move closer. 'He's cool. Seb, Tasha. Tasha, Seb.' She waves a hand between them.

'Hi,' he says, trying not to squirm under Tasha's gaze. Her eyes rake over him, making him feel as if she can read his innermost thoughts.

'You're late,' she says after a moment, turning her gaze back to Jodie.

'Yeah, yeah,' Jodie replies, moving past Tasha into the building. 'Where's my shit?'

'Where you left it.'

Seb stays outside, turning away from Tasha and looking around the field. It is so quiet, and a sense of peace settles over him that he hasn't felt in a long time. All thoughts of Izzy seem further away here.

Jodie emerges with two large carrier bags. She flicks her long braid over her shoulder as she grins at him. 'Take these, will you? I need to get the chairs.'

He does, holding the heavy bags against his chest while Jodie wrestles two folded deckchairs through the narrow doorway. She sets them up round the side of the building, and Tasha rolls out a large striped blanket beside the chairs.

'Help me with the bench,' she says to Seb, and he places the bags down before following her. 'So how do you know Jodie?' she asks as they grab opposite ends of a metal bench.

'We used to live near each other. We hung out a lot when we were kids.' Tasha makes a noise in the back of her throat. 'You?'

'Community service,' she says, flashing him a grin that brings to mind a wolf baring its teeth. 'She still the same?'

Seb shakes his head. 'I don't know. I just bumped into her today.' They manoeuvre the bench through the door and carry it round the side of the building. 'How did you find this place?' he asks Jodie, who is sitting cross-legged on the blanket, a small rectangular tin open on her lap. He watches her sprinkle small green flakes onto a line of tobacco.

'My boyfriend brought me here last summer,' Tasha answers, collapsing onto one of the deckchairs and opening a bottle of cider with her teeth. 'It's been abandoned for years.'

'Sit down,' Jodie says to Seb without glancing up. 'You're making the place look untidy.'

He perches on the bench, suddenly wondering why he is here. The Jodie he used to know is still there, but she is buried under a harder exterior, one which has been battered by the elements. He should leave, but where would he go? Izzy is gone, and he doesn't want to see his friends, doesn't want to be reminded of everything that has happened over the past few weeks. He just wants to forget.

Jodie licks the paper, twisting it into a perfect cone, before holding it up triumphantly. She digs out a lighter and holds the flame to the end, watching as it catches, a small line of smoke drifting upwards. She puts it in her mouth and inhales before holding it out to Seb.

He shakes his head. 'Not for me.'

Jodie laughs. 'Oh, go on. You look like you could do with a pick-me-up.' But he shakes his head again.

Tasha snatches the spliff from Jodie's hand and takes a long drag. 'I didn't realise you were mates with pussies,' she says, blowing a smoke ring into the air.

Jodie whacks her leg. 'Seb isn't a pussy. He's just not a delinquent like us.'

'Who's a delinquent?' A voice makes them turn. Three boys and a girl have emerged through the trees, ducking beneath the wire fence and walking towards them.

'You're the biggest one, Olly,' Jodie says, laughing. She takes the spliff back from Tasha and holds it out to one of the boys. 'Just in time, as always.'

'I can smell bud from half a mile,' he says, grinning as he takes it from her. He looks at Seb while the others find places to sit. 'Who's this then?'

'This is Seb,' Jodie says. 'Seb, meet Olly, Dylan, Ben. And Kyra, of course.' The girl gives a small wave from where she sits down on the blanket while the boys nod. Olly sits beside Seb on the bench, spreading his legs and leaning back on the cool metal. He holds the spliff out to him.

'He doesn't do drugs,' Tasha pipes up. 'He's a good boy.'

'I'm not,' Seb protests. He doesn't mind weed, has smoked it a few times with his friends, but he doesn't like the way it makes him feel afterwards, when the high is gone and he is left feeling empty.

Olly shrugs. 'No pressure. Not all of us are crackheads, Tash.' Tasha's nostrils flare, her eyes darkening at the slight. Olly turns to Seb. 'So, Seb. Short for Sebastian? "Under the Sea"?' He laughs, not unkindly. 'Where you from?'

'Not seen you around before,' Dylan says, opening a can of beer and cursing as it sprays his leg. 'You one of them posh boys?'

Seb shakes his head. 'I live near Jodie. We knew each other as kids.' It suddenly strikes him that he is doing the opposite of what he has done all his life, reaffirming that he is from the estate on the edge of town that nobody in his circle of friends would ever visit, instead of playing it down. He has always tried his best to fit in with the people who live in nice, semi-detached houses with more rooms than they need and a fridge full of food, who always have the latest phones and brand-new trainers, but he has never fit in, he realises now. He has never been able to keep up.

'We were good pals,' Jodie says. 'Remember when your nan took us berry-picking and we got lost?' She laughs.

Seb smiles, remembering. 'You lost a shoe in the mud.'

'Oh yeah, I'd forgotten about that.' Jodie shakes her head. 'My mum had a fit.'

'Heart-warming,' Tasha says, her voice full of sarcasm. Jodie shoots her a look.

'How about a cider, Sebastian?' Ben says, fishing a can out of a bag. 'We're celebrating.'

'Are we?' Kyra asks, glancing at Ben. He slides an arm around her shoulder.

'Course we are. Our Dylan got off, didn't he?'

'What happened?' Tasha asks Dylan, who shrugs.

'Suspended sentence,' he says, lighting a cigarette.

'Yeah!' Ben says, grinning. 'Fuck the police.'

Seb feels Jodie looking at him. 'Didn't you have the feds at yours the other day?' she asks, leaning back on both elbows.

'Yeah?' Tasha says. 'What did you do, cross the road without waiting for the green man?' She sniggers.

'I didn't do anything,' Seb mumbles, feeling his cheeks heat up.

Jodie clicks her fingers. 'Hang on, didn't something happen to your girlfriend?' She turns to Kyra. 'That girl at your sister's school. Something about a photo?' His stomach lurches. How does Jodie know about Izzy? She gives a shrug as if he has asked the question aloud. 'I saw it on Facebook, Izzy something? She's your girlfriend, yeah?'

'Oh God,' Kyra says, her eyes widening. 'Yeah, that poor girl. A naked photo went around the school or something.'

'Naked photo.' Tasha wrinkles her nose. 'Like revenge porn?' She glances at Seb and his body tenses at the accusation in her eyes.

'Nah,' Jodie says, 'didn't she take it herself or something? Sent it to someone?'

Ben whistles. 'I'd be well pissed off if my girlfriend's nudes went around.' He tightens his arm around Kyra. 'Unless I released them myself. Sometimes girls deserve it.'

'Fuck off,' Jodie says, kicking out at his ankle.

'She probably cheated,' Dylan says with a yawn.

'Did she?' Olly asks, but before Seb can answer, Olly is shaking his head. He passes Seb a bottle of Malibu. 'Females are more trouble than they're worth,' he murmurs, nudging Seb with his shoulder. 'Drink up, mate.'

Seb opens the bottle and drinks, the liquid burning his throat.

'And *males* are a bunch of dickheads,' Tasha mutters.

Jodie looks at Seb, her head cocked to one side. 'Is that what happened? Did you share it?'

Seb doesn't know why he does it, doesn't know what possesses him in that moment to lie, but he nods, and something shifts irrevocably inside him.

32

IZZY

Miranda drives through the city, the car snaking down the backstreets, and pulls into a small car park. She turns to Izzy with a smile. 'I'm so pleased you found the paint you wanted,' she says. 'It's such a lovely pink. Should we decorate this weekend?'

Izzy nods. 'That would be great, thanks.' She thinks of how grown-up her room will look, how stylish, and smiles to herself.

'You're going to love this place,' Miranda says as she pulls up the handbrake. 'It's where your dad and I went on our first date. Well, our first in England.'

'How did you meet?'

'Ah, now there's a story.' Miranda gets out of the car and crosses to the meter to pay for parking. Izzy checks her phone while she waits, sees several notifications waiting for her. She opens them one by one, heart lurching as she reads the messages from new, clearly fake accounts. Why can't they leave her alone? She has blocked so many of these accounts over the last few weeks, has even considered taking herself off social media again, but she knows her mum sees every one of her posts, and besides, she wants to show the world that she is doing okay. That she is moving on. So why can't everyone else?

'Ready?' Miranda asks, slipping the parking ticket onto the dashboard and locking the car. Izzy looks up and pockets her phone, trying to ignore the prickle of anxiety at the words she just read. She won't let them get to her here. She *won't*.

'Ready.'

They walk past the aquarium, the water in the harbour beside them a deep blue, glistening in the morning light. Seagulls cry overhead, and boats bob gently on either side of the walkway. Izzy reads some of the names as they pass. *Grace & Serenity. Seas the Day. Ships & Giggles.*

'Your dad and I met abroad,' Miranda is saying. 'In Brittany. There was an exhibition, and I wanted to buy something for my sister. She's a real art lover.' She flashes Izzy a grin. 'You'd like her. She's quite a bit younger than me, from my dad's second marriage. She's an *influencer*.' She rolls her eyes at the term, but she is still smiling.

'Does she live here too?' Izzy asks.

'Oh, no. She still lives in France, in a house built on our father's land. Close enough to have dinner every evening and not have to do the washing-up. Far enough away so she can escape the third wife.' Miranda winks. 'Anyway, it was Anthony's exhibit, though of course, I didn't know it at the time. He was wandering around, and to be honest I didn't pay much attention to him. I was looking at a painting of a woman riding a horse, thinking how perfectly it would go in my sister's dining room, when he approached me. He asked if I liked horses.' She makes a face. 'Some chat-up line.'

Izzy laughs, picturing it, as they approach a building made almost entirely of glass. Miranda holds open the door for Izzy to enter and a waitress approaches, greeting Miranda by name and showing them to a table in the far corner. The water laps gently against the window, mesmerising Izzy.

'The sourdough bread here is amazing,' Miranda says, placing a menu in front of her. 'I'm going to have poached eggs. And veggie bacon, sod it. Go wild.'

'When did you move to Plymouth?' Izzy asks after they have ordered.

'Anthony lived in Exeter when we met,' she says. 'I'd just put in an offer on the house. My house in Brittany is rented out to holidaymakers, so I rented a small flat in the city until the house was ready, and then Anthony joined me.' She smiles. 'It's funny how things work out, isn't it?'

A tall glass of orange juice is placed before Izzy, a paper straw sticking out of the top. Miranda puts a cube of sugar in her coffee and stirs. They eat in companionable silence for a while, half-listening to the low conversations around them, the sound of cutlery scraping against plates, the clatter of pans coming from the kitchen.

Izzy looks at the ring on Miranda's finger, a plain gold band with an intricate vine pattern etched into it. No engagement ring. 'Where did you get married?'

'In Brittany last year. It was a lovely service, very small and intimate.' Miranda pulls a face. 'I'm sorry you weren't there. You and your sister would have made beautiful bridesmaids. Perhaps we could do something with you both, renew our vows or whatever people do.'

'It's okay,' Izzy says, then, braver now: 'Did you know about me? Us? When did he tell you that he had children?'

'Oh, yes, very early on,' Miranda says. 'He had wanted to contact you for a while, but he didn't know how to go about it.'

'Did he tell you about what happened between him and Mum?'

A pause. 'A little. I didn't like to pry. It's none of my business anyway; past relationships are in the past.' She puts down her cutlery and sips her coffee. 'How is your mum?'

Izzy realises with a pang that she hasn't spoken to her since Saturday. 'I need to ring her today,' she says. 'She sent me a message last night, but I was asleep.'

'She'll be happy to hear from you. Anthony has told me all about her. She's quite a remarkable woman.' Izzy frowns. She has never heard the word *remarkable* used to describe her mother before. Miranda smiles. 'It's difficult to see our parents as actual humans sometimes, isn't it? But your mum has been through a lot, and she's come out the other side. You should be proud of her.'

'Why?' Izzy asks, then flushes. 'I mean, what has she been through? She doesn't talk much about the past. Not even about Dad.'

'I'm sure it's very painful for her to talk about, especially with her children. As a mother, you're expected to be the strong one. The one everyone depends on.'

'Do you have children?' Miranda pauses, and Izzy immediately regrets her question. *How rude can you be*? she scolds herself silently. *How thoughtless.* She is about to apologise when Miranda speaks.

'No. I had a child, once. A boy. His name was Raphael.' Her smile is watery, her gaze faraway. 'He passed away when he was five. Cancer.'

'I'm so sorry.' Izzy reaches out and takes Miranda's hand. 'I shouldn't have asked.'

'Oh, no, Izzy,' Miranda says, squeezing her hand. 'I should talk about him. I never want to forget about him.' She sits back, picking up her coffee again. 'You know, I'm so glad you're here,' she says. 'I know things haven't quite gone to plan, but you are so young. You have your whole life ahead of you. Trust me. Things will get better.'

Izzy nods, trying to hold on to Miranda's words like a drowning woman grasping onto a piece of driftwood. She watches the gentle waves splash against the window, trying to centre herself, trying not to think about the messages she hastily deleted as she leaned against the car. She tries not to think about Seb, and how much she hurt him. She has spent her life feeling as if she is always out of her depth, her legs kicking uselessly against the current. Can things be different here? Can *she* be different? She has to believe the answer is yes.

33

LIV

That day, two things happen that change everything.

The first thing happens just as I'm leaving for work, my phone buzzing in my pocket. *Private number* flashes up on the screen, and I instantly think *police*. Is this what my life has become now, waiting for the proverbial knock on the door?

But it isn't the police. On the other end of the phone is a man who introduces himself as Trevor in a Jamaican accent. And he informs me, in that lovely, rich accent, that he is with my mother, who had been found wandering the streets in her underwear, a large kitchen knife in her hand.

'Where is she now?' I ask, my pulse quickening.

'She's at the hospital now. They're just checking her over.'

'And who – sorry, but who are you?'

Trevor chuckles. 'I'm the postman round that area. I found her outside the Indian restaurant, down the bottom of Bullocks Lane.'

'Jesus. That's... that's ages away from where she lives.'

'I know, I'm her postman too,' Trevor says. 'I'll wait with her until you get here.'

'Oh, no, you don't have to do that,' I say quickly, grabbing my car keys and hurrying out the door. 'What about your round? You must be so late.'

'Don't you worry about me,' he says firmly. 'I've known your mother for some years now, it's a pleasure to wait with her. We'll see you soon.'

As I drive, I wonder at how little I know of my mother's life. She has never struck me as the type of person who befriends the postman or milkman or anyone at all, especially not those who sound like Trevor. She has always been prickly, stuck in her ways in that way that people often brush off at her age, but she has been like it for as long as I can remember.

I find a space and rush to the A&E department, where I ask for Jean Braybrooke. While the nurse checks her records, I wonder, stupidly, why she kept my father's name for all these years, why it never occurred to her to revert back to her maiden name – Taylor, the name I gave myself and Seb – or to even choose a new one, a new identity away from her association with the men in her life. The men who had been in her life and were no longer. Though I suppose it's either one man's name or another, I reflect darkly. I wonder whether that will change for the women of the future.

'Follow me,' the nurse says, standing and moving around the front desk, and I do, my shoes squeaking on the linoleum as I hurry to keep up with her. Mum is in a cubicle, looking very small against the large hospital bed. She has a dressing on her forehead, and another nurse is stitching up a cut on her arm.

'Oh, Mum,' I say, rushing towards her.

She glares at me. 'Who the hell are you?'

The nurse looks up and I try to smile. 'I'm her daughter, Liv. She has... well, she's–'

'Mad,' Mum says, tutting. 'That's what she'll tell you. I'm mad as a hatter.'

'Dementia,' I say, ignoring her. 'She has dementia.'

The nurse nods. 'Take a seat, Liv, we're almost done here.'

'Where's Trevor?' I ask no one in particular as I sit on the uncomfortable chair beside the bed.

'The man who brought her in?' the nurse says. 'He's outside making a phone call.'

'That man assaulted me,' Mum says. 'I told him, I said I'll call the police if you don't unhand me.'

I frown. 'I don't think it happened quite like that, Mum.'

She tuts again. 'You would believe him over me. You like that sort, don't you, Paige?'

I stare at her, my mouth hanging open. I am getting more used to being called Paige – after the initial shock, it's no different to being called Samantha or Brigit or sodding Gertrude – but she has never been so openly rude before, at least not in public. *That sort*. I think of Brad, of how Mum treated him the same way she treats everyone – with contempt. But there was never racism, was there?

I am saved from answering by the nurse speaking. 'There we are, all done.' He stands, flashing me a sympathetic smile. 'The doctor will be along in a minute.'

'Male nurses,' Mum mutters as he leaves. 'What next? A feline prime minister?'

'We've already had one of those,' I say. 'You should remember, you voted for her.'

'Feline,' she says, shouting now. 'Not female. Clean your ears out, Olivia.'

Ah, so she does know who I am. For now.

'What happened?' I ask, leaning forward in the chair. 'Trevor said he found you in the street, quite far away from home.'

'Who?' She tuts again, not looking at me.

'Trevor,' I try again. 'The postman. He brought you here.'

'Where am I?' She sits up then, pushing herself forward on her elbows. 'I don't like this hotel, Margaret, I want to go home.'

'Olivia?' A voice behind me makes me turn around. 'I'm Trevor.'

I stand, holding my hand out. 'Thanks so much for bringing her here, and for calling me. I can't believe... She's not well, you understand.' I hear my voice turning posher, as it does whenever I feel flustered, and blush. 'Thank you, really.'

'It's no problem at all,' he says, shaking my hand. 'Just a little scratch.'

'On her arm?' I begin, then glance down. Trevor's arm is bandaged too. 'Oh, no. What did she do to you?'

He smiles, withdrawing his hand. 'Like I say, just a little scratch. No harm done.'

I feel my eyes start to prickle with tears and try to force them away. 'I'm so sorry,' I say quietly, mortified at what my mother has done. 'She's never done anything like this before.'

'She's in the right place now,' he says, patting my arm. 'Don't worry yourself about it.'

We are interrupted by the arrival of the doctor, and Trevor gives me another smile before heading off down the corridor. I am torn, wanting to run after him and thank him again, but also to get me away from whatever the doctor is going to tell me. I know I won't want to hear it. But I turn and follow him back to Mum's bedside, where she is sitting with her eyes closed, though I know she is not sleeping.

'I'm Dr Shaw,' he says, addressing Mum whose eyes stay closed. He glances up at me. 'Sorry, I didn't catch your name.'

'Liv. Jean's daughter.'

He nods. 'And how long has your mother been diagnosed with Alzheimer's, Liv?'

I think for a moment. 'About eighteen months.'

'Does your mum live with you?'

'No. But I visit most days,' I add quickly. 'I work, you see, and I have a grandson who lives with me.'

Dr Shaw nods. 'I'm sure you're doing your absolute best.' I know the words are meant to be comforting, but I cannot help feeling like they are a criticism. My *absolute best* is obviously not good enough. 'Have you looked into additional help for your mum, for when you can't be there?'

'I don't want strangers in my house,' Mum says, opening her eyes and glaring at the doctor. 'I'm not an invalid.'

'I'm sure you're not, Mrs Braybrooke.' Dr Shaw smiles. 'But everyone needs a bit of help now and again.'

We leave half an hour later, a bundle of leaflets stuffed into my handbag, Mum tutting at how far away the car is parked. *At least she's all right*, I tell myself as we make our slow way across the car park. *At least she isn't hurt badly.* But she could have been, and would it have been my fault? She's been deteriorating for a while now, her memory worsening, and yet I have been too proud and she too stubborn to call in extra help. But I see now that it has to be done.

I spend the day with her, helping her into the bath and washing her like I used to wash Seb when he was younger, like I imagine my mum did with me when I was a child, though I cannot remember it. I carefully rub soap into her back and wash her hair, keeping the water away from the dressings on her arm and forehead. When I stand to help her out, my lower back twinges, and I realise that we may have to make some changes to the house. A wet room, or one of those baths with a door. I try not to think about the cost of something like that.

I make her a late lunch of soup and buttered slabs of bread, and wander into the room opposite the lounge. It is another reception room, small but large enough to fit a bed and a chest of drawers. I think about the leaflets in my bag and make a mental note to see if there is anyone who can help me turn this room into a bedroom for Mum. Could I move in for a while? Seb would have to come too, but where would we sleep? I'd have to clear out some of the rooms upstairs. My heart sinks at the thought. Mum would hate it, but her strength is starting to fail and I keep picturing her lying in a crumpled heap at the bottom of the stairs, alone and in pain. I stand there for a moment, nibbling at my lower lip, anxiety coursing through me until a glance at the clock kicks me into action.

'I'm off now, Mum,' I call from the hallway. She is in the lounge where I left her, a paperback resting in her lap. 'Seb will be home from school soon. I'll see you tomorrow, all right?'

She gives a grunt that I take as assent and I leave the house. And as I'm getting into the car, the second thing happens.

'Hello, Liv? It's John here. I've got Seb with me.'

34

SEB

The afternoon drifts on. Seb feels as if he is going to cough up a lung the first time he takes the spliff, so out of practice is he, but the second puff is smoother, and then he is floating, his body cushioned as he lays down on the grass and watches the clouds drift past. A haze settles over Seb's vision, his usually turbulent mind slowing until he can no longer hear the thoughts fighting against one another, battling to be heard. Instead, he listens to the music playing on Ben's phone, laying back and folding his arms beneath his head. The sky is a light blue peppered with clouds, darkening at the edges as dusk begins to fall. A plane moves across above him, and he wonders where it is headed. Is it landing at Stansted or Luton, or is it carrying people to an exotic destination, far away from here? Seb has never been further than Clacton, the one holiday he vaguely remembers with his parents. Or is that another invented memory, brought about by the photographs his nan keeps in a frame in the hallway?

Another shape moves across the sky, large wings gliding through the air. It is a red kite, Seb recognises it from the books he got as a child one Christmas. He has been seeing them more often lately, flying low over the fields. He remembers pointing them out to Izzy one day, watching her eyes follow the bird as it sailed above them.

Seb feels as if he could sleep here, his body relaxed for the first time in weeks. He has not been sleeping. Whenever he closes his eyes, he sees the suspicion in the police officers' faces, sees the way his nan looks at him out of the corner of her eye. Watching, waiting. But for what?

'Seb,' Jodie says, her face looming over him. 'Earth to Seb!'

'What?' She lays down beside him, her hands clasped over her stomach, turning a piece of glass over and over in her fingers. 'You'll cut yourself,' he says, and she makes a face.

'Have you heard from Izzy?'

He sits up, shaking his head to clear it. 'What?' he repeats. 'Why?'

She shrugs. 'Just wondered.'

Seb lays back down, trying to find the red kite again, but it has gone.

'She's been keeping you on the straight and narrow then,' Jodie says after a moment.

'Who? Izzy?'

'Your nan.' Jodie lifts a bottle to her lips and gulps some of the liquid down. 'She always did think she was better than the rest of us.'

'She doesn't,' Seb protests.

Jodie gives him a look. 'She proper does. My mum went to school with your mum, she was a year younger or something.'

Seb looks at her, wondering why her mum never mentioned it before. Perhaps she'd thought he was too young to talk about his dead mum. Perhaps she'd had nothing good to say. 'So?'

'So,' Jodie says, exasperated, 'your nan was always a bit stuck-up. All *take your shoes off* and *eat at the table* and *mind your manners.*' She nudges him with her elbow. 'Still. Nothing wrong with wanting better for your kids, I suppose.'

Better than what? Seb thinks but doesn't say. He thinks about what Evelyn and Rosa said about his mum, how kind she was. Is Seb like her? Or was he created from that violence, formed not in the womb but four years later, moulded by his father's hands around his mother's neck? Is he bound by those events, those choices which have set him on his path?

A rustle breaks him out of his reverie. He turns to see a figure moving through the trees, heavy boots crushing the grass under foot.

'Oi!' the figure shouts. He is holding something in his hand; as he comes closer, Seb realises it is a pitchfork, the long spikes glinting in the sun. The image is so ridiculous he almost laughs. 'What do you think you're doing? This is private property!'

Dylan starts to laugh then, a low cackle that seems to fill the air. Seb shakes his head, suddenly wishing he were sober, wishing his mind didn't feel so chaotic. The man comes closer and Seb recognises him as the farmer, the one who sometimes gives his nan eggs when he's passing.

Shit.

'Let's bounce!' Ben says, getting to his feet and pulling Kyra up with him.

'Leave them!' Seb says urgently to Jodie, who is folding up the deckchairs. He grabs her hand and they start to run, long grass whipping at their legs as they hurtle towards the fence. He lifts it and lets Jodie climb through, then Olly who is behind them. The others have run in the opposite direction, and he watches as Kyra stumbles, falls.

'Come on!' Olly says, and Seb climbs through the fence, and then they are running again, weaving between the trees, ducking beneath branches and tripping over roots. They run blind, all sense of direction lost, until the ground begins to slope downwards and they are sliding down the bank towards a low river. They jump over it, slipping in the damp mud, Olly falling onto his knees, but he is back up and they are running again, until their feet hit the concrete path and they emerge onto the field behind the tennis courts.

Seb pauses for a moment, looking around. He remembers coming here so many times before, lazing on the grass with the boys. He remembers spending the day in a happy haze, watching the clouds pass overhead, listening to the children shriek with joy as they jumped in and out of the river further up.

He suddenly longs for those days, the days before Izzy, before the photo. Before he saw the flicker of distrust in Michael's eyes the first time Izzy took him home as her boyfriend, before he slammed the door in his face. Before all of it, and before he knew what it meant. Before he failed to stand up for Izzy today, before he was ashamed of who he has become, ashamed of his small council house and his father the murderer and his skin colour which is darker than any one of his friends, which he had pretended not to notice. Until now.

'This way,' he says, and starts walking quickly across the open field, heading for the wooden bridge over the river.

'Oi!' A voice rings out from behind them and Seb recognises John, the farmer, standing in the middle of the bridge. 'Get back here! I've called the police.'

For a split second, Seb is torn. And that's all it takes. While Jodie and Olly run in the opposite direction, Seb waits, believing that he can explain himself to this man he recognises, believing in the values his nan has instilled in him. *Respect your elders. Respect authority.* And then he hears Evelyn's words, her dark eyes fixing him in place. *Don't ever get yourself caught up with the law. They won't see past the colour of your skin.* And then it is too late.

~

Liv is waiting for him, one hand gripping the door frame as he follows John inside, his head bowed. The pitchfork is left in the truck which smelled of petrol and hay. The stern lecture is absorbed in silence, his head still bowed, his hands clasped between his knees. When his nan sees the farmer out, he sits back in the chair, his mind reeling.

'What do you think you're playing at?' she hisses from the doorway. He turns to look at her, suddenly too exhausted to think, to do anything but sit and breathe. 'Drinking? Drugs? Criminal damage? Haven't I taught you better?'

He doesn't speak, just lets her words flow over him like the tide. He cannot explain how he has felt nothing but anxiety since everything happened. And then the frustration, no, the anger, the pure, unfiltered rage when Izzy said it was over, as if he were at fault, as if she hadn't taken a photo of herself and sent it to someone else. And now she is gone, and he is left behind with all of these questions bouncing around inside his head, completely in the dark.

'Seb?' Liv snaps her fingers in front of his face and he jumps. 'Are you listening to me?'

'You wouldn't understand,' he says with more venom than he intended. He gets to his feet and sees his nan take a step back. Something clicks inside his head. 'I'm not him, you know,' he says, quieter now, almost begging, desperate for her to believe him, knowing it is fruitless. All of it. 'I'm not my dad.' And then he turns, going upstairs and closing his bedroom door behind him.

35

IZZY

At precisely twenty-eight minutes past seven, Izzy wakes. It is Monday, the start of a new week, and her first day at school. She can see her new uniform hanging on the back of the wardrobe door, neatly ironed by Miranda at the weekend after they finished painting her bedroom. Her new bag, a dark-purple rucksack, rests against the wall, beside her new shoes.

She is ready. She is not ready.

Her forehead is clammy, her eyes gritty. She had trouble falling asleep last night, anxiety prickling her skin as she tried not to think about all the new people she was going to meet, the unfamiliar layout of the school. Whether anyone would recognise her. And now she is awake, and she isn't sure she can do it, walk into a new school and put herself out there. Not again.

Her alarm buzzes at half past seven. She silences it and shoves back the duvet, padding barefoot towards the bathroom. She washed her hair the night before, after spending the weekend watching videos on how to care for her curls, and as she takes it out of the bobble she is amazed at how defined it looks. It looks nice. *She* looks nice, with her newly shaped brows and freshly cleansed skin. A new version of herself.

She carefully applies some make-up and gets dressed, draping her blazer over her arm and grabbing her bag. Downstairs, Miranda is making pancakes with chopped strawberries and bananas, and the scent of freshly brewed coffee hits Izzy as she enters the kitchen.

'Mum never lets me drink coffee,' she says as Miranda pours her a cup.

Miranda flashes her a look. 'You've been to Starbucks before, haven't you?' She winks when Izzy nods. 'It's okay, I don't mind being the evil stepmother.' But she is anything but. *Mum would like her*, Izzy thinks, surprising herself. The two women are so alike, Izzy thinks her father must have recognised parts of Caitlyn in his new partner. And yet they are different too. Miranda is more laid back, less stressed and focused on appearances. Where Caitlyn worries, Miranda breezes. *Mum could learn a thing or two.*

'Are you ready for your first day?' Miranda asks as she slips a pancake onto a plate and passes it to Izzy.

'I think so.' Izzy spoons up some fruit from the bowl on the table and drizzles some maple syrup over the top. 'I think I've got everything I need.'

Miranda comes over and sits beside her, her coffee cup clasped between her hands. 'It's okay to be nervous,' she says gently. 'It's difficult being the new girl. But you'll be fine.'

Izzy chews, thinking of the message her mother sent her last night, a variation on the same words, and yet they made her feel so different. *Don't be nervous. You'll be fine xx*

Her form tutor is called Miss Anderson. She is young, mid-twenties at the most, with smooth blonde hair and a silver bracelet on her wrist. She looks up as Izzy enters the room, a map of the school clutched between her fingers.

'Ah, Isabelle Bennett?' Izzy nods. 'Welcome to your form room, I'm Miss Anderson.'

'Hi,' she manages, trying to ignore the faces turning towards her. Miss Anderson notices, too, and clears her throat.

'Folks, this is Isabelle. It's her first day, so let's be kind and help her settle in.'

She is seated at the end of the back row beside a girl with short dark hair. 'Hi,' she says, flashing her a shy smile. *You can be anyone here*, she reminds herself. *Anyone you choose to be.*

The girl glances up from her phone and smiles back, pushing her glasses up her nose. 'Hey, I'm Leah.'

'Oh my God, I love your hair!' a voice interrupts. Another girl is leaning back on her seat, one hand steadying herself on Izzy's table. 'Is it natural?'

Izzy feels her cheeks heat up. 'Yeah. I mean, I used a curl cream. There's this method–'

'Curly Girl?' The girl nods. 'I've seen it on Insta. Been meaning to give it a go.' She runs her fingers through her straight hair. 'Does it give you curls if you don't already have them?'

'I don't think so,' Izzy says, 'I think it just enhances what you have.'

'Enhances what you have.' The girl smiles. 'I like that. I'm Katie.' She holds out a hand, and after a beat Izzy shakes it. 'Where do you live?'

'Oh, erm, Mannamead I think? I just moved in a week ago.' She feels herself flush again and silently reprimands herself. *Confidence, Izzy.* 'It's near a big park. It's got a big wooden gate at the front?'

'I know it! I live round the corner.' Katie grins. 'You'll be getting the same bus as me.'

'Oh, my dad's wife gave me a lift this morning,' Izzy says. 'I didn't know there was a bus.' There's so much for her to learn.

'What's she like?' Katie asks. 'The *stepmother*.' She raises an eyebrow at the word.

'She's nice. I only met her a week ago. But she's been with my dad for a few years,' Izzy adds quickly. 'He wasn't... in the picture, until recently.'

Katie nods sagely. 'My mother pissed off and left me when I was twelve. Lives in the Algarve now, the bitch.' She cocks her head at Izzy. 'Where did you move from?'

'Hertford. Hertfordshire.'

'Hertford. Hertfordshire,' Katie mimics, then laughs. 'You sound so posh! Is it in London?'

'Erm, yeah. Not far.'

'I went to London last Christmas, the *stepmother* took me to see *The Lion King*. Have you seen it?'

Izzy shakes her head.

'I saw it at the Theatre Royal,' Leah puts in. Izzy hadn't realised she'd been listening. 'It was brilliant.'

Katie makes a face. 'That's not really a proper theatre, though, is it?' she sniffs. 'You need to experience it on Broadway. It is incredible!'

Izzy looks between the two girls, noting a hum of tension in the air. Katie is slim and beautiful, with her long blonde hair and tanned skin and bright blue eyes. She is probably popular, with lots of friends and invitations to parties and everything else Izzy wants. Then she glances at Leah and sees the Izzy she used to be, and feels a pang of sadness. She notices a paperback poking out of her bag, recognising the cover, and is about to ask about it when the bell rings, and the air fills with the scraping of chairs and chatter as the students leave the room.

'What's your first lesson?' Leah asks as she stands up.

Izzy takes the timetable out of her pocket and checks. 'French.'

'That's with me,' Katie says, reading over her shoulder. She slips her arm through Izzy's and starts to move towards the door. 'I'll show you.'

Izzy wants to say something to Leah, *see you later* or *nice to meet you*, but Katie is leading her across the room and out into the morning sun. 'You want to be careful around her,' she murmurs as they follow the crowd of students finding their way to lessons. 'She's so *weird*.'

36

LIV

We do not speak about what happened.

Seb is avoiding me. He goes to school and I go to work. He does his homework and goes out with friends. We eat dinner together less often, and when we do it is accompanied by awkward, stilted conversation. The space between us is growing, the silence deafening. I feel the tension growing inside the house, expanding, stretching taut like a rubber band. It's only a matter of time until it snaps.

I watch him as he washes up one evening. I take him in, my grandson, the boy I have raised and loved as my own. For the first time, I see the shape of his father in his long legs, his tight curls. Perhaps it was seeing Rosa again the other day, who looks so much like Brad that sometimes it is hard to separate them. Perhaps it was seeing Seb's face change as he towered over me, his eyes flashing. He is growing up, but what is he growing into?

And so we do not speak of it. Days pass, humming with electricity. I wish I had someone to talk to about this, someone with knowledge and experience with teenagers. Surely this is normal teenage behaviour? Lashing out, playing up. Testing the boundaries. Pushing me away. But nothing would change the way I feel about Seb.

Unless he hurt someone, a voice inside my head says. *A woman. Like his father.*

I think of Evelyn then, the way she stared at a fixed point throughout Brad's trial, never meeting his beseeching gaze. I think of how she has condemned his actions, the tears she has shed since learning of what he did. Did she ever doubt that he was guilty? Did she ever shake her head and say *no, no, not my boy. My boy wouldn't do that*. Or did she know, deep down, that he was capable of it? Of such awful, fatal violence. Had she seen it in him before, lurking beneath the mask of her beloved son?

I could never ask her these questions. It is a line I cannot cross, not after everything she has done for Seb. And for me, too. Although she has stuck to the sideline, never encroaching or forcing her way in, I've always known that I can turn to her in times of need.

And, a voice inside my head says, *she can help you now*. She would know the signs, be able to nip whatever this is in the bud. *Brad could help too.* The thought comes unbidden and my mouth fills with saliva, my stomach roiling. No. I will never ask that man for help.

But something is urging me to contact Evelyn again, to consider doing what terrifies me the most. Seb is speaking to his father regularly, I know, through those voicemail thingies, so what's the difference if they meet face to face? How much longer can I keep Seb apart from his dad? These questions go around and around in my head, and all the while, Seb is slipping further away from me.

Sean has been on holiday for a few days, and I am grateful for the break from his judgemental gaze. I have never had any trouble at work before, at least, nothing I couldn't shake off, but Sean seems to have it in for me lately. Perhaps he is one of those men who hates women. Perhaps he is simply enjoying having power over a woman old enough to be his mother.

I shake myself as a customer comes in to pay, plastering a smile to my face as I count out their change. Another customer enters behind them, and as I read the name on the ID she passes through the window, something clicks.

'Jodie,' I say, surprised. 'Nice to see you.'

'Hi, Liv,' my grandson's old friend says. 'How are you?'

Memories flood back. Jodie and Seb were at primary school together, and they used to play football when they were younger. I remember watching them together, their dark curls so similar. I had Jodie over for tea a few times when her mother had a late shift at the hospital and she was too young to stay at home by herself. Then I remember why she hasn't been around for a while, the rumours I'd heard circulating about the man her mum had been dating until recently. Jodie's mum had been at school with Paige, and she was always one of those girls who found herself in trouble. Drinking, bunking off school, boys. She had an abortion when she was fourteen, I remember, and although I am in no position to judge there, she always gave me a bad feeling, as if she was waiting for me to turn my back so she could pinch something or make a rude gesture.

'Fine,' I say quickly to cover the silence. Jodie was different to her mum, I remind myself. She was never like that. She was a sweet girl. 'I'm fine, thank you. How are you? And your mum, is she well?'

'Good, we're both good, thank you,' she says, and I remember her impeccable manners as a child. She was always so pleasant, never failed to say please and thank you.

'First bike?' I nod towards the moped beside pump number two.

Jodie grins. 'Yep. Just passed my test. First time.'

'Congratulations. You managed that quickly.' I remember she is one of the older children in Seb's year, her birthday in September.

'After living in London for a few years, I got used to being able to hop on the Tube or the night bus,' she says, shaking her head. 'It's a different world out here.' She takes the receipt from my outstretched hand, pauses. 'How is Seb? I meant to pop round after what happened the other day, but–'

'You were there?' I interject.

'Yeah. We bumped into each other and I invited him out with some mates. To catch up, you know.' Her expression has a hint of defiance, making my hackles rise.

'Seb doesn't do drugs,' I snap. 'He needs to focus on his education. He's not like...' I trail off, but Jodie seems to hear the rest of my sentence. *He's not like you.*

'He's a big boy,' she says with a shrug. 'He can do what he wants.'

'He's a child.' My voice has risen almost to a shout, my fingers gripping the edge of the counter. 'I don't want him involved in any of that. Stay away from him. Do you hear me?'

But she is walking away, her braids bouncing as she rips open the door and steps out onto the forecourt. I watch her tuck her wallet in her back pocket and put on her helmet, and as she straddles the moped, she turns back and gives a little wave before speeding off.

I can feel myself trembling, surprised at my own anger, how quickly it rose to the surface. Why is it that the ones I love always seem to be drawn towards those who might do them harm? First Paige, now Seb. But then, I realise suddenly, I was the first. Did I set the path for my daughter and grandson to follow? Did Paige learn from me that it is okay for your partner to hurt you, to humiliate you? Did she learn from me that it's okay to kill?

I shake myself. I can feel the dark hole yawning beneath my feet, waiting for me to fall in. I cannot let that happen. I will not.

A glance at my watch tells me it is almost six o'clock, and I grab my bag, jumping when I hear Sean call my name from his office.

'Hang on a minute,' he says, and I turn back into the staffroom and poke my head around his door. He has his feet up on the table, his arms folded behind his head. 'I'm afraid I have to give you a verbal warning.'

I blink. 'For what?'

He raises an eyebrow. 'For leaving work in the middle of a shift, twice,' he says, holding up a finger. 'For leaving at short notice when nobody else could cover you.' He holds up another finger. 'For being rude to a customer today. You're turning into a liability, Liv.'

I flush. How much did he hear? 'The customer was someone I know personally. And as for the other things, they were out of my control, I–'

'Regardless,' he cuts in, 'take this as your verbal warning. Don't do it again.'

I feel something bubble up inside me, forty-nine years' worth of anger and frustration, and I turn away before it spills out like lava, covering Sean and this entire sodding place and turning it all to ashes.

I get home earlier than expected, my fury increasing my pace as I walk home. I almost bump into Seb as he comes down the stairs.

'Oh, hi love,' I say, trying to ignore the tension between us. 'Good day?' He lifts a shoulder and I feel frustration flood me. When did our relationship become so strained? 'I'm going to have a bath, then we can have some dinner. Bangers and mash, how does that sound?'

'I'm going out,' Seb says, fishing in the fridge for an energy drink. 'I'll eat at Josh's.'

'Is that where you're going then?' I ask, remembering my encounter with Jodie. 'To Josh's?'

He gives me a look as he bends down to tie his laces. 'Yep. Do you want to ring his dad and check?' His voice is laced with sarcasm and I feel myself deflate.

'No, no. When will you be back?' He shrugs, picking up a can of Monster and slotting it into his pocket before turning towards the door. I fight the urge to scream. 'Seb?' He stops then, one hand on the door handle. 'You would tell me, wouldn't you? If there was something on your mind?' I try to smile reassuringly at him. 'You can tell me anything, anything at all. You know that, don't you?'

There is a beat, two, my question hanging in the air, before he nods again. 'Yeah, Nan. Course.' And he is gone, the door slamming in his wake.

37

SEB

S eb doesn't go to Josh's. He turns left at the end of the street, skirting down the alley and exiting by the shop. Jodie is sitting on a bench, a cigarette dangling between her fingers. She smiles as he approaches.

'Saw your nan earlier,' she says. 'She gave me a right bollocking.'

He frowns. 'What? Why?'

'I went to get petrol and she was working. She thinks I'm a bad influence.' Jodie makes a face.

Seb sits down beside her, taking the cigarette from her fingers. 'She's not wrong,' he says, and she whacks his arm. An old man with a small terrier walks past, and Seb can't help noticing the look he throws their way. The dog barks at them, two high-pitched yaps that bounce off the concrete, and the man yanks it away roughly.

'Racist dog,' Jodie says with a sardonic grin.

Seb looks up to see Olly emerge from the pharmacy, a white bag in his hand. 'All right?' he says. 'Gotta take this to my brother, then I'll be back.'

'We'll come with,' Jodie says, hopping off the bench. 'How's Barnaby doing?'

Olly grimaces. 'Not great. He's back on the painkillers, can't get out of bed without them.'

'What's wrong with him?' Seb asks as they walk.

'MS,' Jodie replies. 'Olly cares for him.'

Olly glances back. 'Not just me. His girlfriend does most of the work.'

Seb looks at Olly, feels the picture he'd built up of him in his head shift. How many people have hidden parts of their lives, vulnerabilities that nobody sees? He thinks of his nan then, and how deep her pain runs. Lately he's been feeling as if she just wants to control him, to keep him on the path she believes is right for him, but has he misjudged her? Has he been lashing out since everything happened with Izzy? Or is there more to it, more than he can comprehend? He shakes his head, trying to clear his muddy thoughts. He feels as if he is at a fork in the road, both identical from the starting point, but what twists might lie ahead? A fallen tree for him to stumble over, a wall he has to dismantle brick by brick. But how can he know what's waiting around the corner if he doesn't choose a path?

They arrive at a block of flats. Olly enters a code and opens the door, holding it for Jodie and Seb to enter. The entrance hall is cold and dark, the beige floor tiles shining wetly in the low light, and Seb wrinkles his nose at the distinct scent of urine. Olly turns to the third door on the left, produces a key and unlocks it. 'Only me,' he calls, ushering the others inside. 'I've brought some mates.'

A woman comes out into the narrow passageway, drying her hands on a tea towel. 'Go through, he's awake,' she says, glancing at Seb and Jodie. 'Hiya.'

Seb smiles awkwardly. He notices the dark circles beneath the woman's eyes, the lines on her forehead that make her look as if she is constantly frowning. The hallway is bare, with patchy paintwork and a thin carpet beneath their feet. It opens up into a small living space, a kitchenette on one side, two closed doors on the other, a brown sofa in the middle. A small TV perches on top of a large cardboard box, an image of a coffee table on the side, but the coffee table is nowhere to be seen. 'Take a seat,' she says.

Jodie sits on the sofa and Seb follows, feeling the springs sag beneath his weight. 'How are you, Jenny?' she asks.

Jenny sighs as she sits at the tiny dining table, the chair so flimsy it looks as if it will collapse beneath her. 'All right. It's been hard lately, not gonna lie. I've had to sleep in here for the past few nights. My fidgeting causes him pain.' She points at a neat pile of pillows and a blanket stacked on the floor. 'He wakes up screaming most nights.'

'Shit,' Jodie mutters. 'Are you getting any help?'

'From this government?' Jenny snorts. 'Nah. We got a sanction because Barnaby had a hospital appointment when he was meant to go to the job centre. We told them but they don't give a shit. Any excuse to fuck you over.' She shakes her head. 'I had to go to the food bank last week. Humiliating, it was. Proper humiliating.'

Seb absorbs her words, realising that this is another thing he has been shielded from. Money has never been in abundance, but his nan has always made sure that there was enough to eat and the house was warm. How little he knows, he thinks now, of what Liv has done to make sure he was always taken care of. Did she ever go without so that he didn't have to?

'What do you need?' Jodie asks, getting up and walking into the kitchen. Seb is surprised by her forwardness, her apparent ease in this strange flat. But she has been here before, probably lots of times, and she knows what it is like to look after yourself. He remembers her eating dinner with him and Liv while her mum worked the late shift, the back-door key hidden beneath a small statue of an owl. He remembers her creased school shirts, the shoes with worn soles that leaked when it rained. All these things he witnessed but didn't understand, until now.

Seb watches as Jodie opens the kitchen cupboards. They are mostly empty, but for a few tins and some loose packets of crisps. He thinks of his own kitchen, not much bigger than this but more inviting, the small cubbyholes filled with knick-knacks and the calendar full of scribbles, denoting the everyday life of his family. His family of two. He suddenly longs for it, the house he has grown up in, the nan who has given him everything. How has this happened? They used to get on so well together, with a few hiccups like everyone else, but now Seb feels as if something has inserted itself between him and Liv, some truth that wasn't there before, and he can't seem to see a way around it.

'Write me a list,' Jodie says to Jenny, coming back into the living room. 'We'll get you what you need.'

They leave Olly at his brother's after he tells them he needs to stay for a while. As they walk, Jodie kicks a stone along, her hands shoved into her pockets.

'It's so shit, man,' she says. 'How do they expect people to live?'

Seb is quiet, cannot yet find the words he needs to express how he is feeling. Something is bubbling inside him, a mixture of everything that has ever happened in his life, and everything that is still to come. 'How can we help?' he asks after a moment.

Jodie's eyes rake over him as if she is assessing him. 'We get them what they need,' she says. 'By whatever means necessary.'

The implication is clear. Jodie doesn't have any money, at least not enough to help Olly's brother, so she has to find another way. He thinks of the jar his nan keeps in the kitchen, the university fund he isn't sure he'll ever use. But no, he couldn't steal from her, she who has so little. So he has to find another way too.

'All right,' he says, and with that, he takes a step towards one of the paths laid out before him.

38

IZZY

Instead of going home after school, Katie persuades Izzy to go into the city centre with her. 'I need a new bag,' she says as they walk arm in arm from the bus stop towards the shopping centre. 'And I want to get some new hair stuff. You've inspired me to go curly.'

Izzy has never inspired anyone before, and she basks in the golden light of Katie's friendship. They make their way around Primark, Katie picking out items and holding them against Izzy, declaring that she would look *amazing* in this or that, but Izzy doesn't buy anything. She has some pocket money, transferred to her account from her dad for 'whatever teenage girls need', but she doesn't like any of the clothes Katie picks out for her, doesn't think she could pull any of it off.

'I'm skint,' she says instead of telling the truth. 'Maybe next month.'

They go into Superdrug and Izzy finds the hair products Miranda bought for her. Katie buys the whole range, including three different types of conditioner, plus a new eyeshadow palette and a pink lipstick which she gives to Izzy.

'It'll suit you better than me,' she says, handing it over outside the shop. 'Red is more my colour.'

Izzy takes it with a smile, amazed at how forthcoming this girl is, how unashamedly herself. She has taken Izzy under her wing, and she feels as if they have known each other for longer than one day. *This is what real friendship is like*, she thinks as they walk through the city and up towards the sea. *I'd forgotten how good it feels.*

'This is the Hoe,' Katie says as they emerge on top of a hill, coming to stand in the shadow of a war memorial. She laughs at Izzy's quizzical look. 'I know, weird name. I don't know where it comes from.'

Izzy is staring out to sea, the water shimmering beneath the sun like diamonds. Seagulls whirl overhead, crying out to one another, and a group of small children run across the grass chasing a ball, a dog on their heels.

'I love it here,' Katie says quietly, and Izzy looks at her, feeling a change in her new friend. Her eyes are half-closed, a small smile on her lips, and her expression is relaxed, unguarded.

'It's beautiful,' Izzy says, and Katie's smile widens.

'Come on,' she says, pulling Izzy by the hand. 'Let's get closer.'

They head towards the seafront, passing the couples lazing on the grass, bottles of cider open beside them, the families on picnic blankets with half-eaten sausage rolls lying on the grass, tempting the seagulls closer. They follow the path down to a road, stopping at the low wall and looking out across the Sound.

'What's that?' Izzy asks, pointing at a semicircular pool of water to their left.

'The Lido,' Katie says. 'It's usually full of screaming kids, but I used to love it when I was younger.'

'When you were a screaming kid,' Izzy teases, confident in a way she hasn't been in a long time.

Katie laughs, the sound echoing out around them. 'Yeah. I was a little brat.'

'I can't swim,' Izzy confides. 'Neither can my sister.'

Katie frowns. 'At all? Didn't you ever learn?' Izzy shakes her head, and Katie grins. 'I'll have to teach you then. You can't live by the sea and not know how to swim.' She checks the time on her phone. 'We'd better head back. There's a bus in twenty minutes, we should just about make it.'

They turn back, walking up the hill towards the lighthouse.

'Can you go inside?' Izzy asks as they approach it.

'Oh yeah, the view is amazing. We'll do it together one day, you'll love it.'

Izzy is warmed by the promise of another day together. She pauses, turning to snap a photo of the lighthouse, catching the shimmering sea in the background, a boat zipping across the water.

'Let's take a selfie,' Katie says, holding her phone up and wrapping an arm around Izzy's shoulders. Izzy smiles at the camera, her head pressed against Katie's, and it is a real smile, with genuine happiness behind it.

'Send it to me,' Izzy says when Katie lowers the phone. 'I'll send it to my mum.' She flushes, realising this probably makes her sound like a baby, but Katie nods.

'Tell her she's got nothing to worry about. You've got me now.'

'How was your first day?' Anthony asks when Izzy enters the kitchen. She drops her bag on the floor and sits at the table. 'Made a friend already?'

Izzy can't help the smile that spreads across her face. 'It was good. The city is beautiful.'

'I meant to take you up to Smeaton's Tower myself,' he says, opening the fridge and pulling out a pack of mince. 'You know you can go inside?'

'The lighthouse? Yeah, Katie said. We're going to go one day.' Her dad's smile flickers, and she realises her error. 'But didn't you say there are boat trips?'

His smile widens. 'Oh, you'd love it. They go all the way up to the Tamar bridge. We'll go one day, when the weather's nice.'

Miranda breezes into the room, squeezing Izzy's shoulder as she passes. 'Good day?' she asks.

Izzy nods. 'Is it okay if I get changed? Then I can help with dinner.'

'What, no homework?' Miranda says, winking. 'I thought children were buried under homework these days.'

'It'll all be revision now, won't it?' Anthony says. 'Not long until your exams.'

'God, don't mention the E-word,' Izzy mutters. 'I'm so nervous.'

Miranda makes a noise in the back of her throat. 'I hated exams. I always ran out of time.'

'I scraped through mine,' Anthony says with a grin. 'Just about made it to university.'

'And look at us now,' Miranda says, smiling. 'I wouldn't worry too much, Izzy. Exams aren't the be-all and end-all. Most people don't care what GCSEs you have.'

'Or O levels, in our case,' Anthony adds.

'Really?' Izzy can't hide her surprise. 'But Mum says this is the most important year of my education.'

Anthony and Miranda exchange a glance before Miranda responds. 'And she's right to prepare you,' she says gently. 'Qualifications are important. But there's no need to stress about them. There are plenty of options ahead. You're a bright girl, you'll find the right path.'

Izzy feels something shift inside her, a warm feeling spreading out from her stomach. She has never been treated like this before, like an adult. She has never felt like someone who knows her own mind. Like someone who can find her own path.

39

CAITLYN

I wake in the early hours of the morning with a start, my daughter's name on my lips. *Izzy*. The dream is slipping away as I blink at the ceiling, though the anxiety remains, bubbling in my stomach.

Michael's side of the bed is empty, and I remember that he is in Dublin for a few days. Or is it Belfast? I check my phone to find a message from him.

Had to change hotels – some idiot had booked me and Pete into a double room! Will send the details. Izzy will be fine xxx

And I suddenly remember why I fell in love with him in the first place. His confident grin, the way he always knows what wine to have with a meal, and his kindness. He used to be so thoughtful, so careful with the girls. He'd wanted them to like him, and they did. They do. He alone helped Alicia move into halls because I'd hurt my ankle while out jogging. He spent a long weekend laying the patio in the back garden, Izzy fetching the large stones from where they'd been delivered out the front, gritting her teeth as she pushed the heavy wheelbarrow. He built the new chest of drawers in Izzy's room, then spray-painted it white when she decided she no longer liked the look of pine. He used to cook dinner every Friday night, finishing work early and heading to the supermarket for ingredients. He'd light candles and always make sure there was something sweet and decadent for dessert.

I sigh. When did this gulf appear between us all? But I know. It was last year, when the bullying started.

'She's not made of china,' Michael snapped once when I was making a hot water bottle for Izzy, who was lying on the sofa wrapped in a blanket. 'It's normal, kids being kids. It'll blow over.'

The cracks started to appear then, thin at first, hairline fractures that could be covered up with a warm hug and a cup of tea. Our first proper argument consisted of angry words hissed in the bedroom, across the bed where we had slept and laughed and loved together, and was now full of words piled up between us like an impenetrable barrier. The three words that silenced him, that sent him into the spare room for two nights, never spoken again but never forgotten either: 'She's *my* daughter.'

And now she is gone. Living with a father she barely knows, a father who abandoned her when she was still young enough to forget about him. But Alicia didn't forget. Memories are drifting back, of when the girls were young and I had crawled my way up from the bottom of a vodka bottle. Alicia asking where the photos had gone, the photos of Anthony that I took down because they were too painful to look at. Izzy wearing a shirt she took from the washing basket, the shirt Anthony bought when he sold his first painting when we were at university and had left behind, forgotten. I tried to erase him from our lives, scrub him from my mind with a little compartmentalisation and a lot of alcohol, but their memories endured.

I should never have tried to stop them from loving him, I realise that now. And if I'm entirely honest with myself, I know Anthony wasn't solely to blame. He left because he couldn't carry the weight of our secret, my secret, and I have never been able to bring myself to tell the girls the truth. But despite everything, he has still taken her. Izzy. Taken her down to Plymouth to start again, to finish her education and put all of this behind her. If she can.

I play the radio loudly, trying to drown out the quietness of the empty house. Alicia has forgiven me for our argument, a box of brownies sent through the post with a typed note: *This is for you, Mum. Lis xx*

But I am still alone, and I cannot bear the silence, so I sing, loudly and out of tune, as I dig the dust sheets out of the airing cupboard and position them in the downstairs toilet. I've been meaning to redo this room for years; it is the last one to be done since the renovation, and still bears the style of the previous owners, but I have never found either the time or the energy to do it. But now I have both. I feel rested, despite some fractured sleep, and I have nothing else to do today, so I am going to paint over the lime-green back wall I've always hated with a deep forest-green, and freshen up the other walls with a lick of white paint. I unscrew the shelves and lay them in the hall, before grabbing the tins of paint and roller brushes from the cupboard under the stairs.

While the walls are drying, I make a cup of tea and sit at the island, flicking through my phone. Izzy posted something on Instagram last night: a red-and-white lighthouse standing above a grey, shimmering sea with the caption *Smeaton's Tower at Plymouth Hoe*. I double tap the image and go to leave a comment, then pause as I read a comment left by someone with the name Watthe04.

Plymouth HOE lol

I frown, something tingling along my spine as I realise what is happening. They're doing it again. They're still doing it. Someone is still bullying my daughter. After everything, after *everything* she has been through, they are still bullying her.

I feel myself shaking with fury as I tap on the profile. It's locked, of course, with no profile picture. I hit *request to follow* and wait, then on impulse hit *send a message.*

Who are you? I type. *Why are you harassing my daughter?*

I lock my phone with a frustrated sigh, wondering if I have just made everything worse. Should I report it to the police? Could it have anything to do with the investigation? I drink my tea, trying to calm myself down. I'll call PC Willis later, I decide, maybe she will have an update on the case.

I go back into the bathroom and take down the old mirror, replacing it with a new black-rimmed one. I clean the sink and empty the cupboard beneath it, sorting through the half-empty bottles of bleach and emptying handwash into a new dispenser which matches the mirror, then start on the second coat of paint.

By the time I'm finished, the dust sheets gathered up and thrown back into the airing cupboard, the wall fully dry and the shelves back up, the sun has gone down and I hear my stomach rumble. It is too late to call PC Willis, but when I open my phone the Instagram app pops up, a new message in my inbox.

Stay out of it.

I dial PC Willis's number first thing the next morning. She answers on the third ring.

'Hi, it's Caitlyn,' I say. 'Isabelle Bennett's mum?'

'Hi Caitlyn,' she says, a tentative note in her voice. 'How's Izzy?'

'Oh, she's fine. She's down with her dad now, in Plymouth. Started at her new school this week.'

'That's good.' A pause. 'Is there something wrong, Caitlyn?'

I take a breath. 'Yes. Well, I think so. I don't know. There was this comment on Izzy's Instagram, calling her a... a hoe.' I stumble over the word, wincing. 'It came from an account called Watthe04. I messaged it, asking who they were–'

'You messaged them?' PC Willis interrupts. 'What made you do that?'

I swallow, chastised. 'I just... I thought if they knew I was her mum, maybe they'd lay off a bit?' As I speak, I can hear the disapproval in her silence. 'It was probably a stupid thing to do, I see that now.'

'What happened? Did they respond?'

'Yes. They said *stay out of it*. I've tried sending another message, but it's not coming up as "seen" and they haven't replied.'

'You've probably been blocked,' she says. 'That's the way it works on Instagram. The profile doesn't entirely disappear like on Facebook.'

'Oh.' I suddenly realise how little I know about these things. 'Did I... Do you think it could be related?'

She makes a non-committal noise in the back of her throat. 'Ms Bennett,' she begins.

'Caitlyn.'

'Caitlyn. I understand you're worried about your daughter. Bullying is an awful thing to go through and it can have very serious repercussions.' We are both silent as I picture those repercussions: the cuts on Izzy's wrists, the empty blister pack on the bathroom floor. PC Willis sighs heavily. 'I've been meaning to call you actually. Is it okay if I pop round today? There's been a development that we need to discuss.'

An hour later, I open the door to her. She is alone, with no sign of PC Singh.

'I just wanted to have a chat,' she says, giving me a warm smile I'd only seen her give Izzy before, and it catches me off guard. She follows me into the kitchen where I put the kettle on, inviting her to sit down at the island. 'I meant to say before, this is a lovely home,' she says, looking around. 'Did you do it yourself? This part is an extension, isn't it?'

'Yes, we extended the whole of the back out to create this space. The kitchen used to be where the study is now, at the front of the house. It was tiny.'

'You've done a great job. I'd love to get my hands on a renovation project.' She smiles as I place a cup of coffee in front of her. 'I'm a sucker for shows like *Homes Under the Hammer*.'

'I used to love watching that when Izzy was small,' I say, remembering. 'She'd usually have her mid-morning nap around that time.'

'Speaking of Izzy,' PC Willis says, bringing her coffee to her lips. 'She rang me yesterday.'

'She rang you?' I can't keep the surprise out of my voice. 'Why?'

'She wants us to drop the case.'

I stare at her as the words sink in. 'Drop it? But surely... You're not going to, are you?'

PC Willis sighs. 'There's very little to go on. We haven't identified where the photo originated from, and Izzy won't tell us who she sent it to.'

'But surely you can see who has shared it? It's *everywhere*.'

'The trouble with these things is that they spread far and wide, quickly, like wildfire, and it's difficult to pin anything down. Plus,' she says, a wariness entering her eyes, 'the only person we know for certain shared it is Izzy herself.'

I feel my jaw clench at her words. 'She shared a photo of *herself.*'

'A minor.' PC Willis sighs again. 'I know, believe me. I know how difficult this is. But the fact is that anyone sharing graphic images of a minor has broken the law, even if the image is of themselves.'

'This isn't fair!' I shout, my anger suddenly outweighing the need to be polite. 'They are still harassing her, even though she's moved away. Why won't you *do* something?'

'Izzy has explicitly asked me to drop it,' she says, and I want to rip my daughter's name from her mouth. She fixes me with her gaze. 'I understand how you must be feeling, I do, but if the victim does not support police action, and there is insufficient evidence to identify those responsible, my hands are tied.'

'What about her drink being spiked a few months ago, at Sian's party?' I demand. 'Have you even spoken to her?'

'We have, but Sian denied any involvement, and Izzy didn't report it herself.'

'Of course she bloody denied it! Who would admit to spiking someone else's drink?'

'There was no evidence to suggest that Izzy was spiked,' PC Willis says calmly. 'And it is entirely separate to this investigation.'

'Oh, for fuck's sake.' I run my hand through my hair, my nails digging into my scalp. 'I can't believe this is happening. My daughter is spiked, bullied, harassed, and then a nude photo of her is circulated around social media and you're telling me there's nothing you can do?'

'Caitlyn,' she says, her voice soft. 'It is Izzy's decision not to proceed. There must be a reason for that.'

'She's a fifteen-year-old girl! Of course she doesn't want to proceed. She wants to be *liked*, like every other teenager.' I drop my arms, trying to control my breathing. 'She tried to kill herself.' The words catch in my throat, my eyes burning with tears. 'She slit her wrists and took an overdose because she couldn't stand it anymore.'

'I know.' I am surprised by the touch of PC Willis's hand on my arm. She gives a sympathetic smile. 'Believe me, I know. I was a teenager more recently than you were. I remember what it was like. Kids can be cruel. But Izzy will find a way through.'

I tear my arm out of her grip, hot tears spilling down my cheeks. 'How do you know that?' I hiss. 'How could you possibly know that?'

PC Willis stands, her eyes still fixed on mine. 'Because if I can do it, anyone can.'

40

LIV

I open the front door, breathing heavily as I carry the shopping bags into the house. I am soaked from the sudden downpour that started just as I reached the top of the hill, and the plastic handles are cutting into my fingers. The first thing I notice is a doll lying at the bottom of the stairs, Paige's favourite with the long blonde plaits. And then I hear it, the strike of flesh against flesh.

I drop the bags and shove open the living room door, my heart beating wildly in my chest. Harry is gripping Paige's arm with one hand, his other raised, ready to come down on her bare legs. Her face is streaked with tears, her mouth open in a silent sob. And then the red mist descends, and I am across the room in an instant, my arms around my daughter, pulling her away, pushing her behind me. Harry's fury is like a beast rising up before me, but mine is just as fierce, and for the first time since we've been married, I hit him first. I put all of my strength into it and he stumbles back, surprised. His foot catches on something – a toy train left out of its box – and then he is falling, his head cracking against the mantelpiece. And then he is silent, blood pooling across the floor.

I wake, gasping for breath. My forehead is slick with sweat, my mouth parched. I lean over and grab the glass of water from the bedside table, guzzle it down as I wait for my heart to stop pounding. I haven't dreamed of the day Harry died in years.

Paige was seven when I decided enough was enough. He had been hitting me since the day we married. After the wedding, he took me back to our new home, the house I have never left, and accused me of flirting with his best man during the reception. From that day I lived in fear, the life I pictured lying in tatters each time he grabbed me, his face contorted with rage. Until I walked in on him hitting Paige, and I saw red.

The early days of our marriage sound like something from the 1950s, when the men went out to work and the women had fewer opportunities to be anything more than a wife and mother. I married Harry in the spring of 1987, when a woman was prime minister, the first black woman was elected as an MP, and Women's Lib had been fighting against inequality in the workplace and at home. But I didn't really know anything about that. I knew that my teachers had pushed me towards home economics and away from chemistry. I knew that the boys could pinch bums and lift skirts, and the girls would be hauled in front of the headmaster to explain why they had been distracting their male classmates. I knew that my mother had never pursued a career, and though her sister went to university and became a psychology lecturer, the only time her name was mentioned was when they wanted to discuss whether or not she was a lesbian. I knew that if a nice young man was interested in me, I should be grateful and look forward to the life he could give me, not the life I could build for myself. And so I was never taught that I could have it all, only that this, marriage and children and baking and cleaning and a bottle of gin hidden behind the washing powder, was all I could have.

I stayed at home, looking after my daughter, making sure

there was a healthy meal on the table by the time my husband got home from work. The house was tastefully decorated and kept clean and tidy. I would serve tea to visitors in the china set I found in a charity shop, with the teapot that had a tiny fracture beneath the handle. I swept the front porch and kept the hedges trimmed and planted beautiful flowers that would attract the bees to visit. I took the old bird bath from my childhood garden, which had been all but hidden beneath the overgrown shrubbery, vines twisting around the legs, and placed it beneath a tree at the end of our small garden. I saved my crusts and threw them out onto the grass, and watched the visiting birds from the patio, a cup of tea warming my fingers. I took care of my appearance, using minimal make-up and making sure my clothes were always ironed and neat. This was my life, from the age of sixteen, and I had never known any different.

Harry and I were married on a bright morning in late February. It was a Wednesday, because it was cheaper during the week than at the weekend, and the weather was unseasonably warm. My shoes pinched my feet, and sweat began to gather beneath my armpits as we neared the building which I had walked past a thousand times on my way to and from town. Harry was waiting for me at the front of the room, grinning at his best man beside him. His parents were in the front row, his mother in a stylish navy dress that stopped mid-calf, his father in a smart suit. 'You'd think this was a funeral, not a wedding,' Mum whispered too loudly, and I closed my eyes, hoping the music had drowned her out.

It was, I suppose, a lovely day. I sometimes look back at the photo albums, grimacing at Mum's garish red dress which had never seen an iron, smiling at my one and only bridesmaid's perm. Back then, I didn't see the darkness in Harry's eyes. It wasn't until later that I started to recognise it in those wedding photos, the shadow lurking behind his loving gaze. Back then, I was a glowing bride, three months pregnant and utterly in love.

It didn't take long for the bubble to burst.

I remember again that time I turned up on my mother's doorstep, my left eye sunken and bruised, my ribs aching, Paige screaming, *screaming*, as if she could feel my pain every time her father hit me.

'I can't do it,' I sobbed, tears running down my face. 'She doesn't want to sleep. She doesn't want to eat. She only wants to cry.'

'Where's Harry?' Mum asked, lighting a cigarette and leaning against the door frame. She glanced at her granddaughter, who was still bawling, before looking at me. She didn't invite us in, and I didn't answer her question. I went home. I went home to a bunch of flowers sitting in the sink, a *Sorry, H x* scrawled on the card. And I did the only thing I could do. I filled a vase with water and carefully arranged the flowers, placing them in the middle of the dining table so Harry would see them when he got home, and would know that he was forgiven. Until the next time.

Mum never brought it up again, not when Harry's fist left purple bruises on my arms and stomach, not when he knocked out one of my teeth, not when he broke my wrist. My mother could never be accused of being soft-hearted. Despite never preparing me for anything else, she had warned me against this marriage, had even suggested we 'deal with' the pregnancy so I could 'have a proper life'. But at the time, I didn't know there was any alternative. I was following in her footsteps, being a wife and mother when I was still a child myself, and now I understand her disappointment that I hadn't chosen a different path. She had been seventeen when she married my father, and they'd experienced several miscarriages before I came along, by which point my mother had almost given up. She is one of those people who should never have had children, who would have been happier without them, without the lifelong responsibility and burden. Now it is she who is the burden, and here I am taking responsibility for her, forgiving her cruel words, desperate for the love and approval that I fear will never come.

You are a fool, Liv, I think as I close my eyes, hoping for sleep that will not come. *A stupid, old fool.*

I hear floorboards creaking, the sound of Seb's door opening, and I hold my breath, my eyes flying open. The clock on the bedside table reads 02:41. I listen to him creep down the stairs, picture him pausing to slip on his shoes, listening for any sign that I am awake, before the door closes gently behind him.

Where is he going at this hour? I do not want to know. I do not want to think of what he might be doing, and how I am losing him. Instead I picture the mantelpiece in the living room, the bloodstain covered up by a fox statue pinched from my mother's garden. Tim from down the road ripped it out for me a few years ago, after I got his daughter a Saturday job at the petrol station. He plastered and painted the wall, and that was that. The final memory of Harry, gone.

Instead of worrying about Seb, I think of those days after my husband died, when it was just Paige and me. I started working at the petrol station while Paige was at school and, although money was tight, we had never been particularly well off, even with Harry working. We received a small payout from his firm after his death and with my wages, we managed well enough. I would make us 'eggy soldiers' every Sunday, and then we would go for a walk, rain or shine. I couldn't drive back then, so we stayed close, wandering around Panshanger or down to Hartham, following the river into town or even as far as Ware, a picnic packed into my bag. Sometimes she would swim in the pool which no longer exists, or we would feed the ducks along the river with the crusts we'd saved over the week. Sundays were our special days, with no school, no work, no outside distractions. And I lived for them. My daughter was my world, and with Harry gone, I could be the mother I'd always wanted to be.

It is impossible for me to think of Paige without thinking of how she died. I suppose I am not so unlike Brad after all, I realise with a jolt. Who am I to keep him from his son? Who am I to blame him for Seb going down the wrong path? It was me who started it. The sins of the mother, this time.

'It was an accident,' Paige told the police officers who came later, after Harry's body had been taken away. 'Daddy tripped over my train and fell.'

And that's how I got away with it.

41

SEB

The night air is surprisingly warm as Seb walks. A fingernail moon hangs in the sky, wisps of grey clouds passing over an inky backdrop studded with bright stars. His footsteps beat a tattoo against the pavement, one he cannot hear over the music in his ears. It is his father's music, loud and angry and righteous, music which speaks to him now in a way it has never done before.

He meets Jodie on the outskirts of town. She is leaning against a lamp post, smoking, staring up at the sky. It is quiet when he takes out his earphones, the odd car passing by on the dual carriageway beyond. They do not speak. Jodie pushes off the lamp post, dropping her cigarette butt down a drain as they head off. Towards the house Seb has chosen, the friend he has offered up as a sacrifice.

Sian lives in a new townhouse that was being advertised for seven hundred thousand on a huge sign which hung from the railings outside. Her mother runs a salon in town which she calls a *boutique* and charges almost double what others do, and her dad works in the city, something to do with banking, and he is, according to his social media, a firm Tory supporter. Seb doesn't understand politics, but he remembers the Labour sticker Liv stuck on the kitchen window during the last general election, her nodding along whenever Jeremy Corbyn was on the TV. He remembers the look on Liv's face when the results came in, her disappointment palpable.

Sian is an only child, and, he remembers from her party last year, was given the bedroom at the very top of the house, which features a large rounded window at the end. It stands out, even in the black of night, when not even the street lamps light their way. They go round the back, hopping over the gate into the secure car park. There is only a small courtyard garden, the fence low enough for Seb to easily reach over and unlock. As Jodie begins to pick the lock on the back door, he wonders what he is doing. He considers the divide between the haves and the have-nots, and knows which category he is firmly in, but does it give him the right to take what does not belong to him?

But it isn't for me, he reminds himself. *It's for Olly and his brother, for people who deserve better.* And besides, Sian does not deserve what she has. He remembers the way Izzy had snarled at him that Sian had spiked her drink, and why didn't he believe her? But he did. He does. He knows that those girls can be nasty, that they have contributed to the erosion of Izzy's self-esteem. And so who better to seek retribution from? Who better to pay this price? Someone who can afford it, he decides. Someone who has more than they need while others struggle through life.

The door clicks and swings open, soundless on oiled hinges. Jodie turns towards him and grins, her nose ring flashing in the dark, and they go inside, one careful step at a time, led by the torch on Jodie's phone. They are in a small utility room, with an archway leading into a large open-plan kitchen diner. The cupboards gleam wetly in the dark, the appliances modern and pristine. Seb almost bumps into the island, sees four leather stools lined up on one side. He tries to remember the layout from that party, the one Seb had persuaded Izzy to go to, and feels the familiar guilt flood through him. He has been too passive, always trying to stay out of things, never choosing a side. He knows now that it is because he wanted to be liked, wanted to fit in. He had been trying to mould himself into a shape that was unrecognisable, become someone he is not. But that time is over. Things are going to change.

'Through here,' he whispers, lifting an arm towards the door and the hallway beyond. To the right is the front door, the stairs at the other end, and opposite is a closed door. Seb pushes the handle down and steps inside.

A large desk sits against one wall, white with copper hairpin legs. On top are two monitors, screens dark, and several storage boxes lined up on a shelf above. Sian's father's office, where he works from home when he isn't in the city. Seb wonders what it is like, never having to worry about money, being able to work without leaving the house, without even getting dressed or spending money on a commute. It is the modern world, but Seb can think only of his nan and her long walk to the petrol station five, sometimes six days a week, her feet sore, her back aching, all for a pittance. He thinks of his parents then, the way his father was put into a box since he was a child, the same box Seb is starting to feel close in around him. Young, poor, black. Dangerous. *Why not own it?* he thinks. *Make it mine.*

Jodie gives a low whistle, breaking him out of his thoughts. 'Nice place,' she whispers. 'Didn't you say there was a safe?'

'Under the desk.' He crouches, opening a door and revealing a small rectangular safe. He reaches in for it, his gloved hands disappearing into the dark.

'Isn't it bolted down?' Jodie asks, her breath tickling his ear. He shakes his head, remembering Lew playing around with it at that party, pretending to steal it away and staggering under its weight, and she snorts. 'Fuck's sake.'

Seb lifts it from the cupboard with both hands. It is heavy, and he moves slowly so it doesn't scrape. And then it is out, held tightly against his chest.

'What do you think's in it?'

'A laptop at least, I can't see it anywhere else. Maybe some money.'

Jodie nods. 'I can work with that.'

He wants to ask what she is going to do with whatever they find, how she is going to turn a laptop or other tech into cash, but he decides he'd rather not know. He follows her out into the hall, where she stops, looking at the stairs. 'Let's go,' he says, jerking his head towards the back door.

'I just wanna look,' she whispers. 'There might be more. Jewellery and shit.'

The safe seems to grow heavier at her words. He shakes his head. 'This is enough. We should go.'

She raises an eyebrow at him. 'It'll never be enough.' She places her foot on the bottom stair, her steps as light as a dancer, and Seb swears under his breath, putting the safe down on the floor and following her up, dread pooling in his stomach.

The stairs open onto a landing with a light wooden floor and five doors leading off it, all closed except one, which reveals a bathroom with a roll-top bath and walk-in shower, moonlight shining through the distorted glass window. Jodie turns right, towards Sian's bedroom, and Seb follows, his heart in his mouth. Her hand is on the door handle, pushing down, and then the door is open, and they are creeping up the five steps towards the room above.

Seb looks around, his eyes adjusting to the dark. The windows are covered by heavy curtains, the darkness almost absolute as he tiptoes inside. Jodie flicks the torch back on and aims it low, looking around. A chair sits at an angle to a desk, clothes piled high on top of it. One wardrobe door is open, revealing shoes stacked up on top of one another, more clothes dangling from hangers. Jodie trains the light onto the bed, and at the same moment they realise it is empty, they hear a creak, and then a voice rings out behind them.

'What the fuck?'

Jodie turns, almost knocking into Seb as she shines the light at the person's face. Sian is standing in the doorway of an en suite, one hand thrown up to shield her eyes against the light.

'Who are you?' Sian demands, squinting at them. Jodie switches off the light and they are plunged into darkness. Seb runs towards the door, only realising Jodie isn't with him when he hears a crash and turns back. Light is filtering through the window in the en suite, illuminating Jodie as she grabs Sian by the hair and drags her towards the dressing table.

'Jewellery,' she hisses, keeping Sian's head turned away from them both. They have not covered their faces, and Seb knows Sian would recognise him in a heartbeat. 'Money. All of it.'

'Okay, okay,' Sian says, her voice shaking as she opens a drawer. She brings out a small box which she opens to reveal a small stash of notes. 'That's all I have. Who has cash anymore?'

Jodie tugs on her hair and she lets out a squeal. 'Shut up. Where's your phone?'

Sian lifts a hand and points towards the bedside table. 'On charge.' She cries out as Jodie pulls her across the room by her hair, forcing her to unplug the phone. Jodie snatches it from her and puts it in her pocket with the money and jewellery. Seb can do nothing but watch as Sian opens every drawer, showing what is inside. Jodie finds a tablet and pockets it too.

'Please,' Sian says, her voice clogged with tears. 'Please, that's all I have.'

'All you have,' Jodie sneers. 'This tablet would pay for a week's shopping. Maybe two. You're a spoilt little bitch.' She pulls Sian's head back and lowers her mouth to her ears. 'Don't make a fucking sound, or I'll come back and cut your throat, got it?' Seb doesn't hear a reply, but Jodie throws Sian to the floor and runs, Seb on her heels as they fly down the stairs. He lifts the safe, carrying it back through the house towards the back door. He topples a stool as he runs into it, no longer caring how much noise he makes, and then they are out, into the cool night air, the moon their only observer as they disappear into the night.

42

IZZY

She can hear her dad on the phone, his hushed words still loud enough to hear from her place on the stairs.

'What do you mean, she's dropped it?' A pause, then: 'That's outrageous! I can't believe they would do that.'

She knows the conversation is about her, and she knows it is with her mother. She can almost hear Caitlyn's words, the way her voice gets higher when she is frustrated. But Izzy has done what she needed to do. She is choosing her own path.

'I know, I know,' Anthony says now. 'I'll speak to her, see if I can talk some sense into her.'

At this, Izzy rises, padding back upstairs to her room and slipping into her shoes. She grabs her jacket and bag from the hook behind the door and, pocketing her phone, creeps down the stairs and out the front door. She types a message as she walks – gone to Katie's, back by nine xx – and sends it to her dad, knowing that he will be annoyed, not caring. She'd thought he would be different, someone who treated her less like a child and more like the young adult she is becoming. She will be sixteen soon; she is no longer a child, and she refuses to be dictated to by anyone. She has had enough of it.

Katie is waiting at the entrance to the park, holding two bottles of Coke Izzy knows will have been topped up with vodka. It is Friday evening, and Izzy wonders why it has taken her mother so long to call Anthony about her decision. Perhaps she only just found out. Perhaps she had been building herself up to talk to him. Memories have been coming back since she moved to Plymouth, memories she had buried deep down inside her. The torn-up photographs Alicia found in the bin, Anthony's face scratched out. The shirt Izzy took to wearing to bed, which Caitlyn ripped from her one day and threw into a fire in the back garden, the flames crackling as she drank her way through a bottle of gin. *Mother's ruin.*

When Izzy opens her bottle of Coke, the smell of vodka instantly transports her back to those days when she lost her mother. When Caitlyn would stay in bed, a mute, misshapen lump beneath the duvet. When Alicia would make their breakfast; sugary cereal every morning, and burnt toast and crisps for dinner, and they would walk to school together, hand in hand. Nobody asked where Caitlyn was. Nobody cared.

'So,' Katie says, snapping Izzy back to the present. 'What's up? Parental issues?'

Izzy smiles, despite herself. 'You could say that.' She doesn't elaborate. How can she tell her new friend about what happened back in Hertford? The police, the whispers, the photo. The shame. She cannot bear to speak of it. 'Nothing serious. Just dads, you know?' A month ago, Izzy would never have uttered these words. A month ago, she would never have been able to commiserate with someone who was complaining about their father. Before Anthony showed up at the house, Izzy couldn't remember ever having a father.

'Ugh,' Katie says, taking a swig of her drink. 'I *know*. Mine is on my case about my exams all the bloody time. I keep telling him I'm not going to university, but he won't have it.' She flicks her hair over her shoulder. 'And my hair! What have I got to do to get it like yours?' She pouts, holding up a strand.

'No two curls are the same,' Izzy says. 'You have lovely hair, like beachy waves. Fashionable.'

'In 2004, maybe.' Katie laughs. 'I'm going to have to dig the straighteners out soon, it's un*bear*able.'

Izzy smiles. Katie's hair looks fine, but if Izzy had worn her hair like that at her old school, she would have been teased mercilessly. Some people can just pull anything off, and Katie is one of them. 'Keep going,' she says. 'Why don't you stay over tomorrow night? We can do hair masks.'

'Ooh,' Katie says. 'I love a good pamper session. Count me in. Won't your dad mind?'

Izzy shakes her head. 'He's cool.' *When he isn't trying to run my life*, she adds silently in her head.

'We need to discuss your birthday,' Katie says in a sing-song voice. 'When are you going back to your mum's?'

'Two weeks,' Izzy says, trying to ignore the anxiety at the thought of going back. She will have been away for a month by then. She can't believe how quickly the time has gone.

'Okay, so next weekend, I am throwing you a party!' Katie says, clapping her hands together. 'No arguments!'

Izzy's eyes widen. 'But–'

'What did I just say?' Katie laughs. 'Come on, it'll be fun!'

The words echo around her head, reminding her of the last time someone said them to her. *It'll be fun*. But Katie is not Seb, and so far, nobody has shown themselves to be like Abby or Jess or Sian. This is not her old life, and she is not the same old Izzy.

'All right,' she says eventually, a grin stretching across her face. 'Let's do it.'

Katie punches the air. 'Yes! I've got it all planned out. It'll be *amazing!*' Izzy lets herself get caught up in the excitement, thinking of her previous birthdays: the quiet dinners, the awkward silences as she unwrapped her presents, pretending to care about any of it. This time it will be different, she tells herself. A fresh start.

'Oh my God!' Katie stage whispers, lifting a hand and pointing towards the entrance to the park. 'Isn't that Leah?'

Izzy follows her gaze to see Leah walking through the gate, headphones covering her ears, her phone in her hand.

'Should we invite her?' The words are out before Izzy can stop them. Katie looks at her aghast. 'To the party,' Izzy adds quickly, 'it might be nice? I don't think she has many friends.'

'Listen,' Katie says, lowering her voice conspiratorially. 'I've known Leah since we were like six. Our mums used to be friends, before mine buggered off. Leah is... troubled.' She taps a finger against her temple. 'Her dad was banged up in an asylum for years. Paranoid schizophrenia or something. He would shout at the air, and hide in cupboards.' She shakes her head. 'Mental.'

Izzy feels a pang in her stomach. 'That sounds awful.'

'Yeah,' Katie says, leaning back on her elbows. 'But it's hereditary. Who knows what else runs in that family?'

Later, Izzy is cleaning her face when she hears a gentle tap on the door.

'Come in,' she calls, stepping out of the bathroom, her face coated in cleansing oil. Miranda pushes the door open and smiles at her. 'Oh, hang on,' Izzy says, 'let me just finish up.' She rubs the rest of the make-up off with a muslin cloth and quickly cleans her skin with the bar of charcoal soap before drying her face and switching off the light. 'Sorry. What's up?' She pads over to her dressing table and squirts some toner onto a cotton pad.

Miranda perches on the end of Izzy's bed, hands in her lap. 'Your dad spoke to your mum today,' she begins.

'Oh, I know,' Izzy says, swiping the pad across her nose and forehead. 'She told him about me dropping the investigation. I gather from her messages that she's not impressed.'

Miranda makes a face. 'We just wanted to make sure you know what you're doing. That you're happy.'

Izzy throws the pad into the bin and untwists the jar of night cream. 'I do. I am.'

'When you go back up to your mum's, we wondered... Well, would you like one of us to drive you? I could stay in a hotel for the weekend, I've been meaning to go up to London for a while.'

Izzy turns to face her, considering her words. She's been dreading what it will be like to go home, to sit on a train for hours worrying incessantly about what she will find when she gets back there. Will her mum have planned anything for her birthday, knowing that Izzy will be back in Plymouth on the actual day? She feels something loosen inside her at the thought of travelling with Miranda, of having her nearby in case of emergency.

It's only two days, she tells herself. *You can cope on your own.*

'Actually,' she says aloud, 'that would be nice.'

43

CAITLYN

I find Anthony's outrage at Izzy's foolish decision to drop the police investigation rather soothing. It is comforting, knowing that someone is on my side. I tell him what PC Willis told me, reiterating that I think Izzy has been pressured into not taking it any further, perhaps by the people who have been bullying her. Perhaps by Seb.

'I'll speak to her, see if I can talk some sense into her.' And so I leave it in his hands, surprisingly grateful to be sharing the parenting, sharing the burden of how to steer my daughter in the right direction. I think of the girls involved last time, when the bullying got too much for Izzy to take, and feel certain that it's the same people now. Did she ever tell me their names? I try to think back to last year, before everything started going downhill. Who did Izzy spend most of her time with? I sigh. What kind of mother am I, to not even know the names of my daughter's friends?

Michael gets home at nine o'clock that evening. He looks tired, his eyes bloodshot. I wasn't expecting him back until tomorrow.

'I haven't slept yet,' he says, dropping his case in the hallway and going into the kitchen. 'Is there any juice?'

'In the fridge.' I follow him in, sit at one of the stools. 'You haven't slept at all?'

He shakes his head as he pours two glasses of juice. 'Barely. Things were so full-on, time got away from us. And then when I did get to bed last night, there was some kind of awards ceremony in the hotel. Directly beneath my room.'

I make a face. 'In the middle of the night?'

'It lasted until three o'clock.' He rubs his hands over his face. He hasn't shaved in a few days; his fingers rasp against the stubble. 'There's another event on tonight, so I thought I'd just get on the road and get home.'

'Go up to bed now,' I say, reaching out and rubbing his arm. 'You've been working away a lot recently. Maybe you need a break.'

He smiles blearily at me. 'Actually, I was going to talk to you about that. What do you think about going away for the weekend? Just the two of us.'

'You want to go away again?' I laugh. 'I meant you should spend some time at home.'

'Going away with you would be different,' he says, putting an arm around me. 'What do you say? We could leave tomorrow.'

'Where would we go?' I ask. I feel a bubble of excitement; it's been a long time since we took a spontaneous trip away. I'd thought things would get easier when the girls got older, but since Alicia left for university, things with Izzy have only become harder. She has been taking up so much more of my energy, my time, than I'd expected. Does that also make me a bad mother?

'Anywhere you like,' Michael says, bringing me out of my cyclical thoughts. He kisses my hair. 'Within a few hours' drive. Not Cornwall or Scotland.' He makes a face.

'Beach or city?'

'Either. Anything that isn't a soulless hotel room in the middle of an industrial park.' Michael gets up, filling a glass of water at the sink. 'I'm going to get an early night. Book whatever you want.' He kisses me again before he goes, and I suddenly know just what to do.

~

'I'm driving,' I say the next morning as Michael loads our bags into the boot. 'It's a surprise.'

He chuckles. 'All right. Lead on, Macduff.' I fiddle around with the satnav, turning it towards me while I key in the postcode. 'Only an hour and a half?' he says when I click it back into place.

'Don't you start guessing,' I say, pointing a finger at him. 'I want it to be a surprise.'

'All right,' he says again, holding his hands up. 'I'll sit back and enjoy the ride.'

There's some traffic on the M25, but we arrive in Oxford by eleven o'clock. The hotel I've chosen is the one Michael and I stayed in for our first trip away, the first time I'd left the girls overnight. It sits proudly on the River Thames, and our room features dark wooden beams, exposed brickwork, and wallpaper that looks like rows of books.

'Ah,' Michael says as we enter the room. 'This is more like it.' He wanders over to the window, staring out over the water which is gently lapping against the bridge beyond. He looks relaxed, refreshed from his long sleep, and his muscles melt beneath my fingers as I begin to knead his shoulders. He turns and wraps his arms around me. 'Maybe we should try out the bed,' he says, a mischievous twinkle in his eye that I haven't seen in a long time.

We decide to visit the castle first, walking hand in hand as we follow the tour guide through to the old prison, lost in the history of the place. We buy a sandwich from the Castleyard café and share a pot of tea, and I realise just how long it's been since we spent time together like this, just the two of us. I've been so wrapped up in Izzy lately, I've forgotten to make time for my relationship with Michael.

Guilt floods me at the thought. My daughter needs me, what kind of mother am I to begrudge her my time and love? But I am not just a mother or a partner. I am Caitlyn, and I haven't just been neglecting my relationship, but myself too. I need to remember to take care of myself as well as taking care of others. I need to stop spreading myself so thin.

'This is just what we needed,' I say as we wander down the cobblestone streets. 'Some time away.' Michael squeezes my hand, and I smile up at him, feeling as if we are in the first flush of love again. Whatever has happened in the past, I can feel that this is the start of things getting better.

44

SEB

He is drifting.

Seb is lying on his bed, one hand pressed over his still-racing heart. He cannot forget the look in Jenny's eyes when Jodie handed over an envelope of cash, the way her shoulders sagged in what looked like pure relief. Sian will have insurance for the items they took, and she isn't going to miss the one hundred and thirty-five pounds she handed over. And yet, he cannot forget what he has done, cannot put out of his mind the image of Jodie dragging Sian across the room by her hair. He has been ignoring Jodie's messages since, hiding in his room away from everyone and everything. He feels as if he is being pulled in two directions, drifting along on a current he cannot control.

He picks up his phone and opens the app to send his dad a voice note. He wants to see him with a sudden ferocity that surprises him. He has few memories of his childhood, and even fewer of Brad that are not tinged with a hesitancy, as if he is not sure of the man he is remembering. He does not remember the night that ended it all, though he has heard his nan talking about it with Evelyn before. He listened to their hushed voices from his place on the stairs, the words painting a picture in his mind. But the only thing he remembers is the darkness of the wardrobe he crawled into, dresses and coats and trousers closing around him like a cloak, keeping him safe when the shouting started. He does not remember Liv finding him curled up against his mother, his head tucked beneath her chin, her eyes open and unseeing.

His father did that. It is not that Seb ever forgets what Brad did, but when he remembers it like that, when he does not tiptoe around the harsh reality, he feels something tighten inside him. Those words are so simple yet so terrifying: my dad killed my mum.

But he is sorry. Brad has apologised again and again for what he did, in letters in those early days and even now in his voice notes. *I'm so sorry, Seb.* And he never asks for forgiveness. He does not expect it, though Seb wants so badly to give it. For although he misses his mum and wishes she were with him, he knows that nothing will ever bring her back. But his father is still alive, and so there is still a chance for them both. Or so he hopes.

He listens to his father's latest message again, closing his eyes and trying to picture his face as his words fill his ears.

'Hi Seb, it's me. Dad. I don't know why I say that every time. Who else would it be? But just in case, I suppose. Anyway, how are you? How's the revision going? I was thinking of retaking my own exams soon, maybe you can help me. I didn't do very well at school, much to your nan's frustration. Rosa was a right boffin, straight A's she got. Show-off.' Brad chuckles, and Seb tries to breathe him in. 'You'll be the same, no doubt. Mr Clever Clogs. I'm proud of you, I hope you know that. We all are. How is Grandma Liv? Still working at that petrol station? What's new with you? I hope you're not missing out on too many nights out while you're swotting for your exams. A social life is important too – though who am I to judge? I got the balance totally wrong.

Anyway, let me know how things are going. Mum told me she's got you a provisional licence, I can't believe you're old enough to start driving soon! I never learned, neither did your mum, but we managed all right. Still, it'll be good for you to be able to get around. Go off on day trips! I remember going down to Southend with my parents when I was little, Rosa in a frilly swimming costume. She looked like a jellyfish in the water. I wish I'd done the same with you. Anyway, never mind. You've got so much to look forward to. I'm so proud of you. I've said that already, haven't I? But I am. I really am, son.'

Tears run down Seb's face. He covers his mouth with his hand to silence his sobs. What is he doing? Who is he becoming? All his life, he has been steered down the right path, the path that will give him more than his nan and his parents had. Better. He had to do better. So why has he suddenly veered off?

He thinks of Izzy, how everything can be traced back to that one event. It marked the beginning of a change in Seb, opened his eyes to what he had previously been shielded from. That he is untrustworthy, a suspect. That the people around him have been waiting for him to slip up, to show his true colours. That his friendships are tenuous, fair weather, superficial. What does he have in common with them after all? Most of them are white, all of them middle class, with no idea of what his life is like. He has hidden his council house from them, rarely inviting friends over. He has hidden his lack of money, not telling them about the pet-sitting and car-washing and gardening he has done for neighbours so he can attempt to keep up with the rest of them. His phone is a year old now, his trainers older and showing signs of wear. Is that what he looks like? A slightly outdated, scratched imitation of his friends?

The only person he could be himself around, the only one who came home with him and had dinner with his nan, sitting at the wobbly kitchen table and eating from mismatched plates, the only one who seemed to listen, seemed to care, was Izzy. They had been friends since primary school, the only two at the time who did not have a father. They seemed to stand on the outside, apart from the others, but with Izzy, Seb did not feel alone. He felt emboldened. He learned how to be the joker, the one who was always up for a laugh, and though Izzy might have felt as if she were hiding behind him, Seb felt as if she had his back, and with her behind him, he could do anything.

And then she betrayed him. She went behind his back, sending a photo of herself and god knows what else, probably to some rich, white boy who pretended to be Seb's friend. Was it all a lie, a mirage? Did Izzy ever care about him the way he cared about her? He pictures Abby then, the way her lip curled when she found out Seb and Izzy were together. Had he stood up for her enough? No. The realisation hits him in the gut and he turns over, curling up in a ball, his face still wet with tears. He had thought the bullying had stopped, had even, stupidly, arrogantly thought that being with him would make it harder for Izzy to be targeted. He was popular, funny. The one who could get along with anybody, could sell Christmas to turkeys. But the truth was that he hadn't been there for Izzy when she'd needed him. If anyone was to blame, if anyone was at fault, it was him.

He doesn't go to school. He waits for his nan to leave for her early shift, calling goodbye and switching on the shower as she leaves, before turning it off again and going back into his bedroom. He stays in bed, staring at the ceiling until the walls start to press in on him and he finally leaves the house, blinking in the bright midday sun.

He wanders aimlessly, walking the route into town he knows

by heart. He looks up at Sian's house as he passes, as if surprised to find himself here. *Returning to the scene of the crime*, he thinks as he puts his head down and scurries away. He almost bumps into someone, steps back with alarm as he realises who it is.

'Seb?' Caitlyn says, her eyes wide with surprise and something else. Concern? Fear?

He doesn't say anything. He doesn't meet her gaze, flinches away when she puts out a hand to touch his arm, and then he is gone, hurrying back towards home, anxiety bubbling in his stomach. He tells himself that there are a hundred reasons why he might not be at school, there's no reason she would tell his nan. She doesn't know anything. Nobody does. He is invisible.

45

IZZY

Izzy sits in maths, doodling in the back of her book as she listens to the chatter around her. The teacher has stepped out, leaving the class to complete an exercise nobody has even looked at. Her phone vibrates in her pocket and she pulls it out, unlocking it with her thumb. Her stomach lurches as she reads the message and she deletes it instantly, shoving her phone back into her pocket. She thinks of the comment she deleted on the Instagram post of Smeaton's Tower, hopefully before Katie or anyone else saw it. Why won't they leave her alone? She has moved away, has removed everyone from her social media, has changed all her profiles to private. But still they find her. Still they want to hurt her.

'Psst!' She looks up at the noise, sees Katie's friend Chloe reaching toward her desk. 'Katie asked me to give you this.' She passes a folded-up note over.

'Thanks,' Izzy whispers back.

'Have you done number three?' Chloe asks.

Izzy shakes her head. 'I haven't even started. I don't have a clue.'

Steph grins from behind Chloe. 'That makes two of us then.'

'I can't get another detention,' Chloe says with a sigh. 'My dad said I'd be grounded for a month next time.'

'You won't get a detention if all of us don't do it,' Izzy says, looking around the room. Not one person has their head bent over their book, they are all chatting or flicking through their phones.

Chloe smiles. 'That's true.'

The teacher comes back in then, and the room falls silent, phones tucked under desks, bodies turned back to the front of the room. Izzy opens the note, trying not to remember the last time she got passed a note in class, the word blurring before her as she read it. *Slut*. This note won't be the same, she tells herself. Katie is her friend. But so were the other girls, once.

Meet me by the bench out the front, Katie has written. *I've brought my stuff with me. So excited!*

Izzy exhales, smiling, and tucks the note into her pocket. Katie had had to delay their sleepover after her dad decided that they were having a 'family dinner' last weekend. Izzy had tried not to feel dismayed, tried not to think about the possibility that Katie had been lying to her, that she just didn't want to spend time with her, but her fears were averted when Katie had messaged to rearrange for tonight. Her mum didn't let her do much on school nights, but her dad had quickly agreed.

'She only lives round the corner,' he said. 'What's the difference if she sleeps here or there?'

And so it was decided.

After school, Katie grabs her arm as they walk out of the gates and towards the waiting bus. 'I'm so excited to see your house,' she says. 'I've walked past it so many times, I've always wanted to see what it looks like inside. Do you have your own bathroom?'

Izzy nods. 'A small one, but yeah.'

'*So* lucky. My dad has his own en suite, but the stepmother "prefers baths" so I have to share the main one with her,' Katie says. 'I said, why don't I have their room? *I'd* use the en suite. I'd even clean it myself. But no.' She flicks her hair over her shoulder as she digs in her pocket for her bus pass. 'Why are parents so insufferable?'

Izzy laughs. She hasn't found her dad to be insufferable, not yet anyway. Her mum, however, had always been stricter on Izzy than she was on Alicia, and she'd always thought it was because she'd done something, maybe when she was a baby that she can't remember, to upset her mother. Now she knows that's stupid – what could a baby possibly do to make a parent hold a grudge for so long? – but in truth she doesn't know what to think.

They get off the bus and walk the short distance to Izzy's house, Katie chattering non-stop in the way she has that means Izzy can just listen.

'To think,' Katie says as Izzy puts her key in the lock, 'if you hadn't moved here, we would never have met.'

'Obviously,' Izzy says with a laugh.

Katie rolls her eyes. 'But what I *mean* is, how weird fate is, right? For you to move all the way down here, and only a few streets away from me, and get on the same bus as me, *and* be in my form. It's fate. We were destined to be best friends.'

Izzy smiles. 'I like that. You're a poet at heart.'

Katie pretends to slap her as they kick off their shoes in the hall. 'Wow,' she says, looking around. 'The *stepmother* has good taste.'

'The *stepmother* has a name,' Miranda says from the kitchen doorway. Izzy winces, but Miranda is smiling. 'Come on in. Katie, is it?'

'Yes,' Katie says, her cheeks flushed. 'Sorry. Hi.'

Miranda waves a hand. 'Dinner is at six. I've made spicy potato wedges with salad. Izzy didn't say you have any special dietary requirements.'

'No, I'll eat anything.' Katie grins. 'Sounds lovely.'

'Thanks, Miranda,' Izzy adds. 'Can we grab a drink and go upstairs?'

'Of course. There's Coke in the fridge. Help yourselves.'

Izzy grabs two cans of Coke and hands one to Katie as they climb the stairs. 'She's *so* pretty,' Katie whispers. 'Is she like, a lot younger than your dad?'

Izzy shrugs. 'I don't think so. I've never asked how old she is.'

'She looks like, thirty or something. And she really does have good taste.' Katie touches the frame of a painting hanging on the wall outside Izzy's room.

'My dad painted that,' she says, opening her door. 'He's an artist.'

'Is he? You kept that quiet!' Katie follows Izzy inside. 'Oh, my God. This is your room?' She looks around, moving from the bedroom area into what Izzy calls *the snug*. She sits on the sofa and grins. 'You have your own living room! This is mental. My room is barely big enough to swing a cat.'

'Why would you want to do that?' Izzy says, wrinkling her nose.

'It's just an expression, Iz,' Katie says with an exasperated sigh. 'You are funny.' She springs up, so full of energy that Izzy laughs. 'Do we have enough time to do our hair before dinner? My hair takes *ages* to dry.'

Izzy glances at the time. 'Yeah, I think so.'

They stand bunched up together as they wet their hair under the shower, applying the hair mask and giggling as they bump elbows. Izzy hands Katie a polka-dot shower cap, putting a flowery one on her own head, and they laugh again when they catch sight of their reflections in the mirror.

'We look like old dears,' Katie says. 'Oh hang on, I brought face masks.' She runs back into the bedroom and reappears a minute later, a small pink jar in her hands. 'Australian pink clay,' she explains as she opens it. 'It's meant to be *amazing* for your skin.'

They apply it to their skin, giggling as Katie drops some down her front. 'Oh, for God's sake,' she mutters. 'I didn't bring a spare school shirt with me.'

'You can borrow one of mine,' Izzy says. 'I think we're about the same size?'

'You're *definitely* skinnier than me,' Katie says, turning to observe her figure in the full-length mirror behind them. 'Just *look* at my hips!'

Izzy looks. She cannot see anything wrong with Katie's hips, or anything else about her, but she doesn't know how to say so without sounding weird. 'Now we really look like old dears,' she says instead. 'Like Mrs Doubtfire.'

'Mrs who?'

Izzy laughs. 'You haven't seen *Mrs Doubtfire*? Right, that's decided, we're watching it tonight.' In the bedroom, she finds the film on Netflix. 'Better set a timer,' she says, opening the app on her phone. 'For the hair masks.' They settle down on the small sofa together, Katie's legs on Izzy's lap, the warmth surprisingly comforting. They laugh loudly, sharing a bag of Haribo Katie pulls from her bag, until the timer goes off.

Back in the bathroom, they wash their faces before Izzy rinses Katie's hair with the shower head, scrubbing her scalp with her fingertips then applying conditioner and squishing in handfuls of water. 'Seaweed hair,' she says, rinsing it out. 'Here, that's how you want it to feel.'

Katie reaches out blindly and touches a strand. 'Ooh, yeah! It does feel like seaweed. Can I stand up yet? All the blood has gone to my head.'

Izzy laughs. 'Just a bit longer. I always wash upside down, it helps create volume.'

'I'm in your hands, Isabelle!' Katie trills. 'I'm trusting you.'

Izzy rakes the cream through Katie's hair, using her fingers to create clumps, then she applies a gel, gently cupping the strands in her palms and scrunching upwards.

'This won't give me crunchy curls, will it?' Katie asks.

'It will, but we'll scrunch it out once it's dry. That's the trick. Now you can flip your hair over.' Katie stands, tipping her head one side as Izzy scrunches her hair, then the other. 'Okay, I'll just do mine quickly.'

'I'll watch,' Katie says, sitting on the closed toilet lid. 'I want to see what you do.'

Izzy tries not to feel self-conscious as she switches on the shower, pulling down the hem of her top as she bends under the water. She quickly washes and conditions, taking time to squish in plenty of water, before smoothing her hair over with a brush.

'You didn't do that with mine!' Katie protests.

'You have looser waves,' Izzy explains, parting her hair like a curtain to look up at her friend. 'I didn't want to stretch them out. Every curl is different, remember?' Katie nods, and Izzy suddenly feels warm inside. It is nice to be the expert for once, the one leading things. It feels good to be trusted.

Once she has applied her styling products, Izzy steers Katie towards the dressing table, where she attaches the large diffuser to her hairdryer and switches it on. 'We'll just set the cast,' she says over the noise, 'then go down for dinner.'

'Won't we look stupid?' Katie asks, her worried expression reflected in the mirror.

Izzy shakes her head. 'They're used to it. And even if we do, who cares? We'll look stupid together. That's what friends are for.'

46

LIV

I leave work late, walking quickly to Mum's house. Someone from the care company is coming today, to discuss 'Mum's needs'. I hurry up the drive, noticing an unfamiliar car parked there already. A woman gets out and smiles as I fumble with my keys. 'Liv? Hi, I'm Kez.'

'Nice to meet you,' I say, dropping the keys as I reach out to shake her hand. 'Oh, bugger.'

'Have you come from work?' she asks as I retrieve the keys and slot them into the front door.

'Yes, my shift ran over a bit.' I push open the door and call out to Mum before turning to let Kez inside.

'I've not been here long, don't worry,' she says kindly as she passes. 'Wow. This is a nice house.'

'And you'll have none of it,' Mum's voice floats through from the living room door. 'I won't be selling to pay your fees.'

I smile awkwardly at Kez, shuffling past and entering the living room. 'Hi, Mum,' I say, bending down to kiss her papery cheek. She wrinkles her nose.

'You smell like fags,' she says. 'And onions. I hope you haven't made me any for dinner, you know how they upset my stomach.'

'No, Mum,' I say, fighting the urge to roll my eyes. 'I've just got here. I'm making a curry tonight, get some of those nutrients like the doctor ordered.'

'I'm not eating any of that muck,' she says. 'I'll have two boiled eggs.' She looks at Kez then, who is hovering in the doorway. 'Well, come in then if you're coming. You're making the place look untidy.' I can't help noticing the look Kez gives the room as she enters, her gaze flickering over the piles of newspapers and dirty mugs. She sits on the sofa, her briefcase on her lap and her hands folded on top of it as if she is loath to touch anything.

'Tea?' I offer.

'There's no milk,' Mum says. 'The milkman didn't come.'

'Oh, you should've said. I would have brought some from work.' I smile apologetically at Kez. 'Unless you take it black?'

'I'm fine, thanks,' she says, opening her briefcase and taking out some papers. I notice that she has a northern accent, Birmingham maybe? 'I don't really drink tea.'

'Don't drink tea?' Mum scoffs as I sit in the chair beside her. 'Well, what nonsense.'

'Mum,' I scold.

'Don't you *Mum* me, young lady.'

'Right,' Kez says, smiling brightly. 'Jean, it's very nice to meet you. I'm Kez.' Mum tuts in response. 'What I wanted to do today was get an idea of what kind of help you need. Liv?' She turns to me.

'Yes, right. Well, Mum had an... episode, recently, which resulted in a trip to A&E.' Mum tuts again. 'She was diagnosed with early-onset dementia about eighteen months ago now, and it does seem to be getting worse.'

'Who's she, the cat's mother?' Mum says too loudly. 'I am here, you know.'

'I know,' I say through gritted teeth. 'Her mobility isn't great either, getting up and down the stairs is an issue, so I've been wondering whether to turn one of the downstairs rooms into a bedroom.'

'You'll do no such thing,' Mum snaps. 'I'm perfectly fine as I am.'

I ignore her and continue. 'She fell down the stairs a few weeks ago, hurt her hip. I'm worried that next time she might seriously injure herself.'

'I'll seriously injure you in a minute,' she mutters.

'Right,' Kez says, making a note. 'And what about day-to-day activities? Washing, dressing, that kind of thing? Does she need help in and out of the bath?'

'I certainly do not,' Mum says, glaring at her. 'Am I speaking Japanese? I do not need any help, from any of you.' She crosses her arms, reminding me of Paige when she was a toddler and having a stubborn moment. 'What I would like is to be left in peace.'

'We'd just be here to give you a hand, Jean,' Kez says gently. 'With whatever you need. I understand your daughter does your cooking? That's something we can help out with.'

'I suppose you only eat foreign muck as well,' Mum says, and I throw her a look. 'Don't you look at me like that, young lady. There's nothing wrong with liking British food.'

'Sorry,' I begin, but Mum tuts loudly.

'Don't apologise for me either. This is my house and I'll say what I like.'

Kez's smile is becoming strained. 'We'd cook whatever you like,' she says. 'Do the shopping for you too, and some cleaning, laundry. Anything to make your life a bit more comfortable.'

'I'd need some morphine for that,' Mum says crossly. 'Not a cheese and pickle bloody sandwich.'

I sigh. 'Perhaps a tour?' I suggest, and Kez nods somewhat eagerly.

I take her through to the kitchen, noticing the pile of washing-up and grimacing. 'She can't do much herself,' I say. 'Or she often forgets to do things. Like the washing-up.'

Kez smiles at me. 'It looks like you've got your work cut out for you,' she says.

'She's not easy to deal with,' I admit. 'But she's my mum.'

She places a hand on my arm, and I feel ridiculously grateful for her kindness. 'Don't worry,' she says. 'We're here now.'

47

IZZY

That week, Izzy sits with Katie's friends at lunch. They lounge on the field on top of blazers laid out like blankets, plucking blades of grass absent-mindedly. She tries hard to remember everything the girls tell her – whose parents are still together, where they all live, whether they have any siblings – while also trying to be the new-and-improved Izzy, who has interesting things to say and is funny and smart. They try to ask her about her old school and her friends, but she is vague, waving their questions away and asking more about them. Deflecting. She finds that she is quite good at it.

On Saturday, the doorbell rings just as Izzy is pulling on her socks. Her hair is still wet, the gel forming a cast around the curls which she will scrunch out later. She runs downstairs and pulls open the door, where Katie is waiting, her arms laden down with bags and a large square box. Pink ribbon is looped around her wrist, three balloons trailing behind her as she enters the house.

Miranda comes out of the kitchen. 'Hello again, Katie. Let me take that off you.' She slides a hand under the box and takes it from Katie. 'I bet I know what this is,' she says with a wink. 'I'll pop it in the fridge.'

'Thanks,' Izzy says quickly. 'And thanks again for letting us, you know, take over the house.'

'We won't wreck it,' Katie adds. 'And I'll personally clean up.'

'I'll hold you to that,' Miranda says with a laugh. She turns towards the kitchen and the girls follow. 'I've cleared the table, so just set up however you like. Any bottles for the fridge?'

Katie glances at Izzy, who grins. 'Don't worry, they've said it's okay to have a few drinks.'

'Can I live with you please?' Katie says as she opens one of the bags and pulls out three bottles of white wine followed by a two-litre bottle of lemonade. 'My dad barely lets me have a shandy at Christmas.'

'We'd prefer it if Izzy did her drinking supervised,' Miranda says, slotting the drinks into the fridge door. 'Rather than on park benches where she's more vulnerable. Besides, we all did it. Even your dad.' She winks. 'Right, I'll just be upstairs. Shout if you need me.'

Katie grins at Miranda's retreating back. 'I like her,' she says quietly. 'You really lucked out here.'

Izzy opens a cupboard and pulls out two large bowls. 'I know. My mum isn't half as cool.'

'Will you stay here? After you've finished school?'

The question surprises Izzy. 'I haven't really thought about it,' she says honestly. 'Maybe. I'm not sure what I want to do when school's over.'

'Come travelling with me!' Katie says, unrolling a tablecloth with HAPPY BIRTHDAY in multicoloured letters and throwing it over the table. 'I've got it all planned out. Australia, New Zealand, Thailand. Ooh and Bali, there's a turtle sanctuary in Bali that I'm *dying* to volunteer at.'

'Sounds great,' Izzy says, though she isn't sure she wants to go travelling. She'd like to see more of the world, but the idea of being so far away for such a long time makes her nervous. What if something happened and she couldn't get home? What if she lost her passport, or spent all her money? What if a virus swept across the globe, or deadly fires broke out across the continent, trapping her in a country far from home? She shivers, pushes the thought away.

'Right,' Izzy says, after she and Katie have poured crisps into bowls, arranging them on the table. 'Shall we get ready?'

Upstairs, Izzy lets Katie do her make-up, watching as she is transformed in the mirror. A memory flashes into her mind, a memory of another girl's fingers holding an eyeshadow brush, her hand resting on Izzy's cheek as she moved the brush in circular motions, blending it out. A faint smile when she caught Izzy looking at her, cheeks pink.

'You have flecks of gold in your eyes,' the other girl said. 'Did you know?'

'Did I poke you in the eye?' Katie asks, snapping Izzy back to the present. 'You flinched.'

'Oh. No, you didn't.' She pushes the memory away. 'Am I done?'

'Almost.' Katie rifles through the make-up bag, coming up with the lipstick she'd bought for Izzy in town and popping the lid off. 'Just the finishing touches,' she says, carefully applying the lipstick before reaching out for a setting spray. 'Close your eyes!' Izzy obeys, feels the cool mist settle over her skin. '*Et voilà!*'

Izzy opens her eyes and turns towards the mirror. 'Thanks,' she says, a smile spreading across her face. 'I love it. I wish I was as good at make-up as you.'

'Well you've *transformed* my hair, Isabelle Bennett,' Katie says, flicking her hair over her shoulder and grinning. 'I'm so glad I met you.'

'Me too,' Izzy says, and she means it. She hasn't had a friend like Katie in a long time, not since...

The doorbell rings and Katie squeals. 'Party time!'

They race each other down the stairs like six-year-olds, giggling as Katie slips on the bottom step and only just manages to stay upright by grabbing the banister. Izzy pulls open the door, realising at that moment that she doesn't know who is coming, who Katie has invited. 'No boys,' was all her father said when she asked him if she could have a party. 'And we're going to be here.'

'Upstairs,' Miranda had clarified with a smile. 'In reach, but out of earshot.'

She assumes Katie has stuck to the *no boys* rule, and grins at the girls standing on the doorstep. Chloe and Maddie smile back at her, and Steph and Cara let out a cheer from behind them.

'Happy birthday!' they chorus, and Izzy grins back, standing aside to let them in.

'Follow me,' Katie says, sashaying down the hall towards the kitchen. Izzy follows behind, suddenly shy. She doesn't know the other girls well enough yet, and she is anxious to make a good impression. To not make a fool of herself.

Katie is fiddling on her phone while the others sit down on the large sofas, dropping their bags at their feet.

'I love your house, Izzy,' Chloe says, looking around the room. 'It looks like something from a magazine!'

'Oh, it's all Miranda,' Izzy says, tucking her hair behind her ear. 'She has good taste.'

Steph gets up and opens the fridge door to put a bottle of Coke inside. She smiles when she notices Izzy looking at her. 'I've got a match tomorrow,' she says with a shrug. 'I've tried doing it hung-over before, *not* a good look.'

'Match?'

'Steph plays football,' Cara supplies. 'I used to, until I broke my ankle when I was fourteen.' She pulls a face.

'You were better than me,' Steph says, sitting down beside her. 'Always scored, every single match.'

'Yeah.' Cara grins. 'I was, wasn't I?'

Music starts playing from the speakers and Katie claps her hands together. 'Right! Shall we order pizza?'

'Erm, is that even a question?' Chloe says, laughing. 'Pepperoni for me, please.'

'I'll share with you,' Maddie says. 'Can we get stuffed crust?'

'Obviously!' Katie says, typing on her phone. 'Cara?'

'Ham and pineapple.'

'Eurgh!' Maddie exclaims. 'That should be illegal.'

'One pepperoni, one ham and pineapple. Steph?'

'Margherita,' she says. 'With vegan cheese.'

'Well that's even worse,' Maddie mutters, and Steph elbows her.

'One vegan margherita,' Katie says as she taps at her phone. She looks up at Izzy. 'And what's the birthday girl having?'

'Oh, just a margherita please,' Izzy says. 'Can we get garlic bread too?'

'I like your style,' Cara says. 'Get a few.'

A few moments later, Katie pockets her phone, the pizzas ordered. She gets up from her seat and opens the fridge, pulling out two bottles of wine. 'Let's get this party started then, shall we?'

48

LIV

Despite Mum's protests, and her attitude towards Kez during that initial visit, I feel better knowing that someone else will be taking on the burden of her care. I spend the weekend moving furniture from her bedroom downstairs, Maggie and her husband Paul helping since I couldn't get Seb out of bed. At least I know where he is now. At least he hasn't snuck out of the house in the middle of the night again.

I pop in to see Mum again before work on Monday, wanting to be there when the carer arrives, but a car is already in the drive. I let myself in and am immediately greeted with the sound of something smashing against the tiles. I hurry through to the kitchen to see Mum standing on a chair, a plate in her hands, another lying in pieces on the floor beneath her. The carer, Anna, is in the doorway, one hand pressed to her throat.

'What on earth are you doing?' I cry, squeezing past her.

'I will not have strangers in my house,' Mum says. 'Get rid of her now, Paige, or I will smash every piece of crockery in this cupboard.'

I try not to react to the use of my daughter's name. 'Mum,

put the plate down,' I say, taking a step towards her. 'Anna is just here to help.'

'She's here to rob me. She wants my money, but she shan't have it.'

What money? I think but don't say. 'She doesn't want anything. She's a carer. Remember what we discussed last week?' I've said the wrong thing, drawing attention to the fact that she doesn't remember. She drops the plate she's holding and I jump back to avoid the shards.

'I can go,' Anna says quietly, and I turn, annoyed. Has she never dealt with someone like this before? Surely her company cares for many people with dementia all the time. Or is my mother a new level of cantankerous?

'No, no,' I say. 'I'll get her down. She'll get used to things soon enough.' I turn back to Mum. 'Right, come on now. Let's get down and have a nice cup of tea.'

Mum blinks, then looks down at the mess below her. 'Oh dear,' she says, and I just manage to move forward quick enough to catch her as she tries to get down from the chair.

'Come on,' I say gently. 'Watch your step. Anna, can you take Mum into the living room for me while I clean up?'

She nods, taking her arm and leading her down the hall. To my surprise, Mum goes quietly, and I let out a sigh at the mess on the floor. What if this doesn't work? What if she needs twenty-four-hour care? She'd never agree to go into a home, that much I know, but what other option is there?

I try to push the thoughts out of my mind as I sweep up the fragments, wrapping them in newspaper and stuffing the bundle in the bin. I fill the kettle and make two cups of tea, and take them into the living room where Mum is sitting quietly in her chair.

'I didn't know how you take it,' I say to Anna, placing the mugs on the table. 'I've put milk in.'

'Oh, that's fine,' she says, smiling. She looks relieved now that Mum is no longer smashing things up, more in control. 'Thank you.'

'I've got to get to work,' I say, glancing worriedly at Mum. 'Will you be all right?'

She looks at me, her eyes unfocused. 'Where's Sebastian?' she asks. The question surprises me; she doesn't often remember his existence.

'He's at school. Working hard for his exams.'

She reaches out then, her fingers gripping my wrist. 'Don't let him hurt her,' she says urgently. 'You can't let him hurt her, Olivia. Not again.'

My shift goes by in a daze, the same monotony of serving customers and refilling the shelves. Sean is off, thank goodness, so I don't have to look at his sour face. I'm still annoyed at the way he spoke to me when he gave me a warning, the jumped-up little git. I stack the newspapers outside, staring without reading the words until one headline jumps out at me. POLICE ISSUE WITNESS APPEAL AFTER HERTFORD BURGLARY LEFT TEENAGE GIRL INJURED. The picture accompanying the text is grainy, two hooded figures entering a house, but something strikes me as familiar.

'Liv?' Tina's voice startles me. 'Can you give me a hand please?'

I nod, put the newspaper down and go back inside, the image forgotten for the duration of my shift.

My phone rings just as I'm leaving. 'Hey, stranger!' Jackie chirps. 'Long time, no see.'

I try to think of the last time I saw her. Jackie and I met at the mother-and-baby group on the estate – though I suppose they'll be called something different these days. She had a daughter, Tania, around the same age as Paige, who is now living in Birmingham where she works at a refuge. I feel a pang at the realisation that Tania is living a life Paige could have had, with a good job and prospects and a future. Everything that was ripped away from her.

'Hi,' I say. 'Sorry, I know, life! How are you?'

We chat as I walk home, arranging to meet this evening for a drink in town. I haven't been out properly in ages, and I feel excited as I wash my hair and put on make-up. I need to make more time for myself, but with work and Seb and Mum, the days just seem to fly past. I frown as I pluck a grey hair from my scalp. When was the last time I had my roots done? Or my hair cut, for that matter? I used to go down to Jackie's salon every so often, taking advantage of her hefty discount. I shake myself. Plenty of time for all of that. Tonight is about catching up with an old friend.

I go downstairs to find Seb in the living room, scrolling through his phone. He doesn't look as if he's showered today.

'Hi, love,' I say, and he looks up.

'You look nice.'

I smile. 'Thanks. I'm going out with Jackie in a bit. Have you eaten?'

He shakes his head. 'Won't you be having dinner out?'

I pause, thinking of the money left in my account. 'No, not this time. Plenty of food in the fridge. I can make something when I get back.'

'Oh, Nan,' he says, rummaging around in his pocket and pulling out his wallet. 'Have dinner with your friend. You deserve it.' He pulls out two twenty-pound notes and holds them out to me.

I stare at them. 'Where did you get that?'

'Odd jobs, you know.' He shrugs, but he doesn't meet my eyes. 'Take it.'

I do, unable to speak, unwilling to ask him again. I turn once more to look at him before I leave, noticing his flattened hair at the back, the way he is hunched over as if in pain. Mum's words float into my mind. *Don't let him hurt her. Not again.*

49

SEB

He sits on the sofa, thinking of Izzy's mum, the look of surprise on her face when she realised who he was. Would she report him for not being at school? But he cannot find it in himself to care.

There is a missed call on his phone. He taps at the name, listening as it rings once, twice.

'Finally!' Josh says when he answers. 'Thought you'd died. Where were you today?'

'Nowhere,' Seb says. 'Why?'

'Mate, you missed it. It proper kicked off between Sian and Abby at break.'

His stomach lurches at the mention of Sian. 'What happened?'

'So, Sian comes in with a banged-up nose. She hasn't been in all week,' Josh says. Seb holds his breath. 'She's got a black eye too, looks like she's been beaten up. Anyway, Abby says something about Sian liking it rough and she goes mental, jumps on top of Abby and starts screaming like a lunatic. She ripped a massive chunk of her hair out.'

Seb exhales. 'Jesus. I didn't know she had it in her.'

'I know, right?' Josh laughs. 'She was like, wild.'

'Did Sian say what happened to her?' Seb asks tentatively.

'Nah. This happened at break, she was gone by lunchtime. Excluded.' Seb hears gunfire in the background, recognises the game Josh is playing. He feels a pang of sadness. Everything he used to enjoy – hanging out with his friends, quiet evenings with his nan – has gone, and he doesn't know how to get it back.

'We should do something tomorrow,' Josh is saying. 'Cinema? Lew's dad could take us.'

Seb shakes himself. 'What? Erm, no, sorry, I can't do tomorrow.'

There is a pause, the silence expanding until Josh speaks again. 'Is everything all right, mate?' he asks. There is no noise in the background now, the game silenced. 'It's just, you've been a bit off lately. Is it because of Izzy?'

Seb inhales, holds it. How can he explain? He cannot even put his thoughts into words for himself, let alone for someone else. 'I'm fine,' he says. 'Don't worry about me.'

A soft rap on the front door startles Seb awake. For a moment he is confused, looking around the room, until he realises that he must have fallen asleep on the sofa. He checks his phone, seven o'clock. His stomach rumbles as he heaves himself off the sofa, exhaustion weighing down his limbs. He opens the door to find Jodie standing there, a cigarette dangling from her fingers.

'You been avoiding me?' she says, her mouth twitching into a smile, but her eyes are hard.

'No,' he lies. 'Just been busy.'

'Busy with your other mates?'

'No.'

'Look,' Jodie says, putting a hand on the door frame. 'I know your nan doesn't like me, but I also know that she's not here. So why don't you let me in?'

'I was just about to have dinner,' he says, glancing back at the dark, empty kitchen.

She looks at him, tilting her head to one side. 'All right. We'll have this conversation out here then.' She leans against the railing, tipping her head back and blowing smoke towards the sky. 'What happened was a mistake, is that what you want to hear? I've never done anything like that before.'

'Seemed like you knew what you were doing,' Seb mutters.

Jodie grimaces. 'I've done other things, just not like *that*,' she says. 'I got scared. I thought she might recognise you. I didn't know how else to keep her attention on me.'

'So you hurt her.'

'Yeah. I panicked. Guilty as charged.' She holds out her arms as if she is about to be handcuffed. 'But that money did some good. It helped keep a proper ill bloke and his family off the streets. It filled his cupboards and heated his flat. It's not like we did it for a laugh, to just blow on booze and bud.'

Seb doesn't speak. He remembers the fifty pounds Jodie handed him the next day, after she had sold what they'd stolen. He doesn't know how much she gave to Jenny, or how much she kept for herself. He doesn't want to know.

'Besides,' she says, dropping her cigarette butt to the floor. 'It was your suggestion.'

'I didn't want her to get hurt,' he protests, but his words are empty. It *was* his suggestion. He chose Sian, plucked her name out of the air and decided that she should be the one to pay for Olly's brother. And why? Because she isn't a nice person? Because she hurt Izzy? Because she is the embodiment of everything Seb could never be?

'I know,' Jodie says. 'I am sorry. It's not like me. I'm not like that. I swear.'

He looks at her, sees the vulnerability in her eyes. Then a memory comes back to him, something his nan told him before that he has forgotten until now. 'You pushed your stepdad down the stairs,' he says. 'That's why your mum kicked you out.'

He watches something flicker across her face: pain? But it swiftly turns to anger. 'I pushed him down the stairs because he was trying to touch me,' she hisses. 'He fucking deserved it.'

'You think everyone deserves it,' he shoots back. 'I suppose Sian did too?'

'Yeah. Yeah, maybe she did. Maybe she did deserve it. But you know what? That's all on you. I take no responsibility for what happened.' She holds up her hands. 'My conscience is clear.'

A door opens, a neighbour passing by on the path beyond. He hopes they haven't heard anything. 'Just leave me alone,' he says quietly. 'I don't want to get mixed up in anything, all right?'

'Seb?' He closes his eyes at the sound of his nan's voice. She comes up behind Jodie, her brows knitted. 'What are you doing here? Didn't I tell you to stay away from my grandson?'

Panic flares inside him. 'It's all right, Nan, she was just going.' He glares at Jodie, dreading what she might say, what she might tell Liv, but she only shrugs.

'See you around, posh boy,' she says, before turning and walking away.

50

IZZY

The table is littered with pizza boxes, crusts with toothmarks nibbled into them thrown back. Izzy is on her third glass of wine, the most her dad said she could have, and she feels tipsy in a nice, relaxed way. The kitchen is full of chatter and giggling, and Izzy feels almost completely at ease. It is only the six of them, a chilled party unlike any she has ever been to before. She still needs to get to know the others better, but she thinks that this could really be the start of something new. Of happier days to come.

'Picture time!' Katie exclaims, attaching her phone to a selfie stick, and the girls cluster together on the sofa or on the floor below, with Izzy in the middle of it all.

'You have to wear your hat!' Chloe says, reaching for the pink party hat with BDAY GIRL written across the front. She places it on Izzy's head carefully. 'Don't want to ruin those lovely curls.'

Izzy pats her hair self-consciously.

'Are we ready?' Katie says, holding the stick out. 'Say cheese!'

'Cheese!' the girls chorus, grinning widely, Izzy's the widest of them all.

'Send it to me,' Cara says. 'I want to put it on Insta.'

'I'll put it up now and tag you all,' Katie says, typing on her phone. Izzy watches her select a filter and tag the rest of them, before adding hashtags like #birthdaygirl and #izzyssweetsixteen. Katie taps to upload and their phones all buzz at the same time.

'Can we watch the film now?' Steph asks. 'I've been *dying* to see this for ages.'

'Yeah!' Maddie chirps. 'It's meant to be awesome.'

'Which film?' Izzy asks, looking at Katie.

'*Doctor Sleep*,' Chloe answers. 'It's based on a Stephen King book.'

'Oh, yeah, I read that last year,' Izzy says. 'I didn't know they'd made a film.'

'Was it good?' Cara asks. 'Do I need to read *The Shining* first?'

'I don't think you have to, but *The Shining* is good too.'

'I've seen the film,' Steph says. 'It was okay. Very eighties.'

'I'm not really a reader,' Katie says with a wave of her hand. 'The last book I read was probably by Jacqueline Wilson.'

'I used to read a lot,' Izzy says, remembering the days when she would hole up in her room, trying to disappear into fictional worlds. Her Kindle is still full of unread books, waiting for her to need them again. She remembers that she hasn't seen it in a while, and wonders where she left it.

'Has everyone got a drink?' Katie asks, playing the hostess. 'Before I start the film.' Izzy looks down at her glass and is surprised to find it empty.

'Oh no,' Cara says. 'The birthday girl doesn't!'

'Well that won't do,' Katie says, getting up and grabbing Izzy's glass before going to the fridge.

'No more wine for me,' Izzy says. 'I've had enough.'

'No way!' Chloe protests. 'There's still loads left.'

'Just a Coke, really.' Izzy smiles. 'I don't want a hangover tomorrow.'

'Fine,' Katie says, dragging the word out. She grabs a can and hands it to Izzy. 'Right, are we ready?'

'Yes!'

The girls settle into their seats as the film starts, Katie passing around the bowls of crisps. Izzy sips her Coke, only half-watching the film. She is remembering her last birthday, when everything had already started to go wrong. She remembers the awkward meal she had with her mum and Michael, Alicia away on a university trip. They ordered Chinese and Izzy picked at her chow mein, unable to focus on the stilted conversation, unable to think about anything but the messages she would be getting. It was strange, the way she felt simultaneously drawn to and repelled by her phone. She couldn't stop herself checking for the messages she knew would upset her, and yet when she checked and there was nothing new, she felt herself clinging to her phone, waiting, waiting for them to come in, almost as if she wanted them to.

As if on cue, she feels her phone vibrate. She fishes it out of her pocket and unlocks it, clicking on the photo Katie has uploaded. It is a nice one, with none of the girls pulling funny faces or looking away. They are all smiling, they all look happy. Even Izzy.

But the smile falls from her face as she checks her notifications. Wattheo4 has left a comment on the photo.

Nice photo. Who's the piggy in the middle?

And then a second comment beneath it, which makes Izzy's cheeks grow hot.

I've got a better photo to share. Wanna see?

She taps on the comment, realising with horror that she cannot delete it. It isn't her photo, it's on Katie's profile. *Fuck*. She can't ask Katie to delete it, that will just draw attention to it. *Fuck*. She glances up at the group, noticing that Chloe is on her phone too. She looks up and meets Izzy's gaze, and she knows that she has seen it. *Fuck!*

She jumps up, mumbling something about needing the toilet, and runs down the hall, locking the bathroom door behind her. She grips the sink, her fingers turning white as she breathes in and out, in and out. *They can't hurt me here. They can't hurt me here.* Oh, but they can. They have followed her all the way to Plymouth, worming their way inside her phone, inside her head. She will never be free of them.

A tap on the door makes her jump. 'Izzy?'

'Just a minute!' she calls, trying to make her voice light, but she just sounds strangled.

'Izzy, it's Chloe. Let me in.'

She meets her own gaze in the mirror, recognises the look in her eyes. Fear, wild and fierce, like a fox taking refuge in its den. *They'll smoke me out.*

She unlocks the door, opening it slowly to reveal Chloe's worried face. Chloe steps into the room.

'I've deleted it,' she says, holding up her phone. The comments are gone. 'I asked to borrow Katie's phone, to see the other pictures she took.'

Relief hits Izzy like a wave, so strong she has to sit down. She almost falls onto the toilet lid, her head in her hands. Chloe crouches before her.

'You were bullied, before, in Hertfordshire?' she asks. Izzy nods. 'I've been there. I had to move schools a few years ago. It was awful.' She places a hand on Izzy's shoulder, and Izzy is so grateful for her kindness that she feels her eyes well up. 'You should know, that person tried to send me a message. I don't know if they've tried the others yet.' Izzy freezes, not daring to lift her head. 'Don't worry, I told them to fuck off and blocked them,' Chloe says. 'But Izzy, they sent me a photo.'

And Izzy feels everything start to disintegrate.

51

CAITLYN

Everything is going to be all right.

I feel strangely better after I see the photo of Izzy's party, how at home she looks with her new friends. How happy. It has helped me to see the bigger picture, the other side of the coin. Izzy is a fifteen-year-old girl – almost sixteen, I remind myself – of course she is going to baulk at a police investigation. She just wants to make friends. My daughter needs to be protected, but she also needs to be loved, and not pressured into something she doesn't want to do. So it is decided: I will simply love her, show her how special she is, how much I appreciate her.

I blitz the house in preparation for her arrival. She has been gone for what feels like forever, the calls and messages dwindling as I'd feared they would, but I'm keeping track of her on social media. She sounds happier when we do speak, laughing more and even making silly jokes, no longer too self-conscious to step outside of her small bubble. It's almost her birthday, and we are going to celebrate this new chapter in her life.

I book our favourite Italian restaurant and order a red velvet cake from a local shop. On the morning of the day Izzy is due back, I drive into town to collect the cake, managing to nab a space in the car park at the back. As I'm walking round, I almost collide with someone, my head consumed with thoughts of Izzy and this weekend, and I shake myself. I, too, am happier than I have been in a long time, and my head is in the clouds.

Shannon, the shop owner, comes down the narrow staircase at the back of the cake shop, drying her hands on a tea towel.

'Hi,' I say, plastering on a smile. 'I'm here to pick up a cake. For Caitlyn?'

'Ah, yes,' she replies, flicking her long braid over her shoulder. 'Let me just grab it. Take a seat.' She goes back upstairs and I perch on the blue wooden bench, fiddling with a coaster while I wait. She reappears holding a white box, and I rush forward to lift the counter for her.

'Thanks.' She smiles as she steps through. 'Here we are!'

I peer through the plastic window at the cake. The rich creamy icing is swirled into a rose pattern, and a glittery topper with the words *Izzy is 16!* is poking out of the top.

'Wow!' I say with a grin. 'It looks fab.' I take the box from her. 'Thanks again for squeezing me in.'

Shannon waves a hand. 'No worries, I had a cancellation.'

'Lucky for me, I guess.'

She holds the door open for me and I exit the small shop, thanking her again. Izzy is going to love this cake. A memory pops into my head of me and the girls baking cupcakes one weekend morning. The weather was dreadful, lashing rain and heavy, grey clouds, so we stayed in and made a dozen cupcakes, covering ourselves and the floor with flour. They came out a bit lopsided, but they didn't taste too bad. I remember Izzy bringing me the last cake, holding it cupped in her palms like a precious object, while Alicia brought in a cup of tea, concentrating hard on not spilling it. I hadn't wanted to eat it, had wanted to keep it preserved for all time like some relic, as if I had known that those days would soon be gone, those simple, happy days of flour fights and rainy days and a house full of giggles.

I slide the cake onto the front passenger seat, clicking in the seat belt for good measure. The last thing I need is for it to go flying on the short drive home. On the way I think of Seb, of how different he looked the last time I saw him. Maybe he's taken the break-up badly, his pride wounded. I should go round one day, I think decisively. I'd overheard two women talking in the chemist the other day about Liv's mother being taken into hospital. I should take some flowers round, repay the kindness she always showed Izzy.

I put the cake in the fridge and unload the washing machine, shoving most of the wet clothes into the tumble dryer before hanging the more delicate items on the airer in the corner of the small utility room. I get the iron out and go over my favourite top, black with metallic pink dots, ready for the meal this evening. Izzy should be here by about half past six, if the traffic behaves, and the table is booked for eight. Plenty of time.

I hear a key in the door as I'm heading upstairs for a shower. Alicia bursts in, a bunch of flowers crushed in her arms.

'Give those here,' I say, taking the bouquet and her overnight bag from her. 'Good journey?'

'Fine, yeah. Dying for a wee though.' She nods at the flowers as she moves past towards the bathroom. 'They were left on the doorstep.'

I pause, frowning. Was it Liv again? I set Alicia's bag on the bottom step and carry the flowers into the kitchen, peering inside the cellophane for a card. I find it tucked into a fold and pull it out, flicking it open and reading the printed words as I dig a vase out from under the sink.

The vase slips from my fingers, smashing against the tiles. Alicia is suddenly in front of me, her mouth moving, but I cannot hear her over the rushing in my ears, like waves crashing against rocks. She takes the card from me, one hand moving to cover her mouth as she reads.

HAPPY LAST BIRTHDAY, BITCH.

52

LIV

A fist pounds against the front door and I almost leap out of my skin. Hot tea splashes against my wrist and I curse, grabbing a tea towel and mopping it up. At least it didn't splash my clothes; it's my last clean uniform. I haven't managed to do a load of washing yet between working and looking after Mum. My thoughts go to Seb, as they so often do these days, something niggling at the back of my mind. He had been arguing with Jodie when I came home the other night; I could feel the tension between them, so thick that I know something must have happened. But what?

The knock comes again and I shake myself. I open the door to find Caitlyn standing there, her fist raised as if to knock again.

'Oh,' she says, as if she is surprised to see me.

'Hello. Is everything all right?'

Something passes over her face and her mouth twists as if she is in pain. 'Well, no, actually. Can I come in?'

I step back and she enters, following me into the living room where she perches on the sofa, her hands clasped between her knees.

'Has something happened?' I ask, sitting down opposite. 'Is Izzy all right?'

'She's fine. Did you know she's dropped the charges?'

My eyes widen in surprise. 'No. Why would she do that? The police haven't agreed, have they?'

Caitlyn takes a deep breath. 'They said there's little to go on.'

'Oh.' I am silent for a moment, wondering what this means for Seb. Maybe he can move on now. Maybe they both can.

'I just, I wanted to ask. Did you leave some flowers on my doorstep again? Today?'

I blink, surprised at the question. 'No. I only did that the once.'

She sighs, a deep, heavy sigh so full of emotion that it seems to fill the room. 'Someone left a bouquet today,' she says, fumbling in her pocket. 'They sent this.'

I take the folded card from her hand and open it, reading the words inside. HAPPY LAST BIRTHDAY, BITCH. I sit back, the words hitting me like a blow.

'Who would send something like this?' I ask, passing it back to her, my fingers tingling as if it has burned me. 'You can't imagine I would do this?'

She shakes her head, her lips pursed. 'Not you. But maybe–'

'Seb?' I feel my cheeks flush with indignation. 'No. Seb would never do such a thing.'

'Where is he today?' she asks, looking around the room as if he is hiding beneath the plant pot. 'At school?'

'Of course he is at school,' I snap. 'Where else would he be?'

'I saw him the other day, in town. He wasn't in uniform.'

I stand then, anger rising at the gall of this woman. First, she thinks Seb had something to do with her daughter taking that photo, now she wants to accuse him of sending vile messages hidden inside a bouquet? 'He is at school,' I repeat. 'Where he is every weekday. And I think you need to leave.'

Caitlyn rises, and I take in her neat ponytail, her perfectly shaped eyebrows. She must be around the same age as me, I realise. I wonder what she is seeing: a frumpy, middle-aged woman with greying hair and too many wrinkles. My council house with the old, worn carpet I can't afford to replace and windows I haven't cleaned in a while. The differences between us adds to the anger bubbling up inside me. The haves and the have-nots. I'd never noticed it before, not really, but now it is like an additional person in the room, a presence standing between us.

'I'm sorry,' she says, her eyes meeting mine. 'But I think you need to have a chat with Seb. I know it's difficult, going through a break-up, but Izzy has made her decision.'

'A break-up?' I echo, confusion seeping through. 'What do you mean? Has he broken up with Izzy?'

'Izzy broke up with Seb,' she says slowly, something like pity in her eyes. 'Before she moved away. Didn't he tell you?'

I spend the entire shift at work thinking about what Caitlyn said, the look in her eyes as she realised that Seb had in fact not told me about the break-up. Why would he keep something like that from me? Then again, I haven't asked about Izzy lately. I'd assumed it would take some getting used to, her moving away, but once his exams are over and he passes his driving test, he could go and visit during school holidays. Or perhaps I'd thought it would simply fizzle out, as so many teenage relationships do. Izzy is a lovely girl, always polite when she visited, offering to make me a cup of tea, but I don't suppose I'd imagined them staying together forever.

That explains why Jodie is back on the scene. Seb is

vulnerable at the moment, and she has pounced on him. But what could she possibly want from him?

When I leave work, I try to phone Seb, but it goes to voicemail. I try again and leave a message. 'Seb, it's Nan. Ring me back please.' I want to go home to check if he's there, but I need to go over to Mum's.

I pocket my phone, trying to squash down my concerns. Seb is fine. He must have had to do something in town that day before school, maybe pick up a birthday card for Izzy. *Or send a bunch of flowers.* I knock the voice away, horrified. No. Seb wouldn't do something like that. He's a kind, loving young man who would never hurt a fly, even if he is smarting from a break-up. He's a good boy, isn't he?

53

SEB

Seb is in the kitchen washing up when Liv gets home that evening. She dumps her handbag on the table and sighs.

'All right?' he asks when he turns to face her. She looks exhausted, dark circles hanging beneath her eyes. Has he caused this? Has he been keeping her up at night, worming his way into her dreams?

'Yeah fine, love. Just tired.' She smiles, but it doesn't reach her eyes.

'There's some salad left over,' he says, nodding toward the fridge. 'I cooked some chicken too.'

'That's nice,' she says, moving towards the kettle. 'Thanks, love.'

'How's Granny?' he asks, realising he hasn't asked after her in a while. 'Any more streaking incidents?' He tries to inject some humour into his words, but they fall flat. He feels the distance between them, a distance that had not existed before all of this started, and guilt needles at him. He is to blame for this, at least.

'She's fine,' Liv says after a moment, flicking the kettle on and opening the fridge for the milk. She doesn't turn to face him when she speaks again. 'I didn't know you and Izzy broke up. Why didn't you tell me?'

Seb leans against the door frame, hands in his pockets. 'No biggie,' he lies. He can see her face in profile, sees her pursing her lips, knows there will be more.

'She's dropped the charges. Did you know?' Her words hit him like a blow. He shakes his head, bewildered. Why hadn't Izzy told him? 'So I suppose that's one less thing to worry about,' she says, filling her mug with hot water.

'What do you mean?'

Liv glances at him, an expression he can't read on her face. 'Just that,' she says evenly. 'You don't need to worry about it anymore. The police coming here, questioning you. And you can start going back to school.' She raises an eyebrow. 'I know you haven't been going, Seb. And I've no doubt it's got something to do with that Jodie. She's bad news.'

'She's had a hard time,' he says, annoyed at her attitude. She doesn't even know Jodie, not really.

'Hmm,' Liv says, turning back to finish making her tea. 'I don't want any more trouble, Seb. I just want you to do well at school and focus on your future. Whatever that may be,' she adds quietly.

'What's that supposed to mean?' he demands. His fuse is so short these days, but why does his nan insist on nit-picking all the time? She doesn't speak, and he feels his annoyance tip over to anger. 'I knew it. You don't believe me. You don't believe *in* me. Do you really think I had anything to do with what happened to Izzy? She took that photo, and then she dumped me and ran off to Plymouth. It wasn't my fault.' His nan shakes her head, her mouth opening to speak, but he continues, his voice rising. 'You think I'm just like *him*, don't you? Sins of the father.' She stares at him open-mouthed as he slams his fist on the table. 'You've been waiting for it, haven't you? Waiting for him to show himself in me.'

'Hold on,' she begins, but he cuts her off.

'He's paid the price for what he did,' Seb says. 'He's sorry.'

'Sorry,' Liv scoffs. 'Because that's going to bring my daughter back.'

'She was my mother!' he shouts, losing control of his barely restrained emotions. 'I lost just as much as you did! More, in fact. I lost both of my parents.'

'And only one of them was to blame!' Liv says, raising her voice. She folds her arms over her chest, glaring at him. 'He murdered her in cold blood.' She stops, taking a deep breath before continuing, her voice lower now. 'You will not go down the same road as him. I won't allow it.'

Seb takes a step forward, suddenly realising that he towers over his nan, his recent growth spurt putting him a few inches taller than her. He sees her eyes widen as he glares at her. 'I knew it. I *knew* it.' And then he turns, storming out of the room and along the hallway.

'That's it, run to Jodie! Like she's got a bright future ahead of her,' Liv shouts as he grabs his jacket from the hook. 'Get back here! You're grounded!'

He turns then, looks her in the eye, sees the fear and frustration in her face. 'You have no idea,' he says, quietly now, almost sad, before closing the door behind him.

Seb walks fast, his limbs trembling with emotion. He has never spoken to his nan like that, never raised his voice at her. He has never felt the need to, not even when she took away his toys or told him off for being naughty. She has always been fair, with endless patience, and he always knew she was on his side. But not this time. This time they are set against one another, on opposite sides, and a crack is appearing between them.

And it is all because he cannot tell her the truth. He cannot tell her what he did to Sian, and what he found in her room. He has been thinking about it since he saw it and realised what it meant. The pieces are slotting together now; he knows that he has been heading in the wrong direction, has lost his way, but he is on the right track now.

He walks with purpose, his feet pounding against the concrete, to where he knows she will be.

54

IZZY

The journey seems shorter this time, or perhaps it is because she is dreading her return, anxious about seeing her mum in person for the first time in weeks. Will she notice the changes Izzy has made? Will she see this new and improved version, or just see the flaws she has always known?

Miranda is listening to an audiobook, the soft tones of the narrator almost enough to calm Izzy's nerves as the countryside flashes by. Devon, then Somerset, then Wiltshire. How many counties separate her from her old life? How many miles does she have to travel to get away from it all? And now she's going back. Can this new Izzy cope better? Can she ignore the whispers and the worried looks her mother flashes her way?

She remembers her conversation with Chloe in the toilet, the mention of the photo. They wouldn't really share it again, with her new friends? Not after the police were involved. *But I dropped the case*, she thinks, suddenly frustrated with herself. *I could have told them everything, and then maybe it would have stopped. Maybe it would have got worse.*

What if she sees them while she's in Hertford? She cannot bear the thought, feels sick at the idea of facing them again. *It's only two days*, she reminds herself. Two nights in her old bedroom, staring at the mirror she took that photo in. *I'll cover it up*, she decides. *Throw a blanket over it like a Victorian house in mourning.* And she feels a little better after that.

There is a crash on the M25, a three-car pile-up on the other side of the road that, for some reason, slows down their side too. 'What do you reckon,' Miranda says, slowing down and peering at the accident, 'on their phone?'

'Boozy lunch,' Izzy offers. Miranda smiles and they drive on.

On the driveway, before Izzy can even dig her key out of her bag, the front door is flung wide and Caitlyn rushes out, her arms open. Izzy steps into them, surprised to find she has missed these hugs, now that she is encased in one. She glances back at Miranda, who is still sitting behind the wheel. Caitlyn follows her gaze and moves away, bending to speak through the open window.

'Miranda,' Izzy hears her mother say. 'Lovely to meet you at last. Thanks for bringing her home.'

Something flickers over Miranda's face before she smiles. 'My pleasure. I'm staying at the golf club in Broxbourne,' she says. 'Thought I'd treat myself to a little spa weekend. So I'm not far away.' This she directs to Izzy, who nods.

'How lovely,' Caitlyn murmurs, stepping away.

Izzy hears movement behind her and turns to see Michael coming out of the house. He claps a hand on her shoulder and gives a 'Hello, you,' before walking over to the car and sticking his hand through the open window. 'Miranda? Michael. Nice to meet you.' He glances at the back seat. 'Is the suitcase in the boot?'

'I just brought this,' Izzy says, lifting her weekend bag. 'I didn't think I'd need much.'

There is a pause, a ripple in the air around them before Caitlyn smiles.

'Of course. We've only got you for a few days!' She turns to go, reaching out and wrapping an arm around Izzy.

'See you on Sunday,' Miranda calls, and Izzy nods.

'Hang on,' Michael says. 'Aren't you coming with us, Miranda?'

'With us?' Izzy echoes. 'Where are we going?'

'Out for dinner, of course. Mum's booked a table.'

'For the four of us, darling,' Caitlyn says, and Izzy glances at her. She never calls Michael *darling* anymore.

'I'm sure the restaurant can find a spare chair,' Michael says, turning back to Miranda. 'You must be starved, after that long drive. How about it?'

'Oh, I wouldn't want to intrude,' Miranda says.

'Nonsense!' Michael says chummily. 'You'd be most welcome, isn't that right, darling?'

Izzy feels her mother stiffen, her fingers tightening around Izzy's upper arm. Nobody speaks for a moment, Miranda looking between them all, unsure how to respond.

'But of course,' Caitlyn says finally. 'Of course you should join us, Miranda. It would be lovely to get to know you better.'

Izzy is in her room, her still-packed bag dumped on the floor by her bed. The room has been cleaned, all the detritus she'd left lying around tidied away into drawers, with not a speck of dust in sight. The carpet has deep vacuum lines carved into it; Izzy prods at one with her toe, her mind focused on the pyjamas her mother must have laid out on her pillow, not realising that it was Seb who bought them for her. She fingers the pair of light-blue shorts with white polka dots, smiles at the cat on the front of the oversized shirt, lying above the words FELINE SLEEPY. She'd picked them out from the reduced section in Primark and he had paid for them, calling it a Valentine's gift, though they'd said they wouldn't bother.

'It's all overpriced chocolate and glittery cards that pollute the planet,' she'd said, but secretly she'd liked him buying her a gift. She'd never had one before, had never found a card hidden in her schoolbag or lying on the mat when she got home from school. And besides, she'd reasoned, pyjamas are a useful gift. Flowers wilt, chocolates get eaten or otherwise spoil. These she would wear until they faded, or they no longer fit.

And yet she had left them here, shoved to the bottom of a drawer, the memory too painful to remember. But now she is here, she realises that she should speak to him, try to explain everything. She owes him that much, at least.

'Izzy!' Caitlyn calls, and Izzy stands, taking a deep breath before approaching the mirror. She fluffs out her hair, runs a finger under each eye, and straightens her outfit. She is wearing tapered green trousers covered with leaves, and a black, short-sleeved top. She looks good. She smiles, trying to make it reach her eyes, and gives her reflection a nod before leaving the room.

'Sizzy!' Alicia's arms wrap around her as soon as she reaches the ground floor. She hugs her sister back. 'I've missed you!'

'I've only been gone four weeks,' Izzy says with a laugh. 'You're always away for longer.'

'It's all right when you're not the one left behind.' Alicia pulls away and stares at Izzy's face. 'You look different,' she says seriously, and this time, Izzy knows her smile reaches her eyes.

'Are we ready?' Michael says, coming out of the kitchen, swirling his car keys around on one finger. 'You haven't blocked me in, have you, Alicia?'

'Yes, Mike,' Alicia says, rolling her eyes. 'And no, Mike.' Izzy stifles a giggle. Michael hates being called Mike. She suddenly feels warm inside, and she is happy to be carried along on this wave. It's her birthday, after all. She deserves to celebrate.

'Right,' Caitlyn says, bustling into the hallway and slipping into her shoes. 'Shall we go?'

'You look nice, Mum,' Izzy says as they leave the house.

Caitlyn throws her a smile. 'Thank you, sweetie. You do too.'

'Those trousers are *loud*,' Alicia says, poking Izzy in the ribs as she passes. 'Can you hear me over them?'

'What?' Izzy replies, and Alicia sticks out her tongue. They squash into the back seat of Michael's car, reminding Izzy of when they were younger and they would listen to music on shared earphones, the cord dangling between them. She tries to hold on to these happier memories, and not the one when Caitlyn crashed the car, the sisters strapped into the back, the smell of petrol and vodka filling the air.

55

CAITLYN

I find myself smiling for the entire journey to the restaurant. While we wait at the level crossing, Michael reaches out and squeezes my hand, and I feel a rush of love. My girls are home. We are a family again.

Miranda is waiting in the car park, a cloud of smoke hanging above her head. She hits a button on the device she's holding and tucks it into her pocket when she sees us pull up.

'I didn't know she vaped,' I hear Alicia say from the back seat. 'Cool.'

'Addiction isn't cool,' Michael says lightly, and I see Alicia make a face in the rear-view mirror.

'It's better than smoking, isn't it?' I say. 'Anyway, she's a grown adult.' I get out of the car, plastering a smile onto my face. 'You found it all right then?' I ask unnecessarily.

Miranda returns my smile. 'Yes, though I think I scraped my car on the way in.'

'Oh dear.'

'It's a tight turn,' Michael adds, coming up beside me. 'You don't want to meet anyone on the way in or out.'

'Is your car okay?' Izzy asks, her brow furrowed in concern.

Miranda smiles. 'It's fine. Let's call it a souvenir.'

'Shall we?' Michael leads us through the car park, our feet crunching over the gravel. He opens the door and we file into the restaurant, and I realise that I have not counted the steps between the car and the door. For the first time in weeks, months, *years*, my anxieties are quiet, pushed to the back of my mind. Perhaps it is a sign.

After a slight scuffle over the extra person in our party, we are shown to a table in the corner, menus placed before us. The kitchen door opens and the chef comes out, making a beeline for our table.

'Ah, Isabella,' he says in his Italian accent. 'Nice to see you again. The birthday girl, no?' Izzy nods, her cheeks flushed. He claps his hands together. 'A celebratory drink then!'

'Good idea,' Michael says, and the chef goes off into the kitchen.

'She's not quite sixteen yet,' I say quietly.

'Oh, what's a few days?' Miranda says. 'Just a small one won't hurt.'

'Quite,' Michael says, grinning as he picks up his menu.

The chef returns with a small bottle of Prosecco and two glasses. 'For the young ladies,' he says, winking at me as he places a glass in front of each of my daughters.

A waiter takes our drinks orders and I put my menu down, folding my hands over it. 'What are we having then?'

'Are we having starters?' Alicia asks.

'I am,' Michael says. 'The aubergine parmigiana is my favourite bit.'

'Ooh,' Miranda says. 'I like the sound of that.'

'It's superb. You should get it.'

'Izzy?' I prompt. She looks up, her menu falling to the side and I see that she is on her phone. I frown. 'Everything okay?'

'Yeah,' she mumbles, sliding her phone into her pocket. 'I've decided.'

We order, Alicia and Izzy deciding to split a portion of garlic pizza bread. Miranda is telling us about the renovation on her house. I sip my wine, noticing the way Izzy seems to hang off her every word, and feel a bubble of envy that I try to push away.

'There was a disaster with the bathroom,' Miranda says, rolling her eyes. 'The plumbing was as old as the house – eighteen hundred and something – and there was a lot of lead piping.' Michael whistles and rubs his fingers together. She nods. 'Yes, it did cost quite a bit to rip it all out. But it was worth it in the end.'

'We ran into some trouble with our renovation,' I say. 'They delivered the wrong flooring for the kitchen, and then the one we wanted was out of stock. It was like living in a sandpit for weeks, dust got everywhere.'

Miranda chuckles. 'Living on a building site is no fun, I don't think I'd do it again.'

'Miranda just got planning permission for a pool in the garden,' Izzy says excitedly. 'Isn't that amazing?'

'Wow!' Alicia says. 'I'd love to visit.'

'Oh, but you must,' Miranda says, reaching a hand across the table and patting Alicia's arm. 'Perhaps during the summer break. It's your home as much as Izzy's.'

I see something flash across Izzy's face, something that seems to mirror my own feelings. Jealousy. I take another gulp of wine.

'I bet you have some brilliant dinner parties in that kitchen of yours,' Michael says. 'Izzy sent us some pictures.' I think of our own kitchen diner, which is also perfect for hosting, but we so rarely have people over anymore. *Maybe that can change*, I think, *now we have more free time.*

Miranda smiles. 'Yes, I do love entertaining. We often have a full house at Christmas.'

'Christmas!' Izzy exclaims. 'Do you have a real tree?'

'Yes. Usually in the dining room, by the back door.'

'I'd love to see it,' Izzy says, and Miranda glances at me.

'I'm sure we can organise something,' she says lightly, fingering her glass of red wine. A waiter approaches our table, arms laden down with plates. 'Ah! Thank goodness, I'm ravenous.'

'Didn't you order a starter, Mum?' Alicia asks when everyone has been served and the waiter asks if he can get us anything else.

I turn to him with a smile. 'Just a bowl of olives.'

He nods. 'Coming up.'

We eat, Alicia regaling us with stories from university and the horrors of shared living. 'All the mugs were going missing from the kitchen cupboards. It was really peculiar,' she says, tearing off a strip of the pizza bread with her fingers. 'Anyway, we eventually tracked them down in Stuart's room.'

I make a face. 'He didn't bother to wash up the ones he'd used?'

She shakes her head. 'It gets better than that. Turns out he couldn't be bothered to walk the five steps to the toilet either. He'd been using the mugs to pee in.'

'Eurgh!' Izzy exclaims, and Michael almost chokes on his food as he laughs.

'How disgusting,' Miranda says, a hand at her breastbone.

'I hope you threw them away,' I say. 'Or I'll know not to accept a cup of tea next time I'm at yours.'

'Oh yeah, they went *straight* into the bin,' Alicia says. 'We keep everything in our own rooms now.'

'Remember when someone tipped your milk down the sink and used the bottle to store their leftover spaghetti?' Izzy says, laughing. 'Was that the same guy?'

'Weirdly, no,' Alicia replies. 'That was last year. So I've lived with two gross boys so far.'

'Girls only next year, then.' Michael chuckles.

'Have you had any thoughts on where you'll live yet?' I ask.

'You have to secure accommodation quite early on, don't you?' Miranda puts in. 'There are quite a few student houses near us, they always seem to be full.'

Alicia nods. 'I'm going to stay where I am. The rent is cheap and it's a decent area.'

'I hope Stuart's moving out,' I say.

'He already has. He was so embarrassed when we found out, he moved in with his girlfriend a week later.'

Izzy makes a face. 'I hope he doesn't do the same thing there!'

'Not my problem,' Alicia says with a grin.

Our mains arrive, and when we've finished eating I order another round of drinks.

'Can I have another Prosecco?' Izzy asks, turning her wide, pleading eyes on me. I can't help but laugh, remembering when she would do this as a child, asking for *just one more biscuit*.

'All right then,' I say. 'Just the one though. And you're having dessert to soak it all up.'

'What a hardship,' Alicia jokes, elbowing her sister. 'I'll have a rosé please, Mother. With ice.'

'Ice? In wine?' Michael looks horrified.

'It's quite nice,' Miranda says. 'Refreshing.'

Alicia nods. 'See? At least *someone* has good taste.'

A waiter comes to clear the plates away. 'Presents?' I suggest. Michael reaches beneath his chair and pulls out a wrapped bundle. Izzy takes it with a smile, unwrapping the bow carefully and folding back the paper.

'Oh!' she exclaims, revealing a stack of three hardback books. 'I haven't read these yet. Thank you.'

'My turn!' Alicia squeals with delight and fumbles beneath

her seat, bringing out a pink sparkly bag. She places it in front of Izzy with a flourish.

'It's so pretty,' Izzy says, lifting the tag and reading it.

'Open it then!' Alicia prods her sister, and Izzy tears into her present. She pulls out a silver necklace, the word *Sizzy* carved onto a circular pendant. Alicia lifts the chain around her own neck. 'Now we match.' She bumps her *Sissy* necklace against Izzy's and they grin.

'I love it,' she says. 'Thank you.'

'*De rien, ma petite soeur.*'

'I didn't know you spoke French,' Miranda says. '*J'habitais en Bretagne.* My sister still lives there.'

'I'd love to go to Brittany,' Alicia says with a sigh. 'Or Paris. Anywhere in France really.'

'Well,' Miranda says, glancing at me. 'I would have waited until next week, but since we're all here.' She opens her handbag and pulls out an envelope. 'Happy birthday, Izzy.' She passes it across the table with a smile.

'But you've already given me my gifts,' Izzy says.

'There's one for you too, Alicia,' Miranda says. 'So this isn't really a birthday present, I suppose. Just a surprise gift for you both, from your dad and me.'

Izzy gasps as she opens the envelope, pulling out two thin rectangles of paper. Tickets, I realise with a lurch. Two ferry tickets to Brittany.

'Really?' Alicia says, grabbing one of the tickets. 'Yay! This is amazing!'

'Look, Mum,' Izzy says, showing me her ticket, and I force myself to smile widely.

'How lovely, darling.' But inside I am screaming. First, Anthony reconnects with Alicia behind my back, then he takes Izzy to live with him, and now this, a surprise trip to France. How can I ever hope to compete?

56

LIV

I pace the living room, four steps from one end to the other. Such a small room which has always forced me to be tidy. It's a good thing I don't own much, I suppose. A TV in the far corner, sitting on a unit which is older than Seb. One of the doors squeak when you open it, but we don't go in there much anymore. It is full of DVDs, and who watches those these days? It's all Netflix and same day delivery and *on demand*. Is that why Seb is becoming this way? The fast pace of everyday life, so used to having everything now, now, *now*.

My leg bangs into the coffee table as I turn and I stop, reach down to press a hand against the pain. It pulsates beneath my fingers, like a living thing separate to myself. This is what it's like having children – or, in my case now, grandchildren. Sometimes it is hard to distinguish them from you, to identify where they end and you begin. When they cross the road for the first time without holding your hand or go to school for the first time, it is like a part of you has gone with them. And when they are in pain, you feel it too.

I press a hand to my chest and try not to cry. When did it all start to go wrong? A few months ago, Seb was a high achiever, with good grades and a decent future mapped out for him. He had nice friends and a girlfriend who was sweet, if a little shy. I know this photo thing hit Seb hard, but is there more to it? Is that the cause of everything? Or was it because I refused to see what was right in front of me? The sins of the father, Seb said. Have I been inadvertently pushing him towards his father's path?

I shake myself. Seb is not his dad. Seb is his own person, who will make his own mistakes. But how do I drag him back from the brink?

I sit up waiting for him to return, the room growing dark around me. The clock ticks past eight o'clock, then nine, then ten. Now it is almost eleven and my body has stiffened in the chair, moulding itself to the fabric. I need to get up. I need to *do* something.

I go into the kitchen and drink a glass of water, relishing the shock as the cold hits my teeth. I slip into my shoes and check my pockets for my keys and phone, then leave the house, closing the door quietly behind me. He can't have gone far. As I walk, I look through his social media pages, trying to find names that stick out, someone he might be close with, but it is fruitless. My finger hovers over Caitlyn's name but I skip over it, remembering the way she looked at me when she accused Seb of leaving those flowers. Pity. Doubt.

I walk around the estate, searching the empty streets. The park is quiet, a swing moving gently in the breeze. The air is hot, muggy almost, the promise of a storm lingering on the horizon. I hope I don't get caught in it.

I find myself outside the block of flats where Jodie lives. Which number is it again? Her mum will probably be at work, another night shift at the hospital. I peer up at the second-floor windows I think belong to her flat; they are dark, closed tight despite the heat. Is anyone at home?

I'm about to press the buzzer for number twelve when a scream rings out behind me. I whirl around, my heart beating faster. Was it a fox? Another shout and I start walking towards the noise, trying to keep my footsteps quiet. I turn the corner and stop, my fingers gripping the wall. A small group of people, barely visible in the darkness, are standing in the alley. Two figures are leaning against the fence, smoke drifting above their heads, but the others – three? No, four – are closer together, heads almost touching like bucks getting ready for a fight. Their voices are louder now, the air full of hard consonants as they argue. One pushes another, and they stumble back, just avoiding tripping over the kerb. I cannot see who they are; their faces are in darkness, some with hoods up despite the warm weather. A bike lies discarded further along, a bag dropped beside it.

'You don't scare me,' a voice says, a voice which sounds like it belongs to a girl. I feel my fingers tighten on the wall, my nails digging in almost painfully. What is going on?

'You owe us,' another voice says, deeper this time. 'Time to pay up.'

'I don't owe you shit,' the female voice says, louder, aggressive. I see the cherry-red tip of a cigarette butt bounce across the pavement, sparks flying. 'Now fuck off.' The figure starts to walk away, in my direction, and I hold my breath.

A tussle then, feet scuffing against the ground. Someone falls – which one? – and groans, collapsing to the ground. And then they scatter, like ashes on the wind, fleeing in different directions. I listen to their footsteps fade away, echoing against the buildings, and then my feet are moving towards the figure still lying on the floor, their shadow a pool of darkness beneath them. Suddenly I am running, and I almost trip over something, looking down to see my foot caught in some kind of fabric. A hoodie, a familiar logo visible in the low light. I keep going, as if pulled on a string, and as I get closer, my pulse pounding in my ears, for a split second, I feel certain it is Seb, and my legs turn to jelly. I fall to my knees beside him, my mouth open, my hands fluttering above him as I take in the scene before me.

It isn't a shadow spreading out beneath him. It's blood. Shock hits me like cold water, my brain struggling to keep up with what my eyes are seeing. I place a trembling hand on his shoulder, turn him so I can see his face. Relief floods me, closely followed by horror, for it isn't Seb. It's Jodie.

She is bleeding heavily, her eyes closed, and when I place my ear close to her mouth, I can just hear her shallow breathing.

'Jodie,' I whisper, digging out my phone and switching on the torch. 'Jodie, it's Liv. Wake up.' I search for the wound, find it on her stomach. I reach behind me and snatch the hoodie, pressing it against her as I dial 999 with my other hand. 'Jodie,' I say again as I'm put through. 'Jodie.'

She moans, shifting beneath me, and her eyes flutter. The operator answers. 'Ambulance,' I blurt. 'Please.' I tell them where we are, tell them that a girl has been stabbed in the stomach. 'There's so much blood. Please, please hurry.'

I don't know how long I kneel there, my hands pressed against Jodie's stomach, talking to her, trying to keep her awake. I tell her about Paige, about how she'd wanted to be a barrister, or maybe a university lecturer. She'd wanted two children and a house with a large garden with trees she could build a den in for the children. She wanted a dog, maybe two, those sausage dogs she'd always loved. 'She liked their little legs,' I tell Jodie, smiling through my tears. 'She loved fish too, but she didn't like the idea of keeping anything in a tank or a cage. She was kind like that, soft-hearted. Just like Seb.'

'Seb,' Jodie moans, and the breath catches in my throat. 'Seb... kind...'

'Yes,' I whisper, thankful that he was not here tonight, trying not to think about where else he might be. 'Yes, he is.'

I stay with her until the ambulance arrives, the flashing lights turning the world blue. I am reluctant to move away from her, the paramedic gently taking my arm and helping me to my feet. My knees are sore, gravel stuck to my trousers, and I stand stiffly, watching them lift her onto a stretcher.

'Are you family?' a paramedic asks. She has blonde hair tucked back in a neat bun, a stripe of pink at the front, and a large tattoo of a rose on her forearm. I tear my eyes away from it and shake my head.

'But I know her, and her mum. She'll be at work, there isn't anyone else. Can I...?'

The paramedic smiles. 'Of course.'

And I step inside the back of the ambulance, sitting down beside Jodie and holding her hand in mine, trying to stop the tears from falling.

57

SEB

Seb calls her, imagining the phone vibrating on her bedside table, lighting up the room. It goes to voicemail and he tries again, and she answers on the fourth ring.

'Hello?' Her voice is croaky. He has woken her up.

'I'm outside,' he says. 'We need to talk.'

She comes out wrapped in a silk dressing gown, thick socks on her feet. He is waiting by the entrance to the small car park which sits behind the house, and they go into it, hidden from the street beyond. In the dim light he can see the bruises on her face, the dark rings beneath her eyes, and guilt floods him.

'What do you want?' Sian demands, her arms crossed over her chest. 'Do you know what time it is?'

'I want the truth,' he says, fishing out a cigarette and lighting it. The smell reminds him of Izzy and his heart contracts. How little he knew. How little he has understood.

'About what?'

'Izzy.'

Sian drops her gaze. 'That's all over with now. The police have dropped it.'

'The police might have dropped it,' Seb says, blowing smoke into the sky. 'But I haven't.'

'She doesn't even live here anymore. She's old news.'

'Don't you care?'

'About what?'

'About Izzy. About what you've done to her.'

'I haven't done anything to her. I don't even like her.'

Seb watches her face, searching for signs. He doesn't know Sian very well, he realises, not really, but he knows her well enough to tell when she is lying. And she is lying right now. 'Why did she send you that photo then?'

Sian's eyes widen. 'What? She didn't, I–'

'You're the one Izzy sent it to. The one who asked for it.' He looks at her, notices the colour creeping up her neck, her lips slightly parted. Her arms go around herself as if desperate for comfort. 'I saw her Kindle in your room, under the bed. I recognised the cover. How long has it been going on?'

She doesn't respond. She is speechless for once, her words ripped from her by his accusation. But he knows he is right. Everything makes sense to him now – the photo, Izzy dumping him. She never liked him, not in that way, and he is surprised to find that it doesn't matter. He would rather have Izzy as a friend who can be herself, than the Izzy who has been hiding in the shadows, desperate and alone.

'Look,' he says, exhaling. He feels sorry for Sian in that moment, which surprises him too. 'I get it. It isn't easy to come to terms with who you are, if it means being out of the norm. Different. But why share the photo? That's what I don't get.'

Sian hesitates for a moment. 'Abby,' she whispers. 'She found it, sent it on. She said she'd tell my parents about it, that I was...'

'Gay?' She flinches. 'It's not a dirty word, Sian,' he says, his voice gentle now.

'I know. I just... My dad, he wouldn't understand.'

Seb takes a deep breath. 'You know, all my life, my nan has been waiting for me to turn into my dad. Angry, violent. She's tried to keep me away from him, in case his influence turns me into him. But I'm not him. I will never be him.' He fixes her with his gaze. 'My dad killed my mum when I was four. He's been in prison ever since.'

Sian's eyes are wide with surprise at his confession. 'I had no idea. It's not the same though.'

'No, it isn't. But it means I understand what it's like to try to live up to people's expectations of you. I know what it's like to want to lash out.' She looks up and meets his gaze. 'You've been bullying Izzy because she made you realise who you are, because you were being bullied about who *you* are.' She starts to cry then, her head dropping into her hands. Seb moves forward and takes her wrists, gently pulling her hands away from her face. 'You need to put it right,' he says softly. 'You need to make amends.'

58

IZZY

Her mum is drunk.

She watches her stagger as they exit the restaurant, laughing loudly and grabbing onto Michael's arm to steady herself. Caitlyn usually moderates her drinking, since the car crash when she broke her arm and received points on her licence, the girls miraculously unhurt, but every so often, something happens and she reaches for the bottle, searching for the solace Izzy knows she will never find.

They say goodbye to Miranda in the car park, Izzy holding on to her for a second too long before pulling away. Caitlyn chatters the whole journey home, her words slightly slurred, her voice too high, too loud.

'Isn't Miranda *lovely*?' she says, twisting around towards the back seat. 'I can see why you like her. And a trip to Brittany! How nice. How *nice*.' But in her mouth, it sounds the opposite of nice. Izzy doesn't speak, doesn't move. She can feel the tension crackling in the air, her mother's words laced with something she doesn't like the sound of. 'I see now why you'd rather live with *her* than with me.'

Izzy closes her eyes. She feels Alicia shuffle beside her, is grateful when she feels her hand slip into hers. She is reminded of those days when their mother was unrecognisable, a lump beneath the duvet, the air stale and cloying. She used to sneak into her sister's room at night, hiding under the covers with her, or they would creep out onto the landing, hand in hand, listening to their mother cry, the smashing of glass punctuating the sobs. They were too young then to understand, too young to know why their mum was upset, and where their father had gone, but they had felt the change in atmosphere, still feel the ripples of that time all those years ago.

Izzy blames him, she realises, opening her eyes. She blames him as much as she blames Caitlyn for those months lost at the bottom of a bottle. Anthony may have taken her in, may have made her welcome in his home, but how much of that was down to Miranda? Why hadn't he been in touch before now? And why hasn't he spoken to her about it all? It has just been brushed under the carpet, like so many things in her family. She doesn't want to go down this road, is only too aware of where it will end. She needs him, needs the refuge of his house in Plymouth, the new life he has given to her. But can she ever forgive him? Can she forgive her mother?

Izzy turns to Alicia, who is scrolling through her phone, her head down. She wants to ask her sister why she started speaking to him again, how they found one another. Does she resent Izzy for going to live with him? But no, how could she? She knows Alicia told him about the photo, the bullying. She knows this is why he came, appearing out of the blue after twelve years of silence, and despite everything, she is still grateful for it.

'Where is Miranda from, anyway?' Caitlyn says, interrupting her thoughts. 'She said she lived in Brittany, but she isn't French.'

'I don't know,' Izzy says. 'I think her dad moved them out there when Miranda was a teenager. When he remarried.'

'Ah,' she says, nodding. 'Another child of divorce. No wonder she feels so drawn to you.'

Izzy feels a surge of anger. 'That isn't why.'

'No?' Caitlyn turns to look at her. 'Why, then?' Izzy is silent. 'You think you know everything, don't you? You think you know how the world works?'

'Cait,' Michael says, his voice low. 'Come on.'

'What?' She whips her head around to face him. 'What? I'm talking to *my* daughter. Mine. Not yours. Not *his*.'

'Mum,' Alicia says angrily. 'That's enough.'

'Ah,' Caitlyn says again, tapping the side of her nose. 'That's another thing you don't know, isn't it, Isabelle?'

'What do you mean?' Izzy asks, hardly daring to breathe. She turns to look at her sister. 'What is it? What do you mean?' she demands again.

Alicia shakes her head, and Michael mutters, 'Well done.'

'You need to stop drinking,' Alicia says angrily.

'Oh, piss off,' Caitlyn slurs. 'I'm sick of you all dictating my life. *Don't do this, Caitlyn,* and *don't do that, Caitlyn. Watch what you say, Caitlyn. Stop drinking. Don't enjoy yourself.*'

'This is you enjoying yourself, is it?' Alicia says with a bark of laughter. 'You're being a twat.'

'Don't speak to your mother like that,' Michael says, but there is no conviction in his voice. He just sounds tired.

'I'll speak to her however I want when she's acting like this. You're an embarrassment. And a liar.'

'What do you know about lies?' Caitlyn laughs, but it is without mirth. 'You are a *child*.'

'You need to start telling the truth,' Alicia says, her voice low and almost unrecognisable. 'Izzy deserves to know.'

Izzy watches her mother's face change then. She is shaking her head, her eyes wide. 'Alicia, don't–'

Alicia's lip curls. 'If you don't tell her, I will.' There is a beat, a heavy pause before Alicia turns to her sister, her eyes glistening with tears. 'Izzy, it's time you knew the truth. Dad. Anthony. He isn't your dad.'

Shock momentarily stuns Izzy, turning swiftly to anger. Why is Alicia trying to take this from her? The one thing she has that her sister doesn't. 'You're the liar,' she hisses. 'You're just jealous that he wanted me to live with him and not you.'

Alicia shakes her head. 'Poor little Izzy. You don't know anything, do you?' She leans close; Izzy can feel her breath on her cheek. 'You're just like her,' she says, jerking her head towards Caitlyn. 'A drama queen. Attention-seeker.'

The slap comes from nowhere. Alicia's head snaps to the side, her hair whipping across her face. When she looks up, Izzy sees that her cheek is red, and her eyes are burning with fury, but Izzy's fury is burning brighter, smouldering inside her, ready to erupt.

59

CAITLYN

It wasn't an affair. It wasn't even a one-night stand. It was a man I thought I knew, a man I called a friend, who I trusted to get me home safely after a night out.

I told Anthony the truth straight away, unable to keep the horror off my face when I took the test. Pregnant. I knew instantly whose it was. Anthony and I had been going through a bit of a rough patch, struggling to navigate the choppy waters of new parenthood, so we hadn't slept together in a while. When I started feeling nauseous at the smell of coffee, I knew, and the test confirmed my worst fears. I was pregnant with my rapist's child.

I got as far as the clinic, the appointment booked, my mind made up, when Anthony changed it. Again. He caught me outside, dropped down to one knee and presented me with a ring. He'd bought it with the money he'd made from his latest sale, a beautiful landscape of the view from Windmill Hill in Hitchin, the bright green grass turning to the high street with old buildings full of character. We were living in Baldock – Cambridge too expensive now we were no longer students – in a tiny two-bedroom flat above a betting shop. But things were going to change. Anthony was a rising star, and he promised me that he would buy us a house, a beautiful forever home with enough space for our growing family. Somewhere up and coming, both historical and modern and with everything a young family could need. And so we moved to the house in Hertford, with renovation plans big enough to keep me busy while my stomach grew. Busy enough to keep the doubts at bay, for the most part. And we rewrote history.

When Izzy was born, I was relieved that she looked more like me than *him*. Alicia took after Anthony, with her ski-slope nose and freckles, but Izzy was all me. Except her hair. Her curls came from *him*, and I spent the next fifteen years trying to tame them, trying to remove that one trait of his that had won out. Because I couldn't bear to see any of him in her. I couldn't bear the idea of her knowing where she had come from, knowing that she had not been wanted. But she knew. Despite my early promises, whispered in the dead of night as I rocked her back to sleep after a feed. When Anthony left and I fell into a deep hole, I made it clear that Izzy was unwanted. Unwelcome.

Tears slip down my face as I sit hunched against the wall, my phone still clutched in my hand. I have been calling Izzy for hours, her phone ringing and ringing, since she jumped out of the car and ran.

I hug my knees against my chest, unlocking my phone and trying Izzy's number again. It rings out, the impersonal voicemail kicking in. I leave another message.

'Darling, it's Mum,' I say, trying to stop my voice from breaking. 'Can you ring me please? We need to talk about this. Please.'

But she does not call back. I try Alicia, my hands shaking as I find her number.

'Leave me alone!' she shouts, her fury blasting through the

speaker like a tornado. 'Stop fucking calling me. You started this. It's all your fault.'

'Lis, darling, I–'

'No.' Her voice is a whip, silencing me. 'You've gone too far this time.' And then she is gone, her phone switched off or my number blocked, and I sit alone on the cold floor, crying for my lost daughters. What have I done?

⌁

Miranda calls me back after I leave a garbled message on her voicemail. 'Caitlyn, it's the middle of the night. Is everything all right?'

'Is she with you? Izzy?'

'No. I wasn't expecting to see her until tomorrow. What's happened?' I close my eyes, my heart pounding in my chest. 'Caitlyn?'

'We had an argument, and she hit her sister. She ran off, last night. I thought she might be with you.'

'Izzy hit Alicia?' Miranda sounds shocked. 'What were you arguing about?'

I try to find the words to explain, but they stick in my throat. 'Have you heard from her?'

'No. I'll try to call her now. I'm sure she'll be fine, she's probably just gone to a friend's.'

She hangs up and I wait, clutching my phone to my chest. Where could she be? I search through my contacts, looking for names and numbers to call, but it's the middle of the night. Everyone will be asleep. Should I call the police? I go into the kitchen and dig out PC Willis's card, remembering the look in her eyes the last time she was here. *If I can do it, anyone can.* Did something similar happen to her when she was younger? She must be in her early twenties, closer to Izzy's age than she is to mine. Can she help us now?

I dial the number, pressing my phone to my ear. 'Hello? It's Caitlyn Bennett. I'm so sorry to call you at this time, but I need your help.'

60

LIV

I stayed at the hospital until the early hours, clutching Jodie's hand until her mother arrived, eyes bloodshot and full of fear and concern.

'She's okay,' I told her, releasing my grip and moving out of the way. Her mum sat down, reaching out to brush a stray hair from her daughter's forehead. 'She was lucky.'

Jodie tried to sit up as I turned to leave, groaned in pain. 'Liv,' she croaked. 'Seb. He's a good boy. He didn't mean it.' And suddenly everything made sense. Jodie had been protecting Seb, protecting him from whoever wanted to drag him into their dark web, and she had almost been killed for it, murdered by those who cannot see a way out of their darkness. I realised then that I had her all wrong, that there is so much more to her than meets the eye. She is still that sweet child who used to eat at my table, her legs too short to reach the floor, her hair in need of a wash. She is a product of her environment, and she deserves better. But where was Seb when all of this was going on?

I got a taxi home, too drained to walk, and fell asleep as soon as my head hit the pillow, but it was broken sleep, full of shadows and memories I've tried so hard to forget. When I wake again, for a moment I don't know where I am. I dreamed I was in Mum's house, listening through the wall to the sound of Mum crying. My mind goes straight to Seb, and I sit up, pushing back the covers. He must be home, I'm sure I saw his shoes downstairs when I got in. I remember thinking that I would take the day off work and we would talk, properly, and I would listen. I *will* listen, to whatever he has to say.

The doorbell rings as I lift my fist to knock on his door. I frown and move away, glancing at the clock as I go downstairs. It is almost six o'clock, far earlier than I'd expected it to be. I'd only managed to get a few hours' sleep. A wave of exhaustion washes over me and I open the door, expecting the postman. I stare at the woman on my doorstep for a moment, wondering if I am still asleep, still dreaming, until she speaks.

'Is Seb here?' Caitlyn demands. Her eyes are wide and heavy with dark circles, her hair tangled and unkempt. She looks as if she hasn't slept for a week.

'Why?' I ask, bewildered. 'What do you want with him?'

'I need to speak to him. About Izzy.' She goes to push past me and I bring the door closed, blocking her path. That's when I notice the woman standing behind her. It takes me a second to recognise her out of uniform. I feel my eyes widen with shock.

'What's happened?'

'Izzy didn't come home last night,' PC Willis says. 'Has Seb seen her?'

'She's missing,' Caitlyn sobs, her eyes meeting mine, and I suddenly see the despair, the desperation in them. 'We argued and now she's missing. Please. Does he know where she might have gone?'

I feel something inside me release, and I hold open the door. 'Come in,' I say gently. I show them into the living room, watch Caitlyn perch on the edge of the sofa like a nervous bird, her hands twisting in her lap, while the police officer sits in the armchair. 'Why are you here, PC Willis?' I ask.

'Charlotte, please.'

'Are the police looking for her? You're not in uniform.'

She shakes her head. 'I'm just helping Caitlyn for the time being.'

'I don't want the police involved,' Caitlyn says. 'They might scare Izzy away.' She glances up at PC Willis – *Charlotte* – almost apologetically. 'I just want her home.' She puts her head in her hands, and pity floods through me as I turn towards the stairs. The woman must be going out of her mind with worry. But Izzy will turn up. She's a teenager, and she's been through so much lately. She'll just be acting out. I knock gently on Seb's door, wait, knock again.

'Seb?' I call through the door. 'Seb, there's someone here to see you.'

No response. I push the door open and stop, taking in the empty bed. He isn't here. I check the bathroom, knowing I will find it empty, then my own room. Empty.

I run back downstairs and check the shoe rack. His shoes aren't there. I go into the living room, my heart pounding. 'He isn't here,' I say, breathless. 'I don't know... I don't think he came home last night.'

Charlotte stands up, alarm on her face. 'Do you think he might be with Izzy?'

'I don't know. I don't think so. Does he even know she's back?' Nobody answers. I pull out my phone and dial his number. It goes straight to voicemail. 'Maybe his battery died,' I say to myself. 'He'll just be with a friend, I'm sure.'

'Can you call them? His friends?' Caitlyn asks.

'I-I don't have their numbers.' I curse myself for my stupidity, for not keeping a closer eye on him. When Paige was little, nobody had mobile phones. I knew which houses her friends lived at, and could usually find her within five minutes. She didn't go far. But Seb's friends don't live nearby, other than Jodie, and she's still in hospital.

'When did you last see him?' Charlotte asks.

'Last night. We – we argued. He went out. I went looking for him at about eleven, I think. I found...' I pause, not knowing whether to mention what happened to Jodie. I don't want to bring the police to her door. 'Someone was hurt, I found them. I went to the hospital with them and got home at about three.'

'Was he here then?'

'I don't know. I thought so. I thought I saw his shoes. But I can't have done. I was so exhausted, I just went to bed.' Guilt ripples through me. How could I have fallen asleep, when Seb was still out there? I should have gone in, checked on him, had that conversation straight away. I should have known he wasn't here, gone out looking for him immediately.

'Okay,' Charlotte says, breaking into my thoughts. 'I think we should try some of their friends. Maybe they stayed the night. Do you have their addresses?'

Caitlyn nods.

'I know where some of them live,' I say. 'I'd recognise the houses, I think.' I take a deep breath, suddenly overwhelmed. I can't believe this is happening. Izzy and Seb, both missing? They have to be together. It has to be connected. 'I'll just get dressed.'

I'm about to run up the stairs when I hear a key in the lock. I whirl around to see Seb standing there. 'Oh, thank God,' I cry, rushing over and wrapping him in my arms. 'Where on earth have you been?'

'Sorry, Nan,' he says, sounding like the Seb I know, the Seb I have raised and loved, and my heart lifts. 'I'm sorry, for shouting. For everything.'

I pull back, taking in his face. He looks tired, but something has changed in him. Or rather, something has returned, the recent hardness in his gaze no longer there. It is then that I notice someone hovering behind him. For a second I think it is Izzy, but I don't recognise the girl standing behind my grandson. 'Who's this?'

Seb clears his throat. 'This is Sian. We're going to... Well, it's a long story, but–'

'Where is she?' Caitlyn almost collides with me in her rush to get to Seb. 'Have you seen her?'

'Who?' Seb asks. He looks between us, bewilderment in his eyes.

'Izzy,' I tell him. 'She's missing. She came back yesterday from Plymouth. Have you heard from her?'

Seb shakes his head and I hear the breath leave Caitlyn's body, turn just in time to catch her before she falls. 'Izzy,' Caitlyn whispers, her eyes full of fear, and I open my mouth to say something, anything, when another voice speaks.

'I might be able to help.' I look up to see Sian taking a tentative step forward. 'I think I know where she is.'

61

IZZY

Izzy walks.

Her thighs burn, her feet throbbing as she walks along the towpath. The water is calm here, gently lapping against the canal boats, but Izzy knows it is deep and vast, with things hidden beneath the murky surface. She climbs the steps and ducks under the tape that screams KEEP OUT, feels the wooden bridge beneath her feet. They are repairing it, the path closed to pedestrians, and the bridge rocks under her weight. The water is tipped with white foam here, like the waves she saw at Plymouth Hoe, moved by the rushing waterfall at the end. She swings one leg over the railing, then the other, feels the wood peeling beneath her fingers.

She cannot swim.

Her phone is switched off, so she does not know the time, but it is early, the sun still low in the sky. She is hidden here, invisible from the main towpath. She and Sian used to come here sometimes, when it was quiet. It was their special place, where they could be themselves. She looks up at the office building to her left, knows that if someone looked out of one of the windows they would see her, see what she is about to do. But there is nobody there. It is early, and the world is still waking up. They are not looking for her.

She tips her head back, looking up at the pale-blue sky. Clouds drift overhead; a bird circles above her, wings outstretched. A red kite. Seb taught her how to spot them. She closes her eyes against the wave of pain. She cannot bear to think about how she has hurt him, how she always hurts everyone around her. Why is she so selfish? Alicia was right: she is a drama queen. An attention-seeker. Why else would she take that photo? Why else would she go out with a boy she wasn't attracted to? She has hurt Seb, treated him with disdain by stringing him along, lying to him. She has hurt her mother, knowing she would find her with her wrists cut and doing it anyway. She has hurt her sister, her hand flying out and cracking against her cheek. She has destroyed all of her friendships, twisted everything and turned it to dust.

For the first time, she allows herself to remember that night, the sleepover at Abby's house that marked the end of everything. Abby and Jess were asleep, or so Izzy had thought when she'd crawled into Sian's sleeping bag, their bodies pressed together, minty breath filling the space between them. The softness of Sian's lips, the way she traced a finger down Izzy's cheek like she always did, her touch light as a feather. It was risky, the first time they had allowed themselves to be close away from here or the privacy of Sian's bedroom, her parents out or downstairs, none the wiser. But Izzy had been craving Sian's touch all evening, had fizzed with delight when Sian slipped her hand into hers while they watched a film, hidden by the darkness.

And then Abby had woken up and saw them together, laughing at their protestations. Sian pushed Izzy away, fear in her eyes as she turned her back, her words designed to sting, to take the focus off of her. And it worked. Izzy was cast out, no longer a friend but someone to torment, to hate.

Izzy the outcast, she berates herself silently. *Stupid, pathetic, hated Izzy*. It is her fault that she is in this mess, no one else's. And only she can end it.

She takes a deep breath. The water rushes in her ears, the waterfall pounding against the surface in time with her heart. She releases the railing with one hand, feels herself shift forward. Her breath catches in her throat as she wobbles, regains her balance. *Do it*, a voice inside her head says. Abby, who has been sending her the messages for months, who won't leave her alone. *Jump*.

'Izzy!' The word rises above the water, above Abby's voice in her head. Her eyes fly open to see two figures running towards her, ducking beneath the tape, their feet pounding on the bridge. She turns slightly, twisting her head to see who it is, and then her foot slips, and she is falling.

62

SEB

P C Willis drives, Seb squashed in the middle between his nan and Izzy's mum. Caitlyn is picking at the skin beside her thumb in a way that reminds him of Izzy, and makes him want to reach out and take her hand, but he doesn't. Instead he turns to Liv.

'I've been a shit,' he says. 'I don't know how you put up with me.'

She smiles sadly, shakes her head. *Not here*, she mouths. *Later.*

Seb nods, knowing that it doesn't have the same meaning as it used to. Later, they will rebuild their bridges, close the gap which has widened between them. Later, he will tell her how he is back on track, how he never meant to go off course, and she, though he does not know it yet, will tell him about what happened to Jodie, and that she understands now where she went wrong. They are in harmony once again.

Sian is directing PC Willis from the front seat. 'I don't know if you can park there though,' she says as they take a side road.

'I can park anywhere,' PC Willis says, and Seb almost laughs. She is younger than he first thought, different without her uniform and severe ponytail, closer to his age than he expected. Perhaps he got her wrong, as he has got so many things wrong. Perhaps she isn't so bad after all.

'Izzy!' Caitlyn cries, pointing at the figure on the bridge as PC Willis pulls the car over. The breath catches in Seb's throat at the sight of her. *We're not too late.* They scramble out of the car, running towards her. She turns her head as they run along the towpath, and then, suddenly, she is gone. Seb rushes forward, watching in horror as Izzy's head disappears under the water.

'No!' Caitlyn cries.

'We can't all go on there,' PC Willis shouts over the rushing water. 'It might collapse. It's not safe.'

'Izzy!' Caitlyn screams, trying to push past her. 'She's my daughter!'

While the two women are wrestling, Seb locks eyes with Sian and they begin to run forward in unison, ducking beneath the tape. He hears his nan shout his name, but he ignores her, kicking off his shoes as he runs, preparing to dive in after Izzy, but Sian is faster. She is up and over the railing before he can blink, jumping into the water with a splash. He remembers watching Sian during their swimming lessons, back when they were too young to recognise the things that divided them. She was a good swimmer, and she always helped the teacher hand out inflatables. He doesn't know why this memory flashes through his mind as he watches Sian dive beneath the surface, her legs kicking against the current, but it feels important. His eyes dart around, searching for them, but the water is like a dark, one-way mirror; he sees only his silhouette reflected back at him, the bridge cutting the weir in half.

How long have they been down there? Ten seconds? Twenty? He tries to count the seconds, doesn't pause for long enough in between them, starts again. He glances back at the path below, sees PC Willis coming towards him, his nan holding Caitlyn in her arms, though whether it is for comfort or restraint he doesn't know.

'I'm going in after them,' PC Willis says, her shoes already off, but then there is movement, something bursting out of the water. Izzy gasps, spluttering as Sian pulls her towards the edge.

'Grab her!' she shouts, and PC Willis runs over, scuttling down the side, stones skittering beneath her feet. She leans forward and takes Izzy's arm, pulling her up and out of the water. Izzy lies on the cement block, still gasping, her body convulsing like a fish. She must be freezing. Seb runs to the edge, takes off his hoodie and hands it to the officer, who wraps it around Izzy, chafing her arms up and down.

Sian treads water while they help Izzy to her feet, guiding her back towards the bridge. She pulls herself out, kneels there for a moment, the cement block soaking beneath her.

'Are you okay?' Seb asks Izzy, repositioning the hoodie around her shoulders.

She nods, her chest still heaving up and down, her body trembling. She turns as Sian clambers back over the railing, her body dripping. 'Thank you,' she whispers, her eyes brimming with tears. 'You saved my life.'

'It was the least I could do,' Sian says, her chin wobbling, her voice full of barely contained emotion. 'Since I was the one who pushed you.' And Seb feels something shift in the air, a wrong righted, a chapter ended, and a new one beginning.

63

LIV

SIX MONTHS LATER

oday's the day. The big five-oh. I open the card Seb has propped up against the kettle with a smile. He was up and out early this morning, helping Jodie move into her new flat. She has healed well, though she says the scar still itches when it rains. I look out at the dreary November sky and hope she isn't doing much heavy lifting.

A piece of paper falls out of the card, fluttering to the counter. I open it, bemused.

To Nan,
I've made pancakes for your breakfast – they're in the blue-lidded tub in the fridge – and there's fresh strawberries. Don't forget the whipped cream!
See you at Granny's for lunch.
Happy birthday.
Love, Seb xxx

I smile, carefully fold the note back up and tuck it into my dressing gown pocket. In the fridge I find everything he promised, and set about making myself a cup of coffee to go with it.

The post comes as I'm finishing my breakfast. A large pink envelope sits on top, my name printed in familiar block capitals. But this isn't the one I open first. I skip over it to find the letter I have been waiting for, ripping it open and pulling out the sheet of paper, glancing over it before stuffing it into my handbag. That's for later.

I open the pink envelope, smiling at Evelyn's words. *P.S. Lunch at mine next Sunday?* she's written at the end. *Yes*, I think. *Why not?*

I place my cards on the windowsill in the living room, five in total, before going upstairs to get ready. I fluff out my hair and apply lipstick, smiling at myself in the mirror. I don't look half bad, I think, for a fifty-year-old.

I drive to Mum's, listening to the radio, singing along to the words that remind me of when Paige was young and we would dance to Kate Bush in the kitchen, her feet on top of mine, our laughter drowning out the music. I smile, a hand pressed against my chest, feeling her with me. 'You'd be proud of me, Paige,' I say aloud, glancing in the rear-view mirror, and for a moment I catch a glimpse of her, her long hair blowing in the wind, a smile playing on her lips. 'You'd be proud of us all.'

Anna opens the door, a plastic apron covering her uniform. 'We've just finished getting ready,' she says as I enter. 'She's in good spirits.'

I smile, make my way into the lounge where Mum is sitting in her chair, her feet propped up. Her hair has been washed and styled, thanks to Jackie. She came over with me the other day, doing both mine and Mum's hair as a treat.

'Hello, love,' Mum says, reaching out a hand to me. I take it, feeling her paper skin beneath mine. 'Happy birthday.'

'Thanks, Mum,' I say, leaning down to kiss her cheek. 'How are you?'

'Fine, fine. That lovely girl came over and did my hair. Can you tell?'

'Yes, it looks great.'

'What was her name again?'

'Jackie.'

'Oh, yes. Jackie. You went to school with her, didn't you, Paige?'

I smile. 'Yes, that's right.'

Seb joins us half an hour later, arriving just as Anne is leaving. He's carrying a square box, while Izzy is laden down with two bags. Sian brings up the rear with a FABULOUS AT FIFTY balloon. As I open the door to let them in, I hear a toot and see Caitlyn waving from her car.

Seeing them all together reminds me of that day six months ago, and everything that happened to bring us to that point. It's hard to believe that it happened so long ago, and yet, bizarrely, it feels as if no time has passed at all. But I can see it in them, these three young people. They have half a year's experience on them; it has moulded them, shaping them into the adults they will become. Izzy has forgiven Sian, Sian has forgiven Seb, and I have forgiven myself. For we have all been at fault, at one point or another. I was always looking for Seb's father in him, waiting with bated breath for the inevitable to happen. I was too quick to see the bad in him, too quick to believe that he might be capable of such cruelty. And so, in the end, it was me who pushed him in that direction, ensuring my fears became a reality.

The biggest surprise has been Sian. I had only ever heard

about how cruel she had been to Izzy, but now she seems like a changed person. She spent the summer doing my mum's garden, hacking away at the years of neglect and transforming it into a little bit of paradise she can enjoy. She volunteers at the local food bank, and spends her weekends cycling to raise money for charity. She has purpose now, I suppose, something to focus on other than the secrets she was desperate to hide.

We went with her to speak to her parents, Caitlyn and I. Caitlyn wanted to explain about the bullying, about what Abby had been doing, but also to support Sian in coming out. 'I don't see why anyone should have to "come out" in this day and age,' Caitlyn said to me afterwards, and I'd silently agreed. But it went well, better than Sian had expected. Just as it should be.

And I was there to apologise for what Seb had done. He'd explained it all to me – the burglary, the assault – and we'd spoken to Jodie when she came out of hospital, the truth behind it all finally revealed. I couldn't condone such behaviour, no matter the intentions behind it, and so Seb had to own up and accept whatever consequences came his way. Thankfully, after everything that had happened, Sian's parents decided not to involve the police, but Seb has been working unpaid in her mum's salon every Saturday ever since, answering the phone and greeting clients. He quite enjoys it, actually. He's even thinking of going to college to train as a hairdresser.

I wave at Caitlyn as she drives away, stepping aside to let the trio inside. They file into the lounge, Seb placing the large box on the coffee table. Izzy brings out paper plates and a bottle of Prosecco, filling plastic cups with the bubbles and passing them round. Mum takes hers with a little chuckle. 'Fizz, well,' she says. 'This is a special occasion.'

And it is. It might be my birthday, but the special part is that we are all here together.

'I need to go,' Izzy says later, once slabs of cake have been demolished. 'Miranda is picking me up soon. Thanks for having me, Liv. Happy birthday.'

I smile as she kisses my cheek. She is still living with Anthony, despite the revelations. It must have been a difficult conversation, one that is no doubt ongoing, but Izzy seems to be more settled now too. They are all spending Christmas in Plymouth this year, even Caitlyn. They are an unusual family, but it seems to be working, now they are free of secrets and no longer hiding in the dark.

Sian leaves too, promising Mum that she will be back in the morning to finish painting the new wet room. Mum pats her hand, smiling, and I realise that she seems happier than I have ever seen her. She is a calmer version of herself. The dementia is a dark cloud on the horizon, but for now we will enjoy what we have.

I close the front door after them and take Seb aside, pulling the envelope out of my bag. He takes it, pulling out the paper inside. I tap my finger against the words printed along the top: VISITING ORDER. He looks at me, his mouth dropping open in surprise.

'Really?'

I laugh. 'Yes, really. Tomorrow, if you want to, that is.'

He hugs me tight, reminding me of when he was small and would cling to me, his tiny legs wrapped around my waist. I breathe him in, my boy, and hold him close.

'I can't wait,' he whispers. 'Thank you.'

Seb may want to forgive his father, may be desperate to have him in his life, but I know I could never forgive Brad for what he has done. I am not as strong as these young people who continue to amaze me every day. I do not have it in me to forgive him for taking my daughter away. But I can no longer keep Seb from his father. For better or worse, he needs him in his life.

Only Seb will suffer if I try to keep them apart. And as we take our seats opposite him in the prison the next day, my palms sweaty with nerves, Brad's eyes clear in a way I've never seen before, a sheepish smile on his lips, I know that Paige is here with us, and I know that she would be proud.

64

IZZY

'Izzy!'

She hears her name being called, turns to see a figure running out of the building towards her. The air is cold, the promise of Christmas just around the corner, and the wind bites at her cheeks as she waits, moving aside to let the flow of students pass her. It is the last day of term, and the midday sun casts Katie's short new curls in a golden hue as she approaches.

'Aren't you getting the bus?' she asks when she catches up, her breath frosting in the air between them.

Izzy shakes her head. 'Not today. I'm meeting Miranda in town. We're picking up Dad's Christmas present.'

'Is it socks?' Katie asks with a wry grin. 'That's what I always get my dad.'

'It's not socks,' Izzy says with a laugh. 'It's–'

'Oh,' Katie interrupts. 'Isn't that Leah?' She raises a hand and Izzy stiffens, the familiar nerves bubbling inside her until she realises that Katie is waving, and then she remembers that first day back in Plymouth after her birthday weekend in Hertford, after the tearful conversations with her mum and Anthony, who drove up when he heard what happened. She remembers Katie turning up with a bag full of chocolate and Prosecco. She remembers her surprise when she found out about Anthony not being her dad, her shrug when Izzy told her the truth about Sian.

'It's the twenty-first century,' she said around a mouthful of Minstrels. 'Who the hell cares about that anymore? Anyway, what happened to *be kind*?' And Izzy had laughed and cried and hugged her new friend, something suddenly clicking into place. She felt the sense of something settling, like a feather drifting to the floor after a long time in the air. She was ready for a new chapter in her life.

The dread had returned when she went back to school, her mind full of worries about what her new friends would think of her after what happened at her party and the photo they had all seen. She wondered whether Katie had told them all about the weir, whether they thought badly of her now. But Katie had squeezed her hand while they sat on the bus, and the rest of them were waiting for her at the school gates. They rushed over, engulfing her in their arms, strands of hair tangling and perfumes mingling, and Izzy had relaxed into them, almost dizzy with relief.

And then there was Leah. She had been reading a book that morning, in her usual corner at the back of the room, and when Izzy sat beside her, she didn't raise her head.

'*Queenie*,' Izzy said, reading the front cover of her book. 'Good choice.' Leah looked up then, blinking as if in surprise. Izzy smiled. 'What are you doing at lunch?'

Leah joined them all on the field that lunchtime, nervously picking at her ham sandwich. Izzy saw the bemused look Katie threw her and took out her phone.

She's not so different to me, she typed. *Be kind, remember?*

And Katie had smiled, her eyes twinkling. She nodded once before speaking. 'Leah, I *love* your bracelet. Where is it from?'

Leah looked startled. 'It was my mum's. She gave it to me for my birthday.'

'Vintage! Cool.'

'Didn't you used to do karate at the church on Mutley?' Chloe said, leaning over and pinching one of Steph's crisps.

'Yeah. I wasn't very good though.' Leah's smile was shy.

'Me neither,' Chloe said. 'I always forgot to bow when I entered. I used to get yelled at every week. Who did you have?'

'Darren, I think?'

'Short, dark hair?' Chloe mimed spikes coming out of her head.

'That's it. He had really hairy feet.'

'Eurgh!' Cara exclaimed while Chloe laughed.

'He did! And his toenails, bleurgh!'

'Why are feet so gross?' Maddie said, making a face.

'Speak for yourself,' Katie said, slipping her foot out of its shoe and pointing her toes. 'I could sell photos of mine online.'

'Fuck's sake!' Steph said, throwing a crisp at Katie. They dissolved into fits of giggles, the type that make your stomach hurt and tears leak out of your eyes, and Izzy had noticed how pretty Leah was when she laughed.

It was that simple. It was that complicated.

'Leah!' Katie calls, jerking Izzy out of her reverie. 'Over here!'

Leah grins as she approaches, taking the halo of tinsel off her head and throwing it at Katie, who catches it in mid-air. 'Thought you'd abandoned me,' she says, smiling as she slips her hand into Izzy's and squeezes.

Izzy squeezes back. 'No such luck,' she says with a grin.

'I can't believe that's our first term at college done,' Leah says. 'It goes so much quicker than school did.'

'I *know*,' Katie says, rolling her eyes. 'School dragged. Now we're surrounded by fun people.'

Izzy laughs before checking the time. 'We'd better go. See you tomorrow?'

'Nah,' Katie says, pretending to examine her nails, 'I've had a better offer.'

'Oh yeah? What, hot chocolate and *Murder, She Wrote* with your dad?' Leah says with a grin.

Katie laughs. 'Yeah, on second thoughts, see you tomorrow.' She whirls around and heads for the bus stop, her hair bouncing around her head.

'I could go for a hot chocolate though,' Izzy says as they walk towards the city centre. 'Costa?'

Leah makes a face. 'How many times? Starbucks all the way.'

'You have no taste.'

They walk hand in hand towards Drake Circus, pausing to look in the shop windows, pointing at a display inside Waterstones. Izzy's phone vibrates and she pulls it out, smiling at the screen.

'Is that...?' Leah asks, eyes widening.

Izzy nods, turning the phone towards her and replaying Sian's Instagram story. A tiny bundle is running across a wooden floor in pursuit of a toy which looks like a cross between an owl and a squirrel.

'I can't believe Sian got a puppy,' Leah says with a sigh. 'I'm desperate for a dog.'

'You should include one in your book,' Izzy suggests. 'The next best thing?'

Leah laughs. 'My characters have all the fun.'

They go to Starbucks – of the two, Leah is the more relaxed one, but this is one argument Izzy will never win – and they order large hot chocolates with marshmallows, the takeaway cups warming their hands as they walk through the shopping centre.

'When are you going to your mum's?' Leah asks, sliding out of the way of a toddler barrelling across the concourse, a dishevelled man chasing after him, a pram dragging along behind.

'This weekend,' Izzy says. 'I'll be back the day before Christmas Eve.'

She thinks of her mother, remembering as she often does the long, emotional conversations they have had in the months since her birthday weekend, sometimes on the phone, sometimes in person. She thinks of her reaction when Izzy told her she was gay, the way she had frowned, making Izzy's stomach tighten with anxiety. 'So?' she said. 'I just want you to be happy, darling.' And Izzy had been unable to stop the tears of relief from running down her face.

One hurdle had been crossed, with a simplicity that surprised Izzy. But then Caitlyn and Alicia came down to Plymouth in September, and they spent the weekend in the kitchen with Anthony and Miranda, drinking endless cups of tea and making piles of used tissues. The room was full of the words they'd kept inside for so many years, the air thick with emotion, but their relationship now is so much stronger than it had ever been. She understands why her mother kept her conception a secret, why she had been so hurt when Anthony left. She finally understands Caitlyn on a level she'd never expected to before. She finally understands why Miranda called her *remarkable* that day at brunch. Her mother is remarkable, full of strength and love and patience. Her sister is too, with her pragmaticism and ability to forgive, and Anthony and Miranda, with their open house and arms, their desperation for Izzy to stay with them, if she wanted. And she did. She does. She has this extraordinary family, with more people than she ever thought she could fit inside her heart. She knows she is lucky to have such remarkable people in her life.

And me, she thinks as they spot Miranda waiting outside a shop for them. *Maybe I'm a little bit remarkable too.*

THE END

ACKNOWLEDGEMENTS

The idea for this novel came to me when I was struggling with another that wasn't quite working. The characters of Seb, Izzy, Liv and Caitlyn arrived almost fully formed, as if they were people who were already in my life and were just waiting for me to notice them. Thankfully, this one seems to have worked, but I couldn't have done it without the support and understanding of my publisher.

This book is dedicated to my nephew, who was not yet born when I wrote these acknowledgements. I am completely useless with children, but I will always strive to make the world a better place for them to inherit, and I will continue to learn and grow in my understanding (though I may never learn how to change a nappy). My thanks therefore to Keisha Corrigan for answering my questions about growing up and dealing with racism. It is a privilege for me to have to ask about rather than live with such things, and any errors or missteps are entirely my own. Thanks also to Herts Black Lives Matter for their showcases and resources, and to everyone who spends their time raising awareness and educating others. You are heard.

Thank you to everyone in the Photos of Hertford, Ware and

surround Facebook group for answering my questions on what Hertford was like in Liv's day, and especially those who sent photos and shared memories of life from the 80s to the early 00s. Thanks also to PC Ricky Carter for his lengthy notes on police procedure - as always, all errors are my own. And to Shannon from Hertford Cake Co and all at Amico di Amici, two of my favourite local places immortalised in this book.

Writing a book is always a collaborative effort, and I am lucky to have such a great team around me. Huge thanks to Ian Skewis, Shirley Khan, Tara Lyons, and all at Bloodhound Books for helping shape my fifth psychological suspense novel. Thank you for having faith in me. Thanks as always to my wonderful beta readers: Michaela Balfour, Chloe Osborne, and Melanie Thomas.

To the Psychological Suspense Authors' Association and The Savvy Writers, thank you for your support and guidance. To Rona Halsall, Lesley Sanderson, and Ruth Heald for your friendship and being there through it all, the highs and lows and everything in between. To the Fiction Cafe Book Club and Skye's Mum & Books for your friendliness and cheerleading. And thank you, readers, for choosing to pick up my books. I really hope you have enjoyed this one.

Finally, to Evie, for being my biggest supporter and giving me 'crumbs' on my early drafts. This was the first novel I completed during lockdown while trying to control a wild puppy, and it wasn't always easy. And by the time this book is published, we'll be busy wrestling with another puppy while I try to write another book, because we are clearly bonkers. But this time, we'll know we can do it.